WAITING FOR THE MAN

A NOVEL

ARJUN BASU

ECW PRESS

Published by ECW Press
2120 Queen Street East, Suite 200
Toronto, Ontario, Canada M4E 1E2
416-694-3348 / info@ecwpress.com

Parts of the chapter "A Big Country" previously appeared, in a very different form, as
"In a Big Enough Country" in joylandmagazine.com.

This is a work of fiction. Names, characters, places, and incidents either are the product
of the author's imagination or are used fictitiously, and any resemblance to actual
persons, living or dead, business establishments, events, or locales is entirely coincidental.

LIBRARY AND ARCHIVES CANADA CATLOGUING IN PUBLICATION

Basu, Arjun, 1966–, author
Waiting for the man / Arjun Basu.

ISBN: 978-1-77041-177-7 (BOUND)
ALSO ISSUED AS: 978-1-77090-516-0 (EPUB); 978-1-77090-515-3 (PDF)

I. Title.
PS8603.A797W33 2014   C813'.6   C2013-907755-3   C2013-907756-1

Cover design: Michel Vrana
Text design and typesetting: Lynn Gammie
Printing: Bang   1   2   3   4   5

The publication of *Waiting for the Man* has been generously supported by the Canada
Council for the Arts which last year invested $157 million to bring the arts to Canadians
throughout the country, and by the Ontario Arts Council (OAC), an agency of the
Government of Ontario, which last year funded 1,681 individual artists and 1,125
organizations in 216 communities across Ontario for a total of $52.8 million. We also
acknowledge the financial support of the Government of Canada through the Canada
Book Fund for our publishing activities, and the contribution of the Government
of Ontario through the Ontario Book Publishing Tax Credit and the Ontario Media
Development Corporation

PRINTED AND BOUND IN THE UNITED STATES

For Jo

WAITING FOR THE MAN

PART ONE

HERE COMES THE SUN

It was as if I were floating. This was what I first noticed. The original thing. This floating business was a sign. Of something going on inside my head. I would find myself off the ground, hovering, and then moving, slowly, effortlessly, seeing my own self encumbered by the normal laws of physics, everyone and everything still governed by the rules and regulations that make things run. I was part of it and was apart. My floating self felt new and improved. Smarter. Fresher. More alive.

But it would never last.

I would be in a meeting, again, thinking up ideas and products, dreaming up the inconsequential things that make the world go round. Thinking up the reasons and pathways and trajectories of desire. Creating desire. And I would leave the meeting. And then I would return. I would hover above myself and observe my own ticks and mannerisms and then return to the normal operations of things. This began happening with an alarming kind of regularity.

It was the floating that started me off. The dreams didn't come until later. And by the time the dreams took over, I was well on the path. My road. To wherever. To this place.

But I'm getting ahead of myself.

I'm a simple person. Everything follows from this truth. Simplicity is a state in which my life has been lived. I grew up in a fake Tudor home in the deepest suburbs of New Jersey, the only child of immigrant parents. I went to a good high school; achieved good grades; attended college; got the degree; landed a safe, conventionally challenging, well-paying, and vaguely sexy job in advertising. Our next-door neighbor knew some people at a boutique agency and helped me get the position. I moved to Manhattan. I was creative. I could make people laugh. I was sufficiently cynical. Engagingly sarcastic. It's the only job I've ever had. The only one I remotely wanted. My father never made me work while I was in school. He wanted me to get good grades. I missed out on flipping burgers, working as a lifeguard, selling shoes, rites of passage in my community. Learning exploitation as a child is a license for abhorrent behavior in the future, I think. I missed that. Being exploited. I worked long hours at the agency, the kind of schedule that precludes a social life. I jumped into this thing and I never thought much about it. I was relatively successful. I was good at thinking up ways to sell things to people. To consumers. To instill want where there had been none. To make the essence of a brand match the core of your being.

I wasn't the kind of person who defined himself by his work. I didn't know many people who did and the ones who did were all older. There is a generational divide in this kind of self-definition, though the quality of the work has more to do with it. Perhaps in our age, there are more jobs but more bad jobs as well. When asked, I did not tell people I was a copywriter or in advertising. Even to the question of "What do you do?" I would describe myself as a frustrated Mets fan, as a drinker of a particular beer, as a lover of uncommon passion. I was sarcastic. I answered this question, as common in this city as "Hello," with sarcasm. I'm not sure if that was shame or a defense mechanism of some sort. It was a sign, surely. What else could it have been?

My work was something that should have offered more. Perhaps I should have accepted what it had to offer. For a long while I did. And it rewarded me very well. And this sense of reward, and the obviousness of it, protected me from the real world. From the real world as it existed around me. I worked within an energy, the kind of energy that came from satisfaction, youth, and the knowledge that we were going to survive the recession, or whatever it was being branded lately, because we were small and nimble and successful.

I was without a plan, I did as I was told, I showed the proper level of ambition. I drank with the right people. I received promotions and raises and these things made me work harder. I figured this was the key to the system. To how things functioned. The circle of life. It's an instinctual way to live. We live unimpressive lives in order to be impressive. And we do impress people. That's the thing. And when we stop treating this with any kind of amazement, one can feel the confirmation of a successful career. One can have things, be the person, wear the clothes. We win. And that's what matters in the end. Winning. Ensuring that everyone knows you have won.

The office was a modern space in that area where Chelsea becomes Hell's Kitchen. Hardwoods and steel and modular desks. Glass. Open. Beams of natural light bathing the place in a modern whiteness. Half a floor in an old building and close enough to my apartment that I often walked home at the end of the day if the weather was right. The agency was growing. Amazingly. Despite everything. There weren't that many of us. Thirty, I think. And that, too, was probably a part of our salvation. Our owners were veterans, refugees from the multinational world; they had experienced the waste and the timesuck of bureaucracy and attempted to avoid it. We dreamed up dreams to move stuff. That's what we called anything we could sell: stuff. We even had George Carlin's great bit about "stuff" running in a loop on a video screen in the reception area. That told everyone we were in on the joke. We were that good. And smart. A bunch of smart people sitting around being smart and doing smart things. And if you signed on with us, we'd do smart things for you, too.

I spun tales. My life appeared more interesting than it felt. To me, at least. It had the trajectory of some chop suey kung fu fighter, flying through the air, impervious to gravity. I was glib and irreverent because I was paid to be and because I could afford it. And because I didn't know better.

I felt like I was contributing to something larger than myself. To the running of the world.

My first campaign was for a government agency public service announcement aimed at exposing racism. That's what the brief said. "Expose racism and its aftereffects." As if racism were hiding somewhere. Whatever. I had studied something about the consequences of hate on human health. And the campaign was simple. A slide:

Racism = Hatred

And then another one:

Hatred is harmful to your health.

And that was it. White letters on a black background. And it was assembled and crafted for television and as posters and was put in the subway and on the sides of buses. My first campaign and I saw it while going to work. And I thought I was doing something noble. And even when my next account was for diapers, and the one after that was for sunscreen, I still felt that nobility. And that feeling of nobility lasted for a long time. Years.

So if the work ever got bogged down in idiocy, as it often did, there was the work, that first campaign, and the idiocy of the moment dissipated and whatever I was doing became important again because I had told the entire city that racism was bad for them.

But self-importance only lasts so long.

And I would go out and would be asked what I did, because you always get asked that, and I would mention that campaign. Everyone had seen it.

But there was only so long I was going to coast on the nobility of my first effort. The creative director at the office, an unnaturally lanky Dutch man who lived on Long Island, threw smaller campaigns at me and dared me to come up with something as intelligent as that first campaign. He would hand me a brief about, say, a new brand of soft drink and say, "Make it sing," and I would have to make it sing. I made up slogans for things that didn't exist, for products that I saw in an elevated light and I would imbue in them qualities that were ephemeral, unshakeable, like mist. I would render a spirituality, an inner life, for inanimate things, like soda. Or running shoes. Or beans. I would develop backstories for cans of beans. Because every brand was a story and every story needed to be told in the right manner. Because a story well told meant our client would sell a lot of beans. And I was the storyteller.

My most successful campaign: I once convinced a brewery to name their new beer "Berlin." Even though the beer wasn't German. They were looking for something Irish and I convinced them to go with Berlin because it sounded cool and the bottle would be cool and cool is something you just don't come across every day. And they bought it. I created an obnoxiously loud, MTV-inspired ad campaign consisting of one word: beer. The TV spot showed a bunch of frat boy types playing touch football and then piling on the local dweeb. Who then yells, "Beer!" Online, you could click on anyone in the pile and they'd yell the magic word. A fraternity in Kansas shot their own version and put it on YouTube. Copycat ads. Viral marketing. A

Twitter campaign with one-word tweets. T-shirts. And that was just half the campaign. Berlin was everywhere, long after the German city had lived its fifteen minutes. The campaign appealed to both urban hipsters and college males. We sponsored jazz festivals and poetry readings. The literati meets the tailgate party. My year-end bonus that year was the source of much envy. The entire Berlin team was written up in trade publications. I spoke at conferences. The agency won an award at Cannes. It was a successful campaign and it elevated the agency and attracted business. Because success is like a pile of shit to a bunch of insects. Everyone wants to eat it, to play in it, to live a little. Because success means more toys. And it means you've won.

So I became the urban hipster guy at the agency. I wrote copy for dog food and created a new market segment: urban hipster dogs and their owners. I made the dogs cool and the owners of cool dogs even cooler. The Kennel Club gave me an award for that one. I created nice things for stupid things. There is an astonishing level of creativity and thought in the movement of objects, of product. Energy. Humanity even. And then one day I suffered from a paradox I noticed more and more around me: the more successful I became the more I hated my work. This seemed cliché and I tried to outrun it. By working even harder. Which was stupid, in hindsight. But a growing paycheck always made up for self-loathing. Especially a healthy paycheck. At least I thought it did.

My neighborhood bar down the street was in a basement space under a lingerie wholesaler. A long counter ran down one side of the room and rickety wooden tables down another, and the light in the bar was always just this side of pitch, and after work I would go there and sometimes I'd stay long and get drunk and I'd talk with the regulars about sports and politics and sex and sometimes that talk would lead to me waking up with someone in my bed, sometimes a nameless woman whom I would find in the morning rifling through my kitchen in a vain search for something edible. I would walk into my kitchen and there she would be in one of my T-shirts and she'd say something like, "You really are a bachelor" or "What do you eat normally?" and I'd shrug and I'd try to bring the conversation around so I could get her name somehow. That's if I cared. When I cared quite a bit, I would ask what she was doing for dinner. But usually I couldn't get them out of my place fast enough.

I was not good at consummating relationships in the sense that I would have one. This caused my mother, especially, considerable grief, because there seems to be something in mothers that makes them want grandchildren the moment their own children move out. This genetic predisposition has obvious evolutionary advantages.

The day I turned thirty-five, I kind of panicked. I had a party at work on a Friday and went out with my coworkers and woke up in a college student's apartment near St. Mark's Place. Then on the Saturday night, my friends took me out and we ended up at my bar and I woke on Sunday with a hangover that felt like it belonged within the landscape of someone not my age. And that night I went to my parents' house and my mother made some exquisite food but nothing felt right in my mouth and my father claimed I was having a midlife crisis and I said, "I'm only thirty-five," and my father said, "Sounds about right," and I could not leave their house fast enough.

And on Monday, my actual birthday, I woke with a start, before the alarm clock had even gone off, and I had to admit that, yes, perhaps my father was right. The age hit me like hay fever. And I asked myself, What did it mean? To be any age? It's supposed to be relative. There are so many clichés about age that to discuss it is boring. And ultimately futile.

Perhaps it wasn't a midlife crisis but it was something and it didn't feel right. It was a crisis. But not a midlife one. It was a crisis of self. I arrived at work and I looked at my desk and the notes on it, and my to-do list, and the timbre of the day was lost on me, sour, off.

I suffered through this for an entire week and this suffering depleted me.

I wondered if I hated myself.

I slept more.

I ate badly. Or worse.

And later that week, I realized what was causing this. Or so I thought. It may have been a "midlife crisis" as my father had suggested, but more than that, I was put off by the normalcy of what was happening. I had a good, satisfying, well-paying job and it wasn't satisfying me. I had just turned thirty-five. I was tired of a lack of significance in my life. I was not proud of the banality of my suburban upbringing, the life as a whole that had brought me to this point, to the paint by numbers aspect of it, the dullness of it, the universality of the problems and the path I had followed. I had chosen this life and now I was thirty-five and I finally realized I was not only nothing special but I was like everyone else. And that was the crisis.

I was fucking boring.

And I saw this and did nothing.

I dove into my work. I helped on the pitch for an anti-persperant aimed at preteen girls.

I hung out at my bar.

I did nothing different. Because I couldn't.

I would walk into the office and sit in on meetings and say things like, "We just need to create a compelling backstory" or "How is the consumer going to be engaged by this?" or "I'm not feeling the feeling we want everyone to feel yet" and I would say this seriously and then we would work some more and laugh at some bad jokes or terribly awful ideas and throw wads of paper at each other or end up talking baseball and then we would go home again.

One day I saw what I had scribbled on my notepad and it said, "Stop sleepwalking."

We ate out and got drunk and came up with brilliant plans.

I turned thirty-six. And then something beyond panic set in. I felt remarkably unhealthy. Sick. Though my health was fine. It was fine because my doctor had told me so. Because I went to see my doctor. Because I was worried. More than that, I felt unhappy. And this was something that went beyond dissatisfaction. This felt like being struck by something big. Like lightning.

I told my parents that I wasn't happy at my job and my mother said, "But Joe, dear, you have a wonderful job," and my father said, "Happiness is overrated, you have a mortgage," and then my mother would offer dessert and she would produce her vanilla panna cotta and that would be that. My father had worked too hard to hear me complain about my work. My unhappiness didn't even make sense to him. He would talk about the carnage taking place on Wall Street and how many people were losing their jobs and their homes and how there was this army of dead people, of zombies, he called them, walking around and drinking coffee in diners and not even going home because they were lost. He used the term "bloodbath" to describe the economy. He hated when anyone used war terms out of context, but he was using war terms. So, no, it didn't make sense to him. And I can see how it wouldn't.

I once told a girl "I want to feel love." These were the words I used. I must have been drunk. I don't even remember when I said this, just that I said it once and I've remembered it ever since. Because it is and isn't true. I have felt love. Just not a lasting kind of love and that never bothered me. I never looked nor was I the kind of person who despaired the lack of it. I hated people who looked for relationships. I had friends who needed someone, always, who always needed that companionship, who found the thought of attending a party or a dinner without someone on their arm to be like walking naked. To be unnatural. They needed someone to constantly speak to, to obsess over, to worry about, to fight with. To love, maybe, though I doubt very much any of them were ever truly in love. Even a fleeting relationship, a coupling on fast-forward, was better than nothing. That was their philosophy. It just wasn't mine.

One night at the bar, I shared a nightcap with Angie, my neighbor. Her father managed my building. And when I moved in, she had helped me with some interior decorating. She told me where my couch should go. She arranged the drawers in my kitchen. She made me dinner.

She had a head of thick auburn hair, with brown eyes and a complexion that was a shade lighter than a latte. Her voice was deep with a lilt that announced her upbringing in deepest Queens. And I was too awestruck by my new status as a New Yorker, by suddenly feeling like I'd arrived somewhere, to ever pursue her. Because I would have. And then I got busy and she was helping her family open up a trattoria in Little Italy and our lives pinballed in different directions. We would meet at the bar at the end of our long days sometimes, and we'd talk and commiserate and get drunk and stumble home and I would say good night to spend my last waking minutes thinking of her.

On this night Angie found me sitting alone at the bar. I was watching the Knicks suffering from egregious badness, and she said, "So I'm noticing."

I turned to her. I smiled. Or tried to. "Can I buy you a drink?" I asked.

And Alex, the stupidly tall, spiky-haired bartender covered in tattoos—and possibly the gentlest guy in the neighborhood—brought Angie her usual rum and Diet Coke. He didn't need to be told.

"I would like to discuss your obvious unhappiness," she said. "Your funk."

"You have me confused with a banker," I said.

She put her hand on my back, and I felt I owed her some kind of admission. "I'm not unhappy," I said. "I'm just in-between."

She took her hand off my back. "You've lost something," she said. "Spark. You're not funny. I don't know. You're not you."

She downed her drink and held it out for Alex. "My father thinks I've been having a midlife crisis," I said. "For a year. He thinks I've been like this for a year."

"You're too young," she said. She watched Alex make her drink. "We're not midlife crisis people. That's just what he's calling it. That's generational."

And I realized I had been diagnosed with something for a year now. "I dislike the whole Boomer thing," I said.

"Your dad's not a Boomer."

"No," I agreed. "He's not. But the Boomers, that's all I think about. Most of the time. At work. And if there's one thing they've done, they've allowed us to see what happens when your entire life becomes a midlife crisis." I finished my beer and Alex gave me another one. He gave Angie her drink and she took a sip.

"You ad people," she said.

"They've shown us how stupid it is to spend your life trying to be something you're not," I said.

"And what's that?" she asked.

"Young," I said.

Angie laughed then. And she touched me again. "Maybe it is a midlife crisis," she said. She took another sip of her drink. It seemed to be too late in the evening for sipping. I took a long pull from my beer. "Or maybe you're in-between, like you say."

"Maybe," I said sighing. "Maybe it's semantics."

The problem was I didn't believe anything. I didn't want to pin my melancholy on age. Because that's what it was. Melancholy. I was listless. I lived my life without living. Without feeling alive.

And that night alone in bed, regretting what had never been with her, drunk most certainly, I started floating.

And then, more alarmingly, I started having these dreams. I

don't know what else to call them. Visions maybe. Nightmares. This thin black man in a floppy straw hat, dressed right out of the seventies, looking for all the world like a TV pimp. Like Huggy Bear from *Starsky & Hutch*. I never watched that show, it was before my time, but I remembered the character and now he was haunting my dreams. And this man, sometimes, later, would ride in on a white horse, a gigantic white horse with a mane that looked combed and neat and clean. A good-smelling horse. Bathed. It smelled supernaturally clean. And the Man had a smile you couldn't outrun. It was the size of the world. I fell into it.

I had the dream every night.

In different permutations. We would talk. Sometimes he would watch me. Stare. From across the room. In one dream, he watched me as I sat in the office and listened to a colleague debate the sexiness of his new iPad. One of my colleagues kept repeating that he didn't need human companionship anymore. His biological imperative had been fulfilled. In another dream, I walked with the Man along the banks of a foul-smelling stream and we debated something archaic, like the reasons behind the British Invasion, or McCarthyism, things I knew little about and cared for even less. Things from another era.

And then I stopped floating. And the dreams came to me at all hours, a bully astride me whenever I closed my eyes. And then, after a week of this, he spoke to me. Or, I stopped speaking to him. He became a kind of monolith. Dressed like a black pimp from the seventies. He was the speaker and I the listener. I absorbed. I saw him walking toward me, slowly, strutting more than walking. I'm sitting on my front steps talking to some neighborhood kids about the inanities of the latest Mets fiasco and I see the Man walking toward me. The kids scatter and he leans close and whispers, *Wait*. And his voice has reverb and echo and sounds vaguely like Isaac Hayes. With that gentle smile, he just tells me to wait. I ask why and he says,

Because. I could smell the horse on him. I'm not sure I knew what a horse smelled like then, let alone a clean one.

And I kept dreaming. Longer dreams. I touched him. And when I did I felt myself falling into him, being crushed and embraced by this good-smelling man. He told me to wait on my front steps and he would come and things would get better. *Things will get better.* That's what he said. Better than what? I asked. But he did not hear me. Because our relationship had changed. My role was not to speak.

I lived close enough to the World Trade Center to think he was talking about life in the most general way possible. I didn't think he was speaking about me. I could see him imparting in me the wisdom for some major civic improvement project. I saw his instruction through the lens of my workspace. Because I never considered my own life. I figured I was living. Even though I knew I wasn't. But that WTC thing, with all the fighting and the politics. I mean, the site was still a tourist attraction. My neighborhood had been through a lot. I breathed in that dust. Somewhere inside of me, I could still taste the burning embers of those buildings and everyone and everything inside of them. That dust lives on in all of us. And through the crazy times on Wall Street right to the crash, that dust lingered, never changing, resilient in its own sad way. I didn't think I needed anything better. I hated my job but everyone hated their job. No. In the dream's promise, I saw something larger than myself.

The next night I had another dream. And then the night after that I had it again. And for another week I had this strange dream of the Man walking up to me and telling me to wait for him. Promising a better world. And one night I was working late, alone in the office, trying to finesse the overall theme for a series of ads for a car company out of China launching an ambitious but poorly planned invasion of America, and I heard the Man's voice. Over the office intercom. I walked around the empty space. Past the light boxes with the black and white photos of the staff. The whiteness of the space. The glassed-in conference room. The rows of blank, humming computers. It was after midnight. And then I heard it again, as clear as if he was sitting across the desk from me. And again, it told me to wait by the steps. It commanded me. Over the office intercom the gentleness of the dream had been usurped by a tone of authority. And the next day, as I lay in bed wondering if I should hit the snooze button for the seventh time, he came again, not in a dream but as a voice that seemed to come in through my window, carried by the wind.

And at that point I became obsessed. I pondered therapy. I started to lose the desire for sleep. Sometimes I'd stay at the bar drinking by myself so I wouldn't have to go home. I became superficial. Even with Angie. How could I explain this? One of my neighbors gave me pills to help keep me awake. Because sleep meant the dream and the dream was a road paved with the outrageous. I couldn't share it with anyone. I didn't dare. Who wants to share their most intimate forms of lunacy? And I heard the Man's voice everywhere around me. Every creak in my apartment building, every kid yelling on the street, every time the wind blew in off the river, everything, every noise I heard was the sound of the Man saying *Wait*. His voice had become the soundtrack to my life.

And then one night, overtired, stressed about selling Chinese cars in America, about making Americans feel the need to own a Chinese car, I realized the Man was talking about me. Because I was alone in my office and I was lobbing crumpled pieces of paper at a wastebasket and pretending I was LeBron, and I was stupid. And instead of seeing these dreams as something deep inside telling me to confront my unhappiness, my little crisis, I took the Man at his word. And being a man of words, I cringed. I saw the Man as someone who was going to help me. I saw the Man and his horse and his mission. He was promising something. Courage maybe. He was asking of me the kind of action that my inactivity had been demanding. He came to me again. I was in mid-jump, sinking the paper ball into the wastebasket, and he said, *The floating stops. Now.*

And that night, I woke from a fitful sleep. And I was crying. I hadn't cried in years, since I had been a boy, and tears were streaming down my face. I was blubbering like a soap opera diva. I went to the kitchen and drank a glass of water. I put my head under the tap. The Man was sitting at my kitchen table. *What are you waiting for?* he asked.

You told me wait, I said. But wait for what?

And the Man stood up then and hugged me. He squeezed me until I had trouble breathing. I struggled under the power of his embrace. *You're waiting for me*, he said. And then he was gone.

And I felt beaten. It was something I just felt. In the shoulders.

I gave up. Maybe it was more like giving in. I think there's a difference. I gave in to the voice, the message of this Man, the constant voice I was hearing, the word that drowned out everything else. I decided I was going to wait. For him. For word. Not because it suddenly made sense, or because the world was both confusing and maddeningly predictable at the same time, or the Mets had opened spring training or my parents were not speaking to each other once again. No. I was tired. I ate breakfast and I took a long, hot shower and I sat down on the steps to my building and that was that. I started to wait.

So here I am, I said. I'm waiting for you.

And the voice came to me and it was pleased. And by the time night rolled around, my course of action seemed to be the most rational, the most logical action I had ever taken. I wasn't going to work for a while, I knew that. I was thirty-six. I was in advertising. I was successful. My parents were proud of me. I had disposable income. The economy sucked. My stocks had been hammered. That loss made me feel adult. I had savings. And I felt an unease about what I did to make all of this possible. I felt dirty doing what

I did. Perhaps it was a lack of maturity. Or perhaps I was hindered by excessive amounts of shame. Or at least a certain amount of self-consciousness.

There were practical matters to sort out. How long would I wait? What would I do if it rained? What would I do for food? And this: was I quitting my job? Or was I going to use up my bank of vacation days? What was the plan? Asking these questions, and considering their implications, I understood this: I had given in to the voice. I surrendered. It had me. The grip of its logic, or the message at least, finally overcame me. In a place where stunned ex-bankers and stock guys still wearing their suspenders walked the streets eating slices of pizza, vacant-eyed, alone; in a world where the bow tie made a comeback; where skanks from the Jersey Shore could become TV stars; and where I wrote ads for a dying media, assailed by technology and the power of a people both numb to their anger and buoyed by it; in this kind of place, giving in seemed logical.

The voice didn't vanish but it wasn't a constant. It wasn't something I could feel all around me. And though I could still feel the Man, I was plagued by an uncertainty that never left my side. And I also realized this: he was waiting, too.

I was stuck someplace, the kind of place that takes the meaning out of things. Wherever I was, joy was being sucked out of me, leeched out. I had to acknowledge that. If everyone around me could feel it, I should, too.

My job was to make people feel unique enough to purchase products everyone else was buying. To create desire where once there was none. Is that even fair?

A day later, I was noticed. A neighborhood kid, a boy who lived across the street, noticed. He asked. Within a few hours, the neighborhood caught on. And I told them, "I'm waiting for the Man." This is New York. This kind of statement just caused a shrug. Angie gave me blankets for the night when I convinced her I wasn't going inside. It was spring and the nights were still cold. She was the only one who tried to talk some sense into me, but I wouldn't listen. She was adorably Italian this way, sexy and motherly and crass and smiling through the rainiest of days. She worried for me. She said so. She said, "You worry me." She was beautiful in that way that all the women in Italian films are beautiful and her worry made her all the more so.

By the next day, I was a fixture. People started to hang out around me. Kids would sit on the steps after school to keep me company. Some would look out for the Man with me, but mostly I just became a place to hang out. I was geography. The old men got their coffees and hung out. Unemployed hipsters came by and texted their friends, who came by, too. And I was the subject of conversation, of debate, the crux of a battery of meaning. Symbolism. The source of something no one understood, but you never knew. Something might happen. I was the subject of impressive conjecture. And the Man zoomed in and out of my consciousness. *Keep at it*, he'd say. And then he'd leave. Sometimes I would smell the horse and know he was around. Watching me. Evaluating.

By the third night, women were handing me leftovers from last night's dinner. They'd say, "Just hang on to the Tupperware, Joe," and they'd leave me alone. Angie would bring me food from the trattoria. Nights I would see her walking toward me, doggie bag in hand. She'd bring me cakes, pasta, paninis, whatever didn't sell. Her chef always seemed overly optimistic about the fish. People were caring for me and not really questioning what I was doing. The world believes, or needs to believe, that New Yorkers are rude and brusque. They need to believe this because they have seen this version on TV and in the movies. But they've never lived here. Not after a snowstorm or during a fierce rain shower or when you show signs of distress. They did not see our strength when the crazies from the other side of the world flew our planes into our buildings.

17

We are a tribe, us New Yorkers, and we can be as civil as anybody. Sometimes more so.

I lost track of time. It got to the point that when someone would ask me how long I'd been sitting on the steps, I'd just have to shrug. The difference between night and day was a question of light and perception. When I slept, the Man would talk to me in my dreams about things like destiny and loyalty. He told me my loyalty would be rewarded. He told me I was doing the right thing and because of this he would do right by me. During the day I would sometimes see him in the small crowd, watching. He drank coffee out of a Styrofoam cup. He would not sit by me. Not while I was awake.

One night Angie sat down next to me and we talked. She said she was getting worried about me. "This was cute and now I'm not so sure."

"Me neither," I said. "But this is something to do." She touched my forehead. "I'm not sick," I told her, backing away.

"You're not crazy, right?" she asked.

She was persistent. She was being a mother without being my mother. She was relentless with concern. And she asked me more and more questions and finally I wanted them to end. I could only handle one type of oppression at a time. "I haven't thought this through," I said. I may have yelled. "I admit it. And admittedly, this is strange and stupid and completely fucked. It's not normal. Yes. I'm conversing with someone in my head. I don't know why I'm sitting here." And then I was yelling for sure. "I'm waiting for a figment of my imagination to come whisk me away. I don't fucking know anything. Isn't that obvious?"

The stupidity of my situation, the trap I had constructed for myself had become obvious to me. And it did feel oddly like a trap. The Man's gaze was like a cage. Forget the logic argument. I had already changed my mind. The confusion, and anger, that would reign over me for so long had set in like a bad storm. Angie cared.

She had always cared about me. Angie was a road not taken. That's what laziness does to you. It obliterates possibilities.

Angie left me alone and I thought, Great, I was getting real used to her doggie bags, and I realized that I couldn't alienate people by jumping all over them for asking simple questions. I apologized to her the next day and she kept bringing me food, but there was no real conversation after that. She wouldn't soon forgive me. She was the first person I hurt in all of this. This whole mess. This thing that brought me here.

PART TWO

IN A BIG COUNTRY

I walked here.

And here is nowhere even by Montana standards. That's not to be insulting. It's just true. It's not New York. And that's a part of this place's charm. It's a selling point. If the concepts of "somewhere" and "nowhere" are human constructs, or at least must be considered in relation to human activity, then this is, indeed, nowhere. Or irrelevant. We'd be considered off the grid if we didn't have electricity. But the power lines come here. They reach this place, webs to a civilization far beyond. In the literal sense, we are very much on the grid. In many other senses, too.

Here is a luxury guest ranch. A five-star spa. In the midst of sky and mountains playing host to wealthy people with a nostalgia for the Old West that only goes as deep as their rooftop plunge pools. Where just running out to go to the store means hopping in a car, or a pickup truck more like it, and hoping your tank has enough fuel to drive a little while. The idea of walking to anything isn't stupid, it's impractical. There's nowhere to walk to.

I didn't walk *all* the way here from New York. Let's get real.

But I walked *here*.

I spent three days walking here and despite my Grizzly Adams appearance, or maybe because of it, I don't know, and my smell and the dirt on my clothes and my shit-covered hair and even though I admitted to walking here, which should have made someone nervous, I managed to talk myself into a job in the kitchen. I found myself a simple job. Peeling. Apples, potatoes, onions, carrots. Edible flora that need peeling. That was my job.

And they gave me a room, next to the bathroom, in a long stainless steel tube full of identical rooms. A trailer of sorts, standing on concrete pillars. And here, the kitchen and waitstaff sleep and fuck and drink and write bad poems and play music and fight and huddle to stay warm during summer nights that always seem to threaten winter. I'm told I'll be receiving new accommodations soon. We've all been told that. We're overcrowded. The difference in the amount of space between the outside and the inside is a kind of cruel irony. Though no one seems to mind. Because there is, here, a general kind of happiness, an odd feeling of being separate from the world's troubles. Of simplicity. Listening to the sounds emanating from the three staff trailers at night is to acknowledge an odd kind of joy. Of freedom.

Not that I felt that joy immediately. I ignored everyone my first few days and nights here, ignored the obvious questions ("So where'd you walk from?"), not talking, not making eye contact, peeling my apples and carrots, eating a lot of fruit and vegetables, taking one shower after the other. Like I was trying to shed my skin. That's what someone said. Had I been more social then I would have told them I was just trying to get clean. I was obsessed by the thought that I was dirty. I couldn't get clean enough. I had much to erase.

When I got here, I would lie in bed in my narrow room, feet propped up on the faux-wood paneled walls, thinking about things like: God. The nature of dreams. The unconscious. The idea of the vision. Immutable things. How could I speak to strangers with these kinds of thoughts and not make them recoil? I was a freak. Self-aware, perhaps, but a freak nonetheless.

I didn't choose this place. Finding it was like stumbling upon a hundred dollar bill. Or, better, winning the lottery. I was anonymous here, just as the land was anonymous to me. So before I became social, I had to do some thinking. Absorb the realities of my life. Assimilate some facts. And then I would go out, smile, be social. Sell myself.

And confront my own happiness. This was something I felt here quickly and it surprised me. My anonymity was reassuring. I smiled. I was a loner who didn't speak to anyone and smiled for no reason. And yet they let me stay.

My station here afforded me a freedom that was hard to describe. After months of living before the world, of scrutiny, of feeling *owned* by others, of being both a construct and a victim of the media, of suffering under the tyranny of something I still have trouble defining, anonymity was like a gift, a return to being me. The joy of being ignored was a joy I had never even imagined. It was a green light to get on with my life, to live again and write new endings to stories unknown.

It wasn't as if these people didn't have access to my story. There were, there are, televisions here. The ranch is hooked up to satellite television. The place is wired. There's Wi-Fi. The media reaches here. It comes in. This place isn't disconnected from the world in that sense. The only thing lacking is standard cell phone reception and they have built this into the PR as a way of selling the place, a "stress-free" environment where the real world need not intrude. Given its proximity to nothing but mountains and tall grass, I imagine the ranch will be "stress-free" for quite a while yet.

I arrived here feeling like a failure. Worse, I felt a comic failure. And I asked myself, got bogged down by this question: is comic failure the true definition of tragedy?

Because I had let people down. People I knew and didn't know. I had disappointed my family. I had spent a summer running toward something but also from something and I had strung the world along. Through no fault of my own. I want to be clear. I didn't ask for the attention. But there are people wandering around, perhaps even close to this place, and I am a possible enabler to their disappointment. This was a fear. Now, after some thought, it's just a worry. A worry I can handle.

And once my fears became worries, once I had started to let things go, I started to socialize. Because I realized, finally, something about happiness. I understood parts of the equation that make up our lives. That freedom from worry, from trepidation, from want, equals happiness. It sounds silly to say, but I had not been a happy man. Only now do I realize how unhappy I was. With the discovery of my happiness, I greeted my coworkers. I became flirtatious. When my fears became mere worries, I began to feel human again. I began to speak. I began to trust people again.

And so this place, the ridiculousness of it, works for me. The Big K Ranch and Spa. Thirty-four rooms, each with a plasma screen TV, stocked minibar, Swiss shower, Jacuzzi, plunge pool, fireplace. Horseback riding, hikes, yoga, full spa with aroma and massotherapy. A lecture series with a guest speaker list that reads like the media guide to a big city PBS station. The head chef published a well-received cookbook. This is the kind of place that generates buzz thousands of miles away. It is a literal oasis, an artfully contrived piece of luxury surround by nothing more than earth and sky.

Guests receive a Stetson upon arrival. Reservations include questions about hat size. The Stetsons are custom-made in Helena. Guests tend to leave with a lighter wallet but buttery skin and a moderately optimistic outlook on life.

I like the idea of optimism.

My most superficial worry, right now, is winter. I've heard about the winters here, about how the wind runs down from the Arctic like a rabid wolf, about how people have lost the use of their facial muscles because they were outside for twenty minutes. I've heard that sometimes it snows here in the middle of August, something I don't want to believe.

And I'm worried about winter because I can't imagine I'm going to leave. And this worry was, is, annoying. How can I assimilate the past if I'm worried about the future? About the weather? This is trivial, isn't it? Had I come all this way to worry about trivia? I had been trivia. I knew from trivia. I already know that I'm going to end up as an answer to some incredibly snarky comments on late night television. Maybe it's happened already. I'm OK with that. A legacy is a legacy. We can't control our stories. No matter how hard we try.

I need to get on with my life. I think I am. This is what I'm thinking: I've decided to be optimistic. And this place breeds optimism. There's something very American about it.

When the sun sets over the mountains, the sky becomes a royal shade of purple. And then the sky turns pink. And the sun is transformed into a dazzling orange producing the sweetest juice. And then the light that covers the peaks is like hearing last call when you haven't had time to finish your first beer. And finally, as the disappointment dies away, you find yourself inside an all-encompassing darkness. Movie theater dark. In every direction the horizon is nothing but a rumor, an imagined place where the dark land meets the dark sky.

You realize how threatening the darkness can be, especially if you've come from the city.

And then suddenly you notice the stars, and the amount of them is enough to make you feel the weight of the universe, the insignificance people have felt since people could think about these things. The horizon is transformed once again and becomes a shadowy line between the star-filled sky and the dark, empty land and you realize it is the sky that looks full of life, full of stuff, in a way so beautiful that it hides its true nature from us, hides the fact that one day the sky will explode and swallow the earth.

This is our setting and it's enough to leave you hurting to breathe. It is a setting where any human emotion has to be understood in the context of the grandeur of the place.

In the city, one never notices the stars. Or the sky. You just don't look. The landscape is not dependent on looking up past the ends of the skyscrapers. In New York, the sky has been obliterated and you don't even notice that it's gone. There's nothing to see.

When I was a kid, we were close enough to New York's electric glow that the sky never really turned black. It was the color of electricity, of a far-off light. And then here, I finally noticed how big it is.

The property sits on one hundred and fifty acres surrounded by grasslands that take you right to the mountains, one of those spots that makes you feel special and lucky and small all at once. It is primitive and primordial and the dichotomy created by the luxury of the place is the point of the whole enterprise.

That's what they're selling. The specialness of being human. Even here.

Thirty-four guesthouses surround a central lodge done up in timbers and whitewash. Inside the lodge, another six suites, two dining rooms, a bar, the administrative offices, a small staff lounge. A library with a fireplace. Off the north end of the lodge, a large barn houses the ranch's horses and behind them, the workers' quarters. One hundred and fifty of us work here.

South of the lodge, between the main gate and the first of the guesthouses, the spa, a large two-story adobe structure with lap pools on the roof. Behind the spa, a fifty-meter outdoor pool. There's another one inside the spa. Further south, five private tents, the most luxurious accommodations on the property. King size beds, claw foot bathtubs, mahogany dressers, dining tables.

No televisions. No stereos. All covered in cream-colored canvas. Personal butler. And behind each tent, surrounded by brush for privacy, open-air showers, a Jacuzzi for two, and a common sitting area where "campers" can enjoy an end-of-day cocktail and munch on popcorn with truffle butter. And off in all directions, but mostly heading toward the mountains, trails leave the ranch like the arms of octopi. Jogging trails, horse trails, hiking trails. One for ATVs. The horses hate the sound of those and a debate has raged about eliminating them. The Japanese love off-roading. They can't get enough of the ATVs. It is part of the irony of this place, the silliness of building a brand and then tearing it down all at once. It is conforming to people's expectations and not the other way around. The brand is confused and so the offer to the customer is as well. Even with the economy in the tank in so many places, the people come. The ranch does well. There's an endless desire for what this place offers. The nightly rates can top $1,000 during the summer. The tents start at $5,000 a night. But now that I've been here a while, I can see it could be more.

Sitting by a campfire near the trailers, you can hear the horses if the wind is blowing right. The breeze is a constant here. It never stops. And I wonder how far the breeze has had to travel. How much further does a wind travel before it lies down in some field to die? Where must it go, what force must it meet, to die? Does it die gently? Or is it eternal? Does my breath end up somewhere, up in the jet stream, to become the eternal wind?

I have taken to whistling. Especially in the darkness. I walk back to the trailer at night and I whistle. If only to confirm my existence.

OH MR. POSTMAN

And then a few days later, a sad, tired-looking guy with droopy eyes from one of the papers came and sat next to me and started asking questions. He carried a pen and notepad, which I found quaint. He also had a laptop, a digital recorder, and a leather pencil case, all in a cheap nylon backpack. His hair was short, the sides speckled with gray. He was from the *Post*, which didn't seem surprising. His name was Dan Fontana, the name of some eponymous character from an old cop show, I thought. But he was media. And I was wary. "How'd you find out about me?" I asked.

Before she'd stopped talking to me, Angie had predicted I would become a celebrity if I kept the wait up and now here was someone from the media, ready to write my story, the first act in the making of celebrity. The *Post* is as good and legitimate a place as any to start this kind of ascent. I knew how this worked. A newspaper story. A blog. Something shared on social media. A few links. Another newspaper. The battle between old and new media. I looked at Dan looking old, a representative of the dying breaths of an industry, perhaps, and I saw the future.

"My brother told me about you," he said. "He owns the pizza shop on the corner."

I had been sending the kids to the corner to buy me slices when the Tupperware mothers were not forthcoming with tastier fare. So at least once a day the kids were buying me slices, and the pizza man had tipped off Dan. That the pizza man's brother was a reporter for the *Post* was beyond humor. The pizza was bad. Just another block away, the pies were made with love. But it was too far for the kids. Because kids are lazy. And to them there is no such thing as bad pizza.

Dan looked like a reporter; his suit was rumpled and creased and pinched at the shoulders. His tie was crooked, as if he'd just taken it out of his pocket and rushed to put it on because of some old-fashioned sense of what looked professional. His shirt wore the morning's coffee. His shoes, however, were spotless. Brown brogues. With an elegant heel and toes that just stopped short of pointy. He was a shoe man. The spotless shoes spoke of a culture behind the facade of the rumpled suit. And of someone not necessarily in the *Post*'s target demographic. Of cultivation. A desire. I understood desire. As any woman will admit, you can tell a lot about a guy by the state of his shoes. Dan's life suddenly interested me. "I'm curious," I said. "I'm curious how it is that you became a journalist and your brother became a pizza man."

Asking reporters personal questions renders their lives strangely meaningless. I've always felt this. Once, when I was a kid, I ran after a mailman and asked him for a stamp. And then laughed. And the face he made was what I was seeing now. Dan's face turned sour. Whether or not he was interested in me then, I don't know. I think I threw his world off balance. Just by asking a question. "How do you mean?" he asked.

I shrugged. "Your brother bought that place, what, seven years ago?"

"He bought it from our uncle," Dan said and I immediately knew that he meant Sal, the man who could make a decent calzone, unlike his nephew, Dan's brother, who put shit for all anyone knew into his calzones. Students bought his calzones. Crackheads when we had them. You drink seven beers and his calzones start to taste decent. Tourists who think everything they eat in New York is superior to what they can get back home order his calzones. I can imagine some out-of-date guidebook wrote them up. There was a time when the eating options in this neighborhood weren't so varied. That's not true anymore. The only culinary limitations now are those imposed by your wallet. The neighborhood has seen glass boxes come. There are now fake speakeasies hosting theme nights centered around, say, flavored gin. There's a hotel down the street and it attracts a lot of Brits with messy hair and Germans in linen suits. This neighborhood got built up and people could keep wearing their aviator sunglasses because they were suddenly cool. Dan's brother was a reminder of what the neighborhood used to be, of the fabric stores and machine parts wholesalers and greeting card shops. Dusty places that had endured and sold goods and services to a local clientele. I could remember rusted out cars here, not so much parked as dumped, used as hiding spots for paper thin guys, feral and wired, selling low-grade dope. That's the feeling you get eating that pizza. I don't miss the grit of the old neighborhood. I like the fact that leggy blond models from Brazil are eating sushi a block away.

"So the joint's a family business?" I asked.

It was early in the morning and Dan needed more coffee. And now he was going to have to go through his family history to get a lousy story out of me. In my boredom, I sensed in Dan an unexpected source of entertainment. Who was it that said comedy was tragedy that happened to someone else? "You could say that," he said.

"And it didn't interest you?" I asked. He wanted to close his notepad, I could tell, but he didn't and that, too, changed my story forever.

"It was my uncle's," he said. "He was closer to my brother." Dan had the air of having lost the battle. I was a two-paragraph story buried between car and futon ads somewhere near the obituaries and this was going to be work.

"And what about your father?"

Dan tapped his pen on his notepad. He sighed. "He's in the mining business."

"Mining?" I said, impressed by the word's implication of wealth.

He could see where this was going. And I saw the Man across the street. He was doing a crossword puzzle and sipping a coffee. "We lived in a good neighborhood if that's what you mean," he said. And I could tell he was a New Yorker, too. He had that air. And so I saw him somewhere, perhaps not Manhattan, but Brooklyn maybe, growing up surrounded by more people like him, like his father, in a solidly upper middle class milieu.

"What kind of mining?"

Dan exhaled. "He didn't actually dig."

"Gold?" I asked.

"Something weird. Like molybdenite. It's an ore. Tungsten. Stuff like that."

"I've never heard of it," I said.

Dan put the recorder in the backpack. "He used to go to Utah a lot when I was a boy. But he had an office not far from here." He pointed north. Which meant the office could have been anywhere.

"What's it for?"

And at that, his gaze bore into mine and he lost his patience. He cleared his throat. "I came here to interview you."

"I heard you," I said. The Man walked across the street to the sidewalk before us. He was going to listen. As if he couldn't already. "Your family situation seems interesting. Two brothers, two wildly divergent career choices. I'm not a philosophical person, but I have time now. There's something to be said for things like fate."

Dan opened his notepad. "Mind if I take notes while we talk?"

"I keep thinking what would have happened if I were, say, a garbage man," I said. And this was true. I was wondering if I would have had the dreams, if I had listened to the Man, had my situation been different. Were my dreams some kind of odd bourgeois affectation? As an ad person, was I chosen because I could sell this?

"What do you do?" Dan asked, trying to steer me toward a quote or two he could use in the article. Trying to do his job.

"Do you think you can convince your brother to give me free pizza while I wait?" I asked. This was shameless, but I was being rational. The more I got for free, the less I would worry about not working. I needed sponsors. I needed the business community to look after my costs. I had no income. And I wasn't getting up to walk to the bank. The thought of not receiving a paycheck gave me a scare. What if I ran out of money? What if I had to call this off because of *economics*? The Man took another sip of his coffee. He looked ready to whistle. "Because if I can get free pizza once in a while, then I can do this for as long as it takes. Neighbors keep giving me free food." I pointed to the small pile of empty multicolored Tupperware next to me. "And I appreciate that. It's the kindness of strangers thing. But moneywise . . . I don't want to touch the investments, the savings. I've never been good at saving and I finally have something put away and, sure, I got hammered, everyone did, and my lack of urgency about this before is finally going to screw me." I laughed. "My parents will kill me if they read that." They saved and cut coupons and treated anything that was "on sale" with the formality of a military funeral. They bought a house in Jersey and my father started his own business and they succeeded. Their story is why millions still want to come here and are willing to die to do it. "I don't care what you write. Really. I make, or made, a very good living, but I'm young. Sort of. Thirty-something's the new twenty-something, right? So I'm in my mid-twenties given that calculation. I haven't always been smart with money. And I guess that doesn't make me all that different from anyone. I don't think I'm old enough to worry about the future." I paused. "Which obviously isn't true."

"What are you waiting for?" Dan asked.

And with this, the Man leaned in. It's annoying, I thought. And I'm sure he heard me. How could he not?

"Isn't this fucked?" I said. I pointed to our audience, to the kids, to the old men coolly leaning over, trying to pretend they weren't listening. Was the Man old? Did he have an age at all? "You should talk to them. They know the story. If you're looking for action, you've come to the wrong place."

"I'll talk to my brother if you help me out here," Dan said. "I need to get something out of you and then I need to be at City Hall. I figure you're a few stories, depending on how long you end up doing whatever it is you're doing. So what if I can get you the pizza? What do I get?" I knew it would come to this. Despite our systems and Adam Smith and supply and demand and the rest of it, life is really about barter. Back scratching. Lice picking. Grooming.

I told Dan about the dream. I described the Man to him. I felt oddly self-conscious talking about the Man while he stood a few feet away from me. I told Dan about the floating. I told him about my job, some of the campaigns I had worked on. He told me he hated the Berlin campaign but congratulated me for it. I told me I liked to drink bourbon, which wasn't true, it wasn't my go-to drink, but it made me seem more interesting. I told him I loved Italian food but that his brother's calzone should be sent somewhere and burned. Dan agreed with me. And I told him that he could ask all the questions he could think up, but nothing would explain what I was doing. "It's not in the realm of explanations," I said.

"I think there's more to you than you realize," he told me when he had stopped scribbling in his notepad.

"Don't flatter me," I said. "I flatter people for a living. I dream up elaborate methods in the delivery of flattery."

He smiled for the first time since he introduced himself. He saw something. That I might play along. "I'm just trying to write a story here." He stood up and put his notepad away. "A small story. I'll go talk to my brother. If he gives you the pizza, what do I get?"

"Unfettered access," I said. "And your brother gets free advertising."

And I think that's when Dan realized that I inhabited the same kind of mind-set; that I saw his paper as just another piece, a prop in the play that was being performed in the city every day, that we were all a part of, in the country, the world, for our own amusement and collective sanity. Or insanity. This was how the world worked. Barter.

Dan had heard of me and decided to make some news. I was going to become a newsmaker. And Dan and I were going to be friendly opponents in a friendly game of "fill up the paper, get the advertising, pay, buy a product, make the owners happy, sell more advertising, repeat." Except the advertising wasn't so much there anymore. It was moving. Money was going in different directions, attention was going in different directions. If traditional media had been a dam, with a giant reservoir of ad dollars holed up behind it, well, that dam was broken. Dan was playing for the losing team. And I felt vaguely sorry for him.

This is what I was thinking as I looked into Dan's eyes, at his *understanding*. And my cynicism, which was never far from the surface, came rushing out of me. People in advertising, journalism, and entertainment are the three horsemen of the cynics.

It says much about the state of things when a simple person sitting on his front steps can take a shot at celebrity. But I know I'm being naive here. We are all celebrities now, aren't we? If you're not, something's wrong with you. My boss used to say that. People become famous for getting kicked in the balls and posting the video online. They get famous for singing badly. For fighting with pneumatically breasted Amazons in tank tops. For being so stupid that people wonder if you're smart. People become famous for wanting to become famous. Wanting to become famous used to be an aspiration and now it's a career.

The middle class of fame is everywhere around us. Angie said this. She said this is how people live their lives now, by watching others live it for them. We have become our own entertainment, she said. Instead of fighting it, instead of making something better, all the producers decided to join in. TV gave up. Publishers gave up. They just threw up their hands and said, "We're too lazy." Reality is packaged for us now. Tragedies have their own graphics and music on CNN. We share our bodies now because people like me sold the idea that people like you could end up in porn.

"That's why I love food," Angie had said. "It's not an Italian thing. It's because you can't give up on food." She told me about visiting France and seeing the *Mona Lisa* at the Louvre. An old man pushed his way next to her and videotaped the painting. And after ten seconds he stopped and pushed his way to the next painting and videotaped that. He was going to videotape the entire museum and watch it on TV back home. Then it would become real. And then she showed me an app for the Louvre on her phone. "He didn't even have to go," she said.

Angie stopped bringing pastas or seafood. Her deliveries evolved into pastry. The tiramisu at her restaurant was light and floated on the palate. It was a wonder of the baker's art. Also, she said the sugars would warm me up at night. And Dan got me the pizza deal.

Meaning very quickly, my diet had become Italian. All I was missing was the wine. I'm waiting for a black man to tell me something I think is important on the steps to my apartment amidst the glass and concrete of the city's fastest-changing neighborhood and I'm eating Italian exclusively. Chinatown wasn't too far from here. A quick jog. Some salt and pepper squid, some slippery sui mai to slide down my throat? Some Singapore noodles or a ma po tofu? Where were the Hispanic ladies? A few pupusas, an enchilada or two, some arroz con pollo. Or how about some corned beef from the deli up the street? Where were the others? A nice Catalan tapas place had opened up close by. There were more sushi places than fish in the ocean. Two Southern barbecues. A gourmet burger joint. Why had only the Italians taken me to heart? And why weren't they giving me anything healthy? Like a salad. Even a creamy Caesar would have been a welcome break. Just sitting there, I could feel my midsection expand. Those years of caring about my looks, the tread-mill at the gym, gone. I was eating a lot of melted cheese.

The deal with Dan and his brother was simple. It was a commercial transaction in the truest, most ancient sense. Dan would return to ask questions until this played itself out. Those were the words he used. And I would have to mention the free pizza. That was it. He would keep tabs on me until something happened. He said I would get mentioned in the *Post* every day until the editors got bored with me. There would be nothing big, a few hundred words, a photo if events warranted, and I would always mention the pizza and the pizza would never get edited out. Perhaps if something interesting happened, he would run an expanded version on the website.

The next day, the paper came out and the crowd grew larger. Mostly locals still, but the radius of the neighborhood seemed to grow. People who lived blocks away were claiming the street as part of their neighborhood. I think they figured that locals don't gawk. You're only a gawker if you're from somewhere else.

The police came by; they figured a crowd meant trouble. I finally told them what I was doing and their confusion was priceless. They had terrorist plots to thwart, murders to solve, chaos to reign in. I assured them I wasn't crazy. Dan even tried explaining the situation. Cops may be the only constituency that takes the *Post* seriously, I've realized.

And for the first time while sitting on the stairs, I developed a sense of worry. I worried that this ridiculous attention would drive the Man away. That he would be scared off. But he remained. Hovering on the edge of the growing crowd. Sometimes, I could only smell him, and I knew he was out there.

But the dreams. They entered my sleeping brain with more promises, all with the same meaning: he would make things better. He emphasized that all the time. And he said this in such a seductive, convincing way that he had me. And he would tell me this in a new place every time. Sitting on the branch of a tree in a silent forest. On a sundeck atop a tall building. Riding a Ferris wheel. I bought the promise. I saw in his message my own improvement. He had created a need I didn't know I had. I was willing to wait to see what he was selling. I was willing to make a purchase from the Man. I was willing.

PIGS ON THE WING

I work in the kitchen. This is what I could manage when I found myself here. That I was employed at all was like some kind of magic. Someone had recently left. I showed up at the right time.

I work in a corner of a large showroom-type space that shines in brushed aluminum perfection. It's a TV kitchen, the kind you might see while zoning out on your couch and say, "I want." It is airy, and the staff—all twenty of us—is never in danger of getting in each other's way.

The kitchen is one of the most obvious clues to me that the idea of roughing it at the ranch is nothing more than a sales pitch. The concrete floors, the high tech ovens, the copper pots—everything shines. An army of ladies cleans the space between meals.

Here is the rugged freedom the West represents. The outside is Ralph Lauren country. The bedrooms are Laura Ashley with subtle Philippe Starck undertones. The kitchen is Martha Stewart but a bit more antiseptic. The influences seem obvious to me.

I spend my days peeling carrots and potatoes, apples and kiwis, in a blank death-mask state, a strange Zen state. One of the sous-chefs keeps inviting me to a regular poker game the staff set up in the main dining room late at night. So far, I have refused. I've never been a big card player. I ignore the joking and laughing coming from the "pigs" as we call them, the lowest of the low in here. The "dish pigs," for whatever reason, work in another room, something that doesn't seem so feng shui to me, meaning we also have "runners" hauling dirty dishes from the busboys and then hauling clean dishes back to the kitchen. The housecleaning staff are called "suck ups" and they are either Hispanic or Native. They hang out with the stable hands and wranglers who, of course, actually like horses and don't mind cleaning up after them. The ultimate act of love is cleaning up after the object of your affection.

In the trailer, our cubicle-like rooms come with a bed, wooden shelves halfway up the walls, and a closet. Each trailer has forty cubicles, twenty on each side of a dark narrow corridor. There are two trailers, set up at right angles. Forty people share six toilets and four showers and with these basics we are expected to remain clean. And presentable. I've heard that during the winter you can see your breath inside.

My cubicle is the last one before the washrooms. To go to work, I have to walk the length of the trailer to the other end, something I'm sure is not to code. During the long walk, I look out for people entering the trailer, because it's impossible to pass another person in a walkway obviously designed for small animals. Pigs, maybe. Because I am at one end of the trailer, my cubicle has two windows. The person I replaced had been here for years and I accepted the inheritance of someone I had never met. My room, then, is a luxury. This has the potential of making me popular.

We eat after the guests have left the Mess Hall—that's the reverse pretentious name for the restaurant—usually around ten. I have been told that the time depends entirely on the number of Europeans staying with us. By eleven, the guests are usually asleep. After a day of riding and roping, hiking, biking, rock climbing (which I don't get—why come to a ranch and go *rock* climbing?), or massages and mud baths and acupuncture and facials and yoga, of listening to seminars by famous motivational speakers, a late night doesn't make sense. Not when the morning bell rings at seven. They still have a morning bell. Another bit of authenticity that is rendered facile the moment a guest receives their breakfast with choice of newspaper before rushing off to yet another session with our Ashtanga-certified instructor. And after paying so much to come here, to miss something because you're tired doesn't seem economical. No one comes here to relax. One guest told me he would sleep after his vacation; he was here to enjoy himself. Experiencing new things is its own form of currency.

This place is a case study in the successful world's work ethic. In rules that have flown right over my head. Perhaps not the rules, but the code. The system is written in code. Whatever system one must live by to make a good living, to earn enough to come to a place like this, is a system I don't understand at the DNA level. I do get it, I know of it, but it doesn't come naturally. The hard work that elevated my parents, the incessant toil that builds places like New York, the round-the-clock activities of the world, its scale, the amount of commerce that is the result of a constant and ceaseless effort, is all amazing, frightening, and, ultimately, tiring. It made me tired. It started to seem pointless. I can see that. Now I can. But I also see the point. The code, finally, has a point, regardless of how silly it might be. Rules are rules. Only the lucky can be smart enough, or rich enough, to avoid playing by them. What was the economic meltdown but a large group of people fudging the rules? It was as if we had all lost the playbook, the keys that unlock the world's riches. All of us grapple with the book, searching for a nugget we can understand.

This may be why I've got my poker face on. The image of me, a man lost in a world he doesn't understand, an outsider, appeals to me. It keeps me out of the center of anything. The center is also, ultimately, tiring.

I'm happy. But I don't know that I'm ready to share that happiness. I'm getting used to the idea of it myself.

I also know this: I won't be able to keep it up. Being out here alone is hard. If it's easy to feel lonely anywhere, and it is, it's especially easy to feel lonely here. I don't want that. I want to feel a part of something larger. Something collective. I want to belong. I want a tribe. I may need to be alone right now, but when I start feeling lonely, I will nudge myself closer to my surroundings. And share the knowledge I have earned.

LET'S DANCE

Dan stopped by every few hours, and within days the charade that was our interviews had ended. "I now understand the decline of the newspaper business," I said.

"There are plans," he said.

"Say that with a German accent and you'll sound sinister," I joked. And he didn't find it funny. "I need to laugh more than ever," I said. "Please see the humor in this."

"I've been thinking about electronic media," Dan said. "This thing has traction."

"I said humor," I huffed. "Not the internet. What about T-shirts?"

"I'm going to start a blog," he announced. "Get some webcams set up. Start up a Facebook fan page, maybe."

"The world has enough stuff," I said.

"Perhaps you should, too." When Dan had an idea, he was deaf to my voice.

"That renders you obsolete. I go new-and-improved and your old-fashioned print goes further along the path of obsolescence." I was surprised he hadn't brought up these possibilities before. Or that he hadn't gone ahead and done it. Who asks permission anymore? The internet means everything is fair game, whether or not the game is fair.

"There's one website devoted to you," he said. "That I've found."

"Only one?" I asked. This information was both surprising and disappointing. "Turn me into a meme, Dan."

"You show up on many sites. But only one devoted entirely to you. It's someone out there." He pointed to the crowd, scanning them. The Man came and went. I imagined him trying out the new Korean BBQ two blocks over.

"Maybe you need to surround me with kittens," I said.

"My feeling is it's just the beginning," he said. "Look in front of you. Traction."

"Or with kittens strapped to the backs of puppies. And the kittens are wearing pearls."

The crowd kept growing, day by day. Some would come with the *Post* in hand. Dan told me he'd done an interview with a blogger covering New York media, a niche that must have been overcrowded and incestuous and boring, a kind of closed loop of friends dishing on friends. But the media thrive on trivia. Or stupid. Sooner or later, this story had a bull's-eye on it. Dan knew it, too. He used the word "traction," but he could have said it's "dumb enough."

Most nights, as I slept on the steps, the Man would enter my dreams. He would ride his white horse down the street smiling, waving his big floppy hat. Or he would strut toward me and pat me on the head, paternally, whispering, *You've been very good*, or something like, *Don't worry, I'm always watching*. Our talks involved a lot of movement. We walked. There was a TV quality to my dreams because of the movement. He spoke slowly and I spoke quickly, as if there were a time limit on my dreams. And there was. Because I would always wake up.

The women of the neighborhood continued to leave their leftovers with me, their Tupperware containers stacked neatly at my feet in the colors of the flags at a Gay Pride parade. The old men stood in front of the steps drinking their coffees, discussing me, politics, the Yankees, the miseries of the Jets, Giants, Knicks, Rangers, Mets, take your pick. Memory unites people in this town and not much else. Loyalties centered on shared conversation. The city is a collective conversation about briefly shared moments. Because it is otherwise constantly changing. My block was a prime example.

We'd gone from rusted out cars to valet parking. From the desperation of crack to the joyless happiness of ecstasy. From bodegas and thrift shops and restaurant supply stores to Scandinavian furniture and fine patisserie. From burnt-out hulls to boutique hotels and investment-grade condos and starchitects and hipsters and cocktail lounges. And my own rising fortunes had mirrored this. Each step in this street's evolution. That I could still afford to live here was perfectly in keeping with the mobility this city offers to a certain type. I'm in the middle space of that Venn diagram between Knowledge Class and Creative Class. That's the kind of working person that can afford this place, barely, even though most have decamped to Brooklyn or even Queens, or for those with kids, to New Jersey. Back to raise more kids like me.

I had a colleague who commuted from Philadelphia.

The other occupants in my building had turned over more than once. Except Angie. Her father owned four restaurants. Plus real estate on Long Island. She was set.

Dan had given me a special "free pizza" pass that looked like a get out of jail free card. It had the cheap look and feel of something done in haste and without much planning. I was told to hold it up if any media ever came by. The newspaper had not yet photographed me. Photos had appeared, but they had been taken from the crowd, anonymously.

Dan asked me, "What do you hope comes of this?"

I didn't have an answer. How could I? "Sometimes I wonder what it is I can see that others can't. In advertising, you're privy to information about consumer behavior, about desires that aren't apparent to most people. But this information is useless to me here. I can tell you you'll probably buy a yellow tie next year. But it doesn't advance your life or mine. You'll buy a tie anyway. I just might know the color or the width or the pattern in advance. I might know where you're going to buy it. Or who's going to make it. Well, so what? I've been sitting here over a week and I'm starting to ask myself what makes me so special. And I'm also thinking who is this African American man in my dreams."

"Do you have anything against black people?" Dan asked, scribbling in his notepad, fishing for an angle, for something to make this ordeal more than it was.

I laughed. "That's pathetic," I said. "You know this and yet you still ask the question. It's not worth it. I have nothing against anyone."

"I'm trying to find the same thing you are," Dan said. "Except this is all going on in your head, so I have to probe. You only let things out on your terms. I respect that. This is a private matter that's become public. I don't have the arrogance to doubt the veracity of your dreams, so if you're having these visions, if the man in these visions is a powerful enough force to make you quit a pretty good job and sit out here like a fool and wait for him, and if you're not even sure who this man is, then I share your questions. Namely, who is this man and why did he pick you?"

Had I officially quit my job? I hadn't done anything officially. "And why did you pick me, Dan?" I asked. "Why do you persist with this story? How far can you take the advertising angle? There's a nice brotherly love angle to this. It feels like it could be a sitcom. Not a good one, but still."

"Your story is different," Dan said. "Anything that's different is newsworthy. That's true everywhere, but it's truer in this city. Especially now. People get tired hearing about crime. Even though it's down, even though TV is full of crime, it's true. It's OK to watch *Law & Order* but in the end, the bad guys always win, right? And people don't really like politics. People are angry out there, sure, but they don't know what they're angry about. Or the budget. The budget hurts people. But their eyes glaze over. And whatever happens in the rest of the world isn't local. Even the UN isn't local. Entertainment is digestible news. Non-threatening. And I won't deny the competition to get a story and make it yours, ours, is intense. Some people say we're losing. The newspeople. Me. Maybe we are. But that means I have to work harder." He paused, flipping through the pages of his notepad, until he found whatever scribble he had been looking for. "Right now, sure, you're a harmless eccentric. No one tires of stories like yours. People like you broaden the experience of living here for everyone else. This is human interest without anyone getting hurt. Human interest is everything. You hear the word 'experience' a lot now. What's reality TV but the rest of us living vicariously through the experiences of a few? Even if the experience is contrived and artificial. Everything is porn now, Joe. And for my brother, this is manna from heaven. This is his feel-good story, too."

That Dan understood exactly what he was doing was equal parts depressing and impressive. Every note Dan wrote down, every plan he hatched, every angle, every calculation, said more about his future than mine. He wasn't writing about me. Not really.

"What else do you cover?" I asked. I've always thought the life of a reporter to be dull in a strange, always on the move kind of way. How many ambulances can you chase, how many fires can you describe, how many doughnuts can you eat with a cop? How many times can you write about another senseless crime before it becomes boring? A lot of reporters made their names during and after the attacks, just for being in the proverbial right place at the right time. They lived in a world where they were expected to do their old jobs while navigating new realities. Dan was like a factory worker at the dawn of automation.

"I cover your basic city stories," he said. "Murder, mayhem, gangs, drugs, lost kids, sex clubs, traffic tie-ups, exploding cars." And so he confirmed my impression of him.

"What would you like to cover?" I asked.

"Why is it that you always end up asking more questions than I do?"

"Last question."

He shrugged. "City Hall? I like politics. I'm not sure. I got into this by being curious, by seeing through the sounds bites and the spin, by a genuine interest in the political process and the politicians. I remember thinking someone like Clinton, well he was perfect. We had this smart guy who acted like some Bubba but could out-think anyone. He jogged to McDonald's. And he manipulated the media masterfully. He got in trouble and he got out of trouble. And that's when we kind of lost our respect for the presidency."

Dan closed his notepad. Again, I had defeated his will to work on this stupid story. Because it was stupid. I'm sure he could see that. "I haven't thought about where I'm going. I don't have a map. I sit at a desk and I write these stories and interview people, I run around town, and my days are long and I never stop to think. Sometimes I wonder what it would be like to cover City Hall and then some kid's been thrown out of a window and some Russian's been gunned down in Brighton Beach and it's a week before I think about what I want to do. Same thing. And when I think about shifting gears, or trying to, I don't have the energy. I'm spent. So I'm saying, OK, next week, tomorrow, next year, this summer, I'm going to inquire about making changes, the feasibility of the thing, I'm going to make a list of what needs to get done, I'm going to think about the possibility of this. And then I don't. I don't even make the list."

This is the stuff of our lives. This is the root cause of our collective anger. My job fatigued me. It was an endurance test for the weary. Dan's missive is the rut we all talk about, the hole, the huge soul-sucking hole that buries you and doesn't let you breathe. This is how people end up becoming managers at Arby's. This is how people end up becoming Willy Loman, how people sometimes fall down and suddenly find themselves on the streets. This is why people are pleased to have a regular paycheck while spending their days complaining about their jobs on Twitter. And when your neighbor loses his job, or his house, well, you resent everything even more, because you know you have little right to complain. You feel petty. And you resent that, too.

For over a decade, life seemed to me something other people did. They lived. I watched. The rest of the world was television to me. Things happened to me but did not touch me. I was free from the kiss that life supposedly bestows upon us. What Dan said told me I wasn't different from him, from others, from everyone who had fallen into a rut and wondered how.

Except, of course, I had done something. People talk about not being able to afford the risk of change. What risks did I take really? Is it a risk to leap from the edge of a sidewalk? I couldn't see how falling would hurt so much. Pain was absent from the calculation.

The Man appeared in front of me. He stood between Dan and me and he said, *Let's take a walk.* And I told him I wasn't tired. *Oh, but you are*, the Man said.

"Where do you want to go with this?" Dan asked numbly, a variation on a question he had asked too many times already.

"This is what I'm doing," I said. "You see me doing it. I'm willing to sit and wait and see what happens."

Dan opened his notepad and wrote this down. His lips formed a quick, sad smile. "And what do you eat?" he asked. "What do you eat while you sit here and wait for your man?" He closed his notepad and put it away. He could not look at me, even as he waited for the expected reply.

PART THREE

STARDUST

Money feels irrelevant here at the ranch. To me. It's not, of course; I understand this. The place is premised on the idea of the possibilities afforded by vast sums of it. But for us, our isolation means there's nothing to spend it on but booze and cigarettes. There's an odd lack of commerce here. The ranch is very careful not to mention the price of anything. Even the bath balms from the spa don't carry price tags. Guests don't hand over a credit card upon check-in. Everything is assumed. And that's a sign of wealth, too.

The closest bar is almost an hour away and the employee lounge carries four brands of scotch, some whisky, some bourbon, two types of vodka, and beer. And once a week, one of the delivery guys brings extra beer and we buy it from him. We save a few bucks this way. When the ranch opened, he worked out a deal with the wranglers and the deal has stuck. He's developed quite a side business and though everyone knows about it, there have been no efforts to shut him down. The GM, the owners, they don't care. They aren't making money off the employee bar. And they need our relative happiness.

The delivery guy's name is Ben. He's a giant, close to seven feet, I think, and he supplies us not only with beer but also with dope and whatever chemical is making the rounds. He'd supply cigarettes also but for some reason the canteen sells them for a cheaper price than he can offer. No one asks Ben where he gets his beer or why his prices are so reasonable but I can imagine someone like Ben has things worked out. He never smiles. He's the stereotype of the stony-faced Indian, Mr. Spock with a tan.

Ben is of this land. There is a certain symmetry in this. Giant Ben born under the giant sky. Everything here is so big, the land is so big, the sky is so big, the mountains are so big, it's difficult not to feel that the world is aligned with something positive. People from this place are optimists. It is ingrained and logical. Our country takes its cues from land such as this. The endlessness of everything that surrounds you here creates a mythology that encourages limitlessness. Thoughts of freedom. I can see that. It's difficult to imagine the end of the world here. This is where I can understand the concept of infinity. I may not be from here but I'm not so dumb as to not see the possibilities that a place like this can will into existence.

In Montana, you look up and the stars are there, magically, an insomnia of stars spreading out toward the peaks.

Ben's deliveries are done in a methodical, joyless manner. He projects an image of disdain for the entire operation and, if his merchandise weren't so vital, some would prefer the long drive to the nearest store to having to deal with him. Watching Ben work is to see a man unsuccessfully straddling the line between stoicism and contempt.

In my room in the trailer, I have a bar fridge, left behind by the previous tenant and for which I am grateful. I can stock it with beer and vodka and a carton of cigarettes. I have taken to bringing back fruit salad from the kitchen. It is my regular breakfast now.

In the mornings, I eat some fruit salad, get dressed, walk to the washrooms, and brush my teeth, wash my face, and head off to the kitchen. I share a smoke outside the service door with some of the dish pigs, go inside, pour myself a coffee, and scan the local paper. I never find anything of importance and I derive an odd sense of comfort from this. The news cycle moves on. Its relentless march forward is one reason certain starlets forget their underwear. It's why the world of PR is so big and getting bigger. Why we pay people to manage and massage reality.

And then I get to work.

The head chef is from Chicago. His name is Tomas Hill. His mother was Czech or Slovak. One of the two. He worked his way through some big kitchens in Chicago until he found the backing of investors and opened up a brasserie just north of The Loop. It bombed. And then he did what chefs do when they need to recover from failure: he went overseas and cooked in a hotel. In Singapore. And away from the pressure and a high stakes foodie culture that tolerates greatness and mediocrity but nothing that merely promises greatness, he thrived. His kitchen became renowned, praised by the very critics who had driven him from the country.

In Singapore, he created the kind of cuisine that should have worked in Chicago but didn't. Because it wasn't of the moment. Because food culture in America is about trends and fashions and not really about food. Because in Chicago, it became cool not to like his cooking.

Vindicated, he looked to return home. But bad memories last longer than good ones. Instead, he wound up here, on a ranch near Canada where the wind can blow the smoke of his creations clear to Mexico. And the food critics love him again. Here, he has been elevated to celebrity. Maybe the critics see in his exile something noble. He has published a cookbook. There has been talk of TV, but he's unsure about that kind of work. And he doesn't want to expose himself to the critics in that way again.

His food is very good. He applies his love of brasserie to classic

American cuisine. It works for a place like this and the clientele adore this, though I don't think he's doing the ranch's brand any favors. He probably sells more porterhouse steaks than he'd like to, but as a Chicagoan, he understands the lure of a good piece of meat as well as anyone. He also sells a lot of bison, something that seems to thrill him. We have a herd of bison next door. Tomas is constantly going on about how fresh the bison is. "It's still moving!" he says every day upon examining the meat.

One joke I dislike: his love of clafouti. He hired a French pastry chef just so he could get her clafouti. It's on the menu every night. The Japanese, in particular, think this is perfect. Ranch. Clafouti. Two Japanese obsessions—Americana and a perceived high-end French culture—in one sitting. And clafouti means peeling an inordinate amount of apples. It is a punch line delivered badly. Apple pie makes more sense to me. A pie in these surroundings, perhaps with some homemade ice cream, would taste better here. But there is no pie when there is clafouti. And there is always clafouti. Every day.

And so, today, for reasons I don't quite understand, I tell him what I think. Because I have had enough of peeling these apples. Today. And forever. And I have said maybe two words since I've been here. To anyone. "More clafouti?" I ask.

Tomas walks into the kitchen and washes his hands. He has his apron slung over his shoulder. "Excuse me?" he says, half smiling. I realize he's never heard my voice.

"Why all the clafouti?" I ask.

He takes his apron off his shoulder and puts it on, over his head, adjusting the back. "Do you have a problem with tonight's menu?"

I sigh. Apples surround me. I have a bucket of lemon juice the peeled apples go into to prevent browning. I am surrounded by peels. All of it destined for the compost. "Who comes to Montana to eat clafouti?" I say. "Everything here is about the West or is trying to be. What's clafouti have to do with it?"

"What's Thai massage got to do with it?" Tomas asks, by way of answer. It's a good answer and it tells me that perhaps I should shut up. And I should.

"Clafouti doesn't fit into the brand of this place," I say. I can't help myself. For the first time since my arrival, I'm questioning my station. "It exists outside of it. The clafouti messes up your menu. There are wagon wheels in there," I say pointing in the direction of the dining room. "Your desserts are brilliant. Your tarts. Your cakes."

"They aren't mine," he says.

"Mathilde's," I say. Mathilde is the French pastry chef.

"And I brought her here because she's brilliant."

"Yes," I say.

"And I don't need to explain myself to you."

"No, of course not."

"Not to be rude," he says.

"It's your kitchen," I say. "You're not being rude."

"Whatever I put on the menu is on brand, as you might say."

"I disagree. Respectfully. There's nothing easy about a brand."

"The Japs love the clafouti," he says.

"It's true. But the Japs wouldn't miss it either. And from what I'm told we don't get so many of them anymore." And this is also true. Even the Japanese are having trouble affording the place.

"They've become almost iconic," he says. "The food writers love them. There's a recipe in my book. The recipe's on the website for this place." He finishes tying his apron. "I like them, too," he says. "Mathilde's clafouti reminds me of my mom's tortes." He walks into his office. What is good food but a pleasant memory? I should appreciate my place. A kitchen is a dictatorship. I need to respect that. Or I could find myself wandering again. Or worse, shoveling up after the horses.

BOTH ENDS BURNING

I had short dreams. I wasn't sleeping well. I was on my front steps and I slept about as well as could be expected. Sometimes my dreams ended abruptly. The Man would get up and leave. And when he did, I knew I was awake.

In one dream we're on an airplane. The Man is a flight attendant. Who smells like a clean horse and wears a floppy straw hat. And he comes over to me and hands me a cup of water. *I like you,* he says. And then the seatbelt sign comes on. And the plane rapidly loses altitude.

The story took up more and more space. Literally. The *Post* gave it four hundred words. It was closer to the front, not a column buried with comics and clairvoyants. And because the story was more prominent, better positioned, more people came to watch me, more eyes waiting for the moment. For a climax. For news. I felt as if I should entertain them somehow, sing perhaps, catch a stack of quarters resting on my elbow, something, over and over until they could feel their time had not been wasted. "No news is bad news," a voice called out from the crowd.

"No news is boring," another yelled.

"Bad news is good news," came the reply. And there was applause.

"You're a very odd, very local celebrity to a very small demographic," Dan said, impressed by the growing success of his little story.

"I'm a niche product," I said.

If nothing else, I understood the compulsion of celebrities to punch certain members of the paparazzi. The intrusion is immense. It is an odd thought to know that when you get up and walk into your own apartment because you have to go to the washroom, others are watching, knowing what it is you need to do; some of them imagining it even. I was a story in the paper that could very conveniently be tracked down and verified, an object of curiosity, a noun. I could have been made of wax, really. I was online. I was the object of blogs. I was not a person. There was a temporal quality to me now. I had become an event.

And no one in that crowd, that growing mass, spoke to me. There was little conversation or interaction. This might have made the intrusion feel less invasive. I would have welcomed conversation. Anything. But they couldn't. Speaking to me would have broken the invisible wall between us. It would have confused subject and object, like web-generated translations from German. Instead, every once in a while they shouted something out at me. Or for the benefit of the crowd. And one shout bred more. And then it would die out and you could hear someone's cell phone ring. And someone would comment about that.

I spoke on the phone from time to time. Usually it was with my mother and explaining this to her was almost comical. She wasn't happy. And that got tiresome. And I turned the ringer off. I was afraid of what my father thought. I kept my phone on vibrate. *I like your mother*, the Man said. He was sitting next to me. And then he wasn't.

Dan left and returned an hour later with some pizza and a photographer. He told me the newspaper had been receiving calls. People wanted to see what I looked like. As if they couldn't find an image online. His editors didn't want to lose their lead on me. They clued in to the posting on the internet. That others had gone places they had not. An editor brought up the idea of a photo essay, some kind of day in the life feature. "This is becoming something," Dan said, the proud papa, lording over his strange creation. "A photo essay. A whole page. This brings you to another level."

"Just what I've been begging for," I said.

"And we're talking about the web," he said. "Creating a presence for you. Pushing the story on the web in a meaningful way."

"I'm not keeping a blog," I said.

Dan shrugged and handed me a slice of pizza. "This is Dick." He gestured in the direction of a small, bald, dark-skinned Asian man. His left eye was fused shut, or so it seemed. I imagined him in a war somewhere in southeast Asia. I saw a jungle, rice paddies, water buffalo. "We're just going to take a picture of you, maybe place some of the kids behind you, and you have to hold a slice of pizza. You don't have to eat it if you're not hungry but hold on to it."

I was hungry but biting the pizza for the camera seemed crass. "I thought mentioning the pizza was enough," I said. "What's next, T-shirts?" To me everything in the world that was possible and laudable and not laudable and smart and not smart culminated in a T-shirt.

Dan thought about this, storing the idea.

I could imagine posters and T-shirts and desk calendars. I could see pizza cutters. I could see apps for smartphones. I could imagine it all. My life was unfolding in ways I had never expected. Were the reality TV people far behind? Was there a TV producer lurking amidst the crowd, trying to figure out the angle? I could choose someone to wait with me. I could assemble teams of young blonds to mud wrestle and dive into pools of Jell-O. I could have a theme song.

"We have a deal," Dan said. The cynicism and weariness. The endless pursuit of cheese. The greed of everything we do. Our facility for ignoring what's best for what's . . . not so best.

Dan was sexed by the way this whole thing was unfolding.

I understood that he wanted to see how big this would become. He saw the money. A payoff. I understood this for the first time. Maybe he fell asleep every night humming that imaginary theme song.

You should smile, the Man told me. I resisted the urge to look around. I could smell him.

Dan directed his one-eyed photographer to ensure that the pizza appeared in all the shots and that I held it in such a manner so as to avoid being cropped by the photo editors back at the office. He moved people away to give Dick room to frame his shots properly. "Okay, now," Dick said, his face behind a zoom-lensed black Olympus digital camera. The thing was a monster. With his good eye looking through the lens, the camera became Dick's eyes. Or eye. It was discomfiting to watch his eye-lens face take the pictures. So I decided to look away. If his face weren't so eerie, Dick could make the perfect spokesperson for a camera company: "I lost my eye in a war. But with the Olympus Mega Zoom, it's like having my eye back." Well, that would have been the first draft. The first idea floated in a meeting that would last into the morning and would include copious amounts of beer and takeout. A campaign for something so major would require a lot of billable hours. Research. Phone calls. Walks. More beer. Arguments about things that were way beyond our mandate. Discussions about Plato's Cave. Anti-Semitism in Vichy France. The math on Wilt Chamberlain's claim of bedding 10,000 women. And then the what-ifs: What if we had cameras thousands of years ago? What if the camera had been invented later? What if New York had been founded on Staten Island? Billable hours. Spent arguing about the Mets and how the older guys loved saying "Mookie Wilson" and what is it with that franchise and whether it really is impossible to love the Yankees if you're from anywhere else but here. We would commission research into the history of photography. We would bring in professional photographers to talk about their craft. We would eat a lot of takeout. We would surf porn on the internet. And then we would present our ideas and the client would say, "I want this," and we'd do it and charge for everything.

"This way please," Dick said.

"What's wrong with your eye?" I asked.

Dick looked at Dan, baffled, as if to say, The thing can talk?

"Just take the shot," Dan told him. "He asks lots of questions." He looked at me, exasperated, flushed with energy. "Don't hassle him."

"Is Dick incapable of speaking?" I asked.

"I speak," he said, shooting.

Dan pushed back at the crowd. Their interest in Dick grew. The presence of a professional photographer with an array of lenses added a legitimacy to the proceedings that had been lacking. Anyone can have a decent camera. But Dick was a professional. There were undoubtedly bloggers in the crowd seriously envious while looking forward to putting Dick out of business.

They closed in. "Stay back!" Dan yelled. And the crowd pushed forward.

Dick was struggling to maintain his position. He really was a small man. I saw him as Vietnamese. I always picture the Vietnamese as being a short people. Or at least slight. I don't know if that's true. It may be an impression I have from movies. Or from restaurants.

Dick shot a few more photos. "Okay," he told Dan.

"Take some more," Dan ordered.

You can do it, the Man told me. I've seen your smile.

"Take pictures of us," someone from the crowd shouted. "We've been waiting as long as him. And we're on our feet!" The camera changes us instantly, the belief that being caught on film, or on TV, even in the corner of an image, is our only road to recognition. Validation. To the fleeting immortality that is fame. Old media still owns a legitimacy that new media can not possess.

"We're more interesting than that dumbass!" another voice said.

"And better looking!" added another.

Dan grabbed his photographer by the shoulder just as Dick was shooting another picture. It was like he was being pulled out of the streets during the fall of Saigon or something. Dick protested but within seconds they were gone, their jobs done, and the crowd watched the two of them run to a waiting car, jump in, and drive off.

The buzz of Dick's visit was everywhere. It was a buzz, that's exactly what it sounded like. It was a noise of a hundred discussions. It was the noise of being the only one at a party with no one to speak to, the noise of my invisibility.

In the morning, I was on page four of the *Post*. The photo wasn't large but everyone who read the paper saw it. Page four is not a page most people skip. It implied a kind of prominence. Everyone on the street had copies of the *Post*. Kids came by with it, opened it to page four, and asked me to sign it. I signed T-shirts and ball caps and pieces of torn-up paper and greasy napkins. More people brought me food. An old Japanese lady brought me a wakame salad, which was a godsend. A hot dog vendor set up shop on the sidewalk across the street. A burger truck parked on the block. And then a dumpling truck. I was creating commerce. People were being drawn to me just to take a look. I was a spot to click into on location-based social networks. A new kind of proper noun. People took their own pictures. They brought their kids, posed them in front of me, took a picture, and left. They brought their guitars and sang, their cases open in front for change. I was creating busking opportunities. They came with sandwich boards proclaiming the Second Coming. They came with their sketchbooks to draw. They came selling balloons. Girls started flashing me. Older people brought lawn chairs.

I awaited the arrival of porta-potties.

All of this happened in one day. All of this the result of a photo in a third-rate newspaper. My musings on the death of print had been overblown. I suspected they always had been. The very thing that makes the web so powerful—its democracy—is the same thing that makes people distrustful of it. And so while we bemoan elitism, we want our leaders.

I awaited the tour buses.

And I wondered where were all these people when the story first appeared in the paper. Does anyone read anymore? I had an idea for a newspaper with no writing. Just photos with captions. Take *USA Today* to its logical conclusion.

Dan set up webcams. He brought four. Three were focused on me, one on the crowd. "We're live," he said and beamed. "Like those eagles with chicks." The tap-tap of his laptop was permanent now. He had three smartphones. He had two blogs going: one for the *Post*'s website and one he had created himself. "It's cool with the editors," he said. "They can appreciate the possibilities. They see what I see." Apparently, hits on his *Post* blog were impressive. Photos of me were all over the web now. There were people in the crowd chronicling this. Debates fired up. Dan also had all the social media angles covered. I had a Twitter account that Dan "curated," he said. But everything on it would be stuff I'd said. My Facebook page had almost 10,000 fans. Dan came across one website for agnostics that was running a special series of reports about my meaning. "What *do* you mean?" Dan asked, smiling.

"Agnostics aren't intellectually honest," I said.

I saw the Man eating a hot dog. He waved, shrugging. What was *he* waiting for?

More reporters showed up. *Newsday*. AP. Some radio stations. A British journalist from the BBC. And finally, almost two weeks after I had started waiting for the Man, even the *Times* sent someone. But only for the website, not for the print edition. I wasn't yet fit to print and for that I was thankful. And every reporter who wanted to interview me brought with them a slice of pizza. This was the tragedy. Pizza. Some of it was quite a lot better than Dan's brother's, but the implication, the commentary about me that each and every slice implied, was demoralizing. The medical community says it is healthy to eat fruit and when you ask for an apple, people think you're crazy. I craved an apple. I told people this. Instead, they would hand me another slice of pepperoni, the grease running off the cheese, onto my hands, dripping onto the pavement. My pants especially, were covered in grease stains.

And yet, they still fit. My pants. My shirts felt comfortable. I had put on some weight but not what you'd expect from a diet clogged by pizza. Somehow, this made sense to me: my world had changed and, like some old Tex Avery cartoon, the laws of physics had changed as well. I could get thrown off a cliff and return in the next frame unscathed. That night, I dreamed that the Man gave me an apple. We walked down a path in the middle of a forest. *Get ready*, he said. For what? I asked. And he laughed. *Just be ready*, he said again. And then I was awake.

Dean & DeLuca sent me a box of apples. And they sent out a press release about it. And a PR girl came and instructed me on what to say about the apples—they were organic and came from upstate—and how much this meant to the chain.

And no one asked about the apples.

PAPA'S GOT A BRAND NEW BAG

Tomas loves the Cubs. He grew up in Wrigleyville. And though his father tried to raise him in some kind of Church of Stan Mikita, Tomas was a Cubbie. That's what the staff calls him. He lives a half hour south of the ranch in an old barn he had restored by a local husband and wife architect–interior designer team who have since gone on to host a TV show. They moved to L.A., signed a lucrative deal, and are set to become a ludicrously asexual design empire. Their work is Style for People with No Time. It is a kind of Wonder Bread interior decorating, inoffensive until you know there's more to the world. Tomas is extremely proud of his barn. It's been featured in magazines and coffee table books. And will be on TV soon, he's sure of it.

Every morning, Tomas drives to the ranch in his vintage BMW 700 and that's when our toil kicks in to a higher gear. I work every day from six in the morning to eight at night. Two shifts. Six days a week. I don't plan on peeling fruits and vegetables for the rest of my days. But I don't mind it now. It clears my head. It allows me to think. To understand. To once again become a part of the world.

My work station is small but ergonomic. The place is designed in such a way as to prevent excessive bending. Everything I need is within reach. I fill buckets with peeled fruits and vegetables. Apples. Always apples for the godforsaken clafouti. Bananas. Kiwi. Kumquats. Tomas loves kumquats. Apparently this love is seasonal. Potatoes. So many potatoes. But when he's making his "dirty" mash, my job is to peel the potatoes badly. That is, leave some skin on. Which is what I'm doing.

I hear Tomas walk into the kitchen. Like Norm entering Cheers, his entrance is met with rounds of "Cubbie!" On most days, he walks into his office to change while speaking to the executive chef, an impossibly thin black guy from Phoenix named Carlos. Then the inspections.

Today, he walks over to me. Everyone watches. He stares them down until they return to their tasks. "I've been thinking about the clafouti," he tells me.

I put down a potato. "I didn't mean anything by it."

"I was speaking to Athena last night," he says. This would be our general manager, a Greek woman from Thessaloniki. Her heavy accent, combined with her love of all things western, makes for an eloquent statement about the benefits of globalization. She is tanned and beautiful with a head of thick dirty-blond hair. Light brown eyes offset her honey-colored skin. She favors white cotton shirts and blue jeans. She could be a Ralph Lauren model. Most staff think that she and Tomas are an item.

"She's with you on this stupid anti-clafouti thing," he says. "On our brand." He shrugs at this, as if I'd been a party to some debate and had won. "She knows you have advertising in your background."

"How?" I ask.

"How what?"

"How does she know?"

Tomas shrugs again. This is something I hadn't noticed before. Our chef is a shrugger. He is insecure. Now his shrugging is going to distract me. "I told her."

Had I ever told him? "And I've told you?"

"When you were hired, yes," he says. "You told me. Well, you told Carlos. I think you told Carlos. You even told him some of the specifics. Like that beer. Berlin? That was yours, right?"

I had also told Carlos about the cat food and the diapers. The relevance my past has to peeling apples and potatoes still mystifies me. "Yes," I say. "I'm surprised he told you anything."

"Me, too," he says. He smiles. "Anyhow, you used the word 'brand.' Her ears perked up."

"Lovely," I say. There's too much respect for that word. It has ruined people and products and entire countries and has made a lot of really dumb people very rich. It is a word that has lost meaning. Very few people know what it means, but everyone uses it. The word is the start of every prayer in every agency in the world. Sell the brand, make it indispensible, reap the rewards. Once you have a client talking about brand you know you've won.

"She'd like to have a discussion about this," he says. "Perhaps tomorrow night. In her apartment. The three of us."

He speaks slowly as if in code. For all I know he's just told me we're going to enjoy a threesome in a hot tub.

"About what?" I ask. I'm here peeling the roughage and getting on with my life.

"Everything," Tomas says. "I don't know. I opened my stupid mouth and now she wants to have this meeting and that's all she told me. And if I know her, she's going to talk, we're going to listen, and it will feel long. So OK?"

He walks away, into his office, his den. And then I'm smiling. I'm smiling because I have bested the chef with his girlfriend and the idea is stupid. I'm smiling because of the inanity of my situation, how a few months ago this would have seemed a stranger dream than the ones that got me here. I'm smiling because Yogi Berra might have been right about the fork in the road. Perhaps I won't be peeling potatoes for much longer. Perhaps there's an odd logic to this. Perhaps. I pick up a potato and peel it extra dirty.

WISHFUL THINKING

Dan wanted to give me a cell phone. I already had one and I had shut it off and I said no. "Who refuses a cell phone?" he asked.

"No," I repeated. I found it intrusive, which was silly, I knew that.

Dan's blogs detailed my every breath, trip to the can, sneeze. What is privacy when someone can tell the world how many bites it takes for you to devour a slice of pizza? He told me someone had set up a Tumblr account that showed me eating pizza exclusively. It was timed. There were stats. About me eating pizza. "You're my mouthpiece," I told him.

He said the *Post* was starting to feel a very paternal sense of ownership over me. I understood that. I only had to think of how I felt about Berlin. The beer, not the city. Whenever I saw a poster or a display case or someone drinking one I thought, That's my beer. I helped put that beer into that person's hand. I sold that thing. I sold this idea. I crafted desire in a stranger. I had a dumb idea that was quite brilliant. We went to Berlin, the city, just to get a photo op for Berlin, the beer. The Germans were flabbergasted by the chutzpah of the thing. I couldn't tell if it made them more or less anti-American. So I understood the *Post*'s thinking. It terrified me. "I can stop this right now," I said.

I heard someone in the crowd laugh, and I was pretty sure it was the Man.

Dan typed this into his laptop. "No, you can't," he said. He didn't even look up from his keyboard.

The crowd was reaching tremendous proportions. The block had filled in with bystanders and media and commerce. A group of people awaiting a spectacle. The cops had closed off the street now during the days. They even threatened to arrest me for causing a disturbance and were chased away.

The Man walked up to me and said, *I like that this is bothering you.* And then he disappeared into the crowd.

My wait was being seen in a theological light. This was perhaps inevitable. Every day another priest, father, rabbi, nun, saffron-robed Buddhist monk, mufti, you name it, every day more of them showed up to catch a glimpse of the guy who had acted on a vision, and they would try to articulate for me what I had seen. According to their beliefs. I had never uttered the word "God" in any of the interviews I had granted and yet the religious somehow knew who the Man was. It is this certainty that has always annoyed me about the religious. Even the Man's horse was significant, an object of debate. A horse showed up in much of the world's mythologies apparently.

There were theological precedents to my actions. I was told how often something like this had happened in the past, how adherents were gathered through the actions of others. A philosophy student from NYU, who also happened to be a practicing Hindu, brought me up on Plato, the Aristotelians, the Academy. I heard about Chinese monks and Buddhist sages and Jewish mystics and Christian thinkers. A priest from Baltimore told me there's no Christ without Paul. And then he looked at Dan. And Dan may have blushed.

The Hare Krishnas were in the crowd.

Evangelicals. Fundamentalists of all stripes. Colonies of Hasidic men, praying, bowing so quickly they resembled those drunken dunking bird toys from the seventies. The amount of prayer around me was startling. Dan said the paper had received inquiries from the Archbishop.

"Of what?" I asked dumbly and Dan didn't answer.

The Man came and sat next to me then. *Don't look for love*, he said.

One night, each person in the crowd looked like a bobblehead doll. I was starting to hallucinate. I was starting to lose whatever sense of humanity I may have possessed. And I understood how removed I felt from the whole thing, the event. I was at the center of an event that I was not even a part of anymore. I felt alienated from my own narrative. The story of my life had been taken from me.

"This is your fault," I told Dan the morning after another dreamless night. "All for your brother's pizza. You and him have issues or something and I'm paying for it."

"If you think I did this just to win some free publicity for my brother, you're as simpleminded as you claim to be," he said. There were no notepads open on his lap. He no longer interviewed me. The laptop lay open on a corner of the balcony. The wait was the story now, the crowds, the police, the people who hovered around me hungry for the meaning of it all. "I saw something that maybe you didn't," he said.

"I never said I was simpleminded," I said. "Simple, yes, but not simpleminded."

"You have a story. These people are interested in it," he said with a dramatic wave of the hand.

Tour buses started coming around. The police presence was constant now. Members of the force had been assigned to me. I had been waiting for the Man to tell me what to do for three weeks. I felt I should be more embarrassed by it all than I actually was. The ridiculousness of my situation was going to be a tattoo. I would forever be known as the guy who . . . what, what was I doing? I would be the waiting guy. The guy who waited. I would have an official name.

Dick became a fixture, an official photographer. The *Post* ran more and more photos of the unfolding event. Their website was updated hourly. Dan told me my pages—the photos, his blogs, the news—were receiving tremendous traffic. I wasn't a hit, he said, but something more like a sustained minor sensation. He said this without irony. He had taken to speaking directly into the cameras. His personal blog now had a sponsor. There would come a time when an entire section of the paper would be devoted to me. I feared the inevitable TV special.

Dick and I had never had a conversation; he had made no attempt to speak with me. He was very professional this way. I looked at his obscene eyelessness and figured his story to be far more interesting than Dan's and infinitely more interesting than mine. The further you had to travel to get where you are, the more interesting the story. "What's with Dick's eye?" I asked Dan.

"He doesn't talk about it. I'm assuming he lost it in Cambodia."

And now I saw Cambodians as small as well.

"He doesn't talk much at all," Dan said. "No one in the office really knows him. He's been here at least fifteen years, and his English still sucks. That's the impression you get. The other photographers suspect he can speak English perfectly but chooses not to."

I wanted to speak to Dick. He had hovered around me for almost two weeks and I hardly knew what his voice sounded like. I wanted to know about his eye. I wanted the backstory. "I would like to talk to him," I said. "Have a conversation. Two humans learning about one another."

"He's working," Dan said. "Don't bother him."

"I'm interested. Just like I was interested in you." Before the crowd in front of me was nothing more than Dan's wildest dream.

A crowd where it was not uncommon to see white robed imams discussing the nature of divinity with Hasidim, strangeness captured by Dick and printed on the front page of this morning's *Post*.

Dan scanned the crowd to find his photographer. He waded into the mass. The crowd parted for Dan as he searched for the one-eyed Cambodian. In the distance, I could hear the drums and bells of the Hare Krishnas. I could hear sermons of brimstone competing against those of treacle. Hipsters with guitars playing songs in minor chords. I could hear the sounds of cheap digital cameras clicking; kids laughing, playing with balls and balloons that the sidewalk capitalists had set up about us and had sold to parents. I could hear orders being delivered to cute blond girls manning the food trucks. I could hear the discussions, the debates, the cops speaking into their shoulder-harnessed walkie-talkies. I could hear it all. And I could hear my heart, too. I was sinking into myself. The less real my life became, the more I sensed my own body and the less it seemed to work or even matter. The more people my wait attracted, the more in tune I was to the voice of the Man in my head. I felt him watching the crowd and sharing my bemusement. I could hear his horse running above the sound of the crowd. I could hear the reality of him. But more than that, I could feel him. He was sitting inside me. Looking out.

Dan dragged Dick toward me, a quizzical look on his one-eyed face. "Don't worry," Dan was telling him before pushing him to me. Dick was so slight he fell on me like a piece of paper blown by the wind.

"That's great," I said. "I didn't say you had to manhandle him."

"I think he's afraid of you," Dan said. We were speaking as if Dick were deaf. Or worse, as if he wasn't there at all. "Ten bucks if you get the story."

"And if I don't?" I asked. I was Dan's new toy. He was a big child playing with an expensive toy. I was going to line a lot of pockets with money. "Just ten bucks?" I said, as Dan waded back into the crowd.

I tried to face Dick. He eyed me warily. I smiled and held out my hand. "My name's Joe."

He looked at my outstretched hand and blinked. He transferred his camera to his other hand and took mine and shook it. "I know," he mumbled.

"I feel the need to explain myself to you," I said.

Dick shook his head. He looked down at the ground. He was uncomfortable and I immediately felt guilty for making him feel so. He transferred his camera back to his right hand. He put it to his face and looked in the lens and snapped a shot of the crowd. "How many rolls of film you think you've gone through so far?" I asked, realizing it was a digital camera.

He took another shot. "Digital."

"Of course," I said.

He adjusted the focus on his lens. "Film's still better," he said in perfect, heavily accented English. "You have more control. You feel like a real photographer. It's more artistic. More everything." He pronounced "more" to sound like what you would do to your over-grown lawn. He snapped another picture. "Except with digital, the photos get to the office right away. Remotely. There's no running around. It's faster. And no chemicals. I'm old enough to miss the chemicals."

Dan would owe me ten dollars. But what did money mean to me? "What do you think about all of this?" I asked.

He put the camera down. His face was disorienting. I'd be lying if I didn't admit that. You look at someone in the eyes. Looking at Dick's face was like being on a lurching ship. You lost your balance. "Crazy," Dick said. He scrunched his nose. "Americans are fuckin' crazy."

The skin that had formed around his empty eye socket was a garish mixture of purple and green, the kind of color combo you could put on bubblegum and sell to little boys. I now realized the socket was empty. I don't think Dick had stood this close to me before. Why hadn't he invested in a glass eye? Or a patch? Or sunglasses? "You don't think this would happen where you come from?"

He almost smiled. "Where I'm from was crazier," he said. "That was political. The killing. The shooting. Cambodia's better now. It's more normal." He picked up the camera again and scanned the crowd, looking for, what? What do photographers look for before deciding to snap the shutter? How was his photography affected by his mono-vision? Surely it must have shaped the way he saw the world, in the broadest sense.

"Did you lose your eye in the war?" I asked. I imagined him as one of the wretched lumps at the reeducation camps I saw in *The Killing Fields*.

Dick snapped a photo. It was of Dan. He was interviewing a young girl. She was holding a doll.

"I'm curious," I said. I shrugged apologetically. "I'm curious about people's backstories. My parents have tremendous backstory. They traveled a long way to end up in New Jersey. And you've traveled a long way as well, and I'm guessing your story is more interesting than mine. I'm sure of that."

Dick ignored me and focused yet more attention on his camera. He was overcompensating. He fidgeted with the lens, flicked switches, reached into his bag, and pulled out an airbrush.

I raised my shirt to show him my belly. The crowd hushed up. Dick's head turned slowly and he looked at my naked torso. "See this scar?" I said, pointing to the tiniest of scars just south of my belly button. "When I was thirteen, I tried to break up a fight and someone nicked me with a steak knife. Only took three stitches to close. My mother kept crying about how it could have been a lot worse. The kid who did it could have really stabbed me. He held back. I think. It gave me some bowel trouble." It hadn't, but I thought admitting this kind of problem would help Dick open up.

Who wants to admit to bowel trouble? "And it gave me an excuse to lift up my shirt for no reason," I added.

I put my shirt back down. Dick stared at my torso, his eye transfixed by who knows what. I could only imagine what those viewing the scene through the webcams thought of the display. The crowd started to mumble and very soon the clatter that I had grown used to was back. It drowned out the noise of city, that background chorus that lets people here know they're alive. "I was stabbed, too," Dick said.

"In your eye?" I said, grimacing as I imagined the pain.

"I was at a work camp," Dick said. *The Killing Fields* came storming back into my head. I saw Haing Ngor eat a lizard. And, for whatever reason, I saw John Malkovich developing film in a makeshift darkroom. Dick lifted his camera again, scanning the crowd. "I asked for food. A young soldier, maybe twelve years old, he stabbed me. Just because I asked for food. I was so hungry. I was hungry all the time but that day I was just stupid hungry." He snapped a photo. "Like I said, it was crazy. Everybody died. My whole family. My wife. My son. My mother and father. Two brothers." He sighed and snapped a photo. "But not me." He put his camera down. "I guess I'm lucky," he said softly. "After the war, I went to Vietnam. Then Hong Kong. Then here. I was sponsored by a church in Kentucky. I got a job. And then I moved here and got a better job. I found a new wife." He shrugged again. "But no children. I can't do that again. I don't trust enough, you know? To bring another kid into the world. No way."

Dick nodded. He took another photo. He checked something in his camera and picked up his bag, slinging it over his shoulder. He faced me and took a quick photo. His eye was dead. I was looking inside Dick and saw emptiness. "People tell me I'm lucky," he said. "All the time with the good luck. But sometimes good luck is also bad. And sometimes bad luck is the best luck of all." He shook my hand and held it. "Are you crazy?" he asked.

"I hope not," I said. I smiled. He let go of my hand. "I'm as normal a man as you'll find. I'm not so sure about them." I pointed to the audience.

He turned around and walked into the crowd, his camera leading the way, everyone mugging for the photographer, demanding the one-eyed survivor take their picture and make them immortal, a feeling Dick would never desire unless accompanied by the power to change the past. I was full of admiration for him. And sympathy. And I felt amazingly lucky. Despite his feelings about the word.

Dan sat down next to me. "So?" he asked.

"Anyone who can say they've been stabbed by a boy for asking for food has a profoundly better story to tell than everyone else," I said.

And then I felt tired. I felt crushed by the expectation of the crowd. For the first time, I felt like going to bed. I would wave to the crowd and close the door and never look into their expectant faces again. The show would be over. Canceled. I was exhausted. I closed my eyes.

And then from deep inside me I heard his voice. *Very soon*, the Man said. I couldn't smell him anymore. He was not around me anymore. I could feel that. But I could feel something more profound. He was inside me. As if he had ditched the crowd and gone into hiding. Back to where he had come from.

I wanted the Man to make a bed appear magically before me. I wanted simplicity. I wanted a world where I wasn't surrounded by "more" and "better" and "99%" and "free" and especially not "lite." I wanted a world where every word wasn't parsed for meaning, where focus groups didn't decide the fate of perfectly fine products and movies and political slogans. I was hungry. I opened my eyes. Dan was sitting there typing away on one of his phones. He was writing the story I would read in the paper the next day. Or on his blog in about six minutes.

"Get me a slice of pizza," I told him, "and then go home."

"You're getting testy," he sang without glancing up.

Of course I was. I was annoyed. I was annoyed with sleeping

on concrete steps night after night. I was annoyed with the growing circus of idiots hanging onto my every breath. With the hot dog vendors and taco trucks and newscasters and preachers and cameras and folk singers and toy sellers and sticky-fingered kids and Tupperware and Dan. I was annoyed with Dan. With his brother and his awful pizza. I was annoyed with how helpless I felt because of the Man. Because of his power over me. I missed my job. I had to admit that. I missed waking up and going to work and thinking up pithy slogans for canned fruit and expensive campaigns that would convince Americans that they needed a better mattress.

I desired such a mattress. I closed my eyes again. I was so tired. *Go*, the Man said. *Follow me.*

I turned to Dan. "Am I getting a slice or what?" I was scared. I finally had to admit I was frightened. What did it mean to go? Where? When? How long could I keep this up?

What was wrong with me?

Dan stood. "The usual, I'm guessing," he said, by which he meant one slice of pepperoni and one of sausage. He sighed. "Nothing's stopping you from just going inside and falling asleep," he said. "Except that voice in your head."

"Sleep? I would love that. It's all I think about. My most depraved fantasies right now don't go beyond a soft surface on which I can be blissfully horizontal. But that would be anti-climactic," I said frowning. "Don't you think?"

Dan was as curious as I was. He was interested in the story, in its arc, and how it ended. I just wanted it to end. I wanted to climb up the stairs and sleep and shit and eat and be normal. I wanted to fall onto my couch and watch baseball on TV, run to the fridge for a beer during a pitching change, fall asleep sometime during the eighth inning, and wake up to the happy chatter of late night salesmen around my head.

I wanted closure. I did not want to go anywhere.

THE SIGN

A shooting star streaks its way across the sky. And then it's gone. And I remember once my father told me that shooting stars weren't stars at all. They were meteorites, or tiny bits of asteroids or comets, burning up on entry into the earth's atmosphere. We're wishing upon something that is either dying or is about to cause death, he said. And I was too young to have understood the full meaning of his words. My father never taught life lessons. He just spoke his thoughts aloud and sometimes you caught the nuance. A shooting star is the wrong term, he said. Yet almost every culture calls it a star. I remember these things but I'm still not sure if they were ever important.

In the night's darkness, the line that separates the peaks of the mountains from the sky is rendered invisible, a rumor, the only clue to the demarcation the sudden absence of stars. At night, walking the grounds, the sounds of the ranch are adrift in the wind. The braying and snorts of the horses. The laughter of guests and workers alike. The opening and closing of doors. But there are moments when all is silent. When the artifice disappears and the music of silence is a spell broken only by the gusts of wind. Sitting in the grass outside, staring at the stars, surrounded by nothing and everything at once. By silence. By a literal hum that is the earth. At times like this, you can hear the earth whipping through space. Another form of sensory overload.

And being a city boy distrustful of silence, I seek out noisy corners of the ranch. The stables. A brook that runs across the western edge of the property. The bar after the guests have retired for the evening.

I scan the sky, willing another shooting star into existence, another chance to wish for something. Though lately I don't know that I would wish for anything. Because I haven't felt the need.

I walk by the stables toward the main building. Athena's apartment is on the second floor, above the library. I think about my mother and that perhaps I should write to her. Something larger than a random email on a made-up account saying, "I'm OK. Don't worry." I can imagine my father, stoic, perhaps drinking a bit too much scotch, but satisfied with the contact—and still seething that I quit such a good job. After my last promotion, he had given me a long, deep hug and said quietly into my ear, "You've made it." What would he say now? What would they say if they could see me, away from the filter of the media, just me, their son, thousands of miles from home, peeling fruit?

I walk up the dark wooden stairs and knock on Athena's door. Tomas answers, a sweat-stained Cubs cap on his head, a glass of red wine in hand. He steps aside to let me in. Athena sits on a large black leather couch, her feet curled up under her. She's drinking white. "Hello, Joe," she says warmly. She has a large mouth with large whitened teeth and the effect of her smile can be blinding. Against her copper skin even more so. It is as if a light pours out of her mouth. It is a physical truth that may make men weaker in her presence than they already are. Athena is a beautiful woman. To deny it would be to expose yourself to a dangerously universal ridicule. And then once you have assimilated her beauty, or at least made the attempt, she speaks, and you realize she is the kind of worldly, infinitely interesting person that only sprouts from places that always seem to be within five miles of the sea. Tomas clears his throat and it's obvious I've been staring.

He walks to the couch and sits down close to Athena. The distance he chooses shows both nonchalance and, I'm thinking, a kind of insecurity. That he even feels this way about me is flattering. As far as I'm concerned, he's the lion king here. The threat I may imply is all in his head.

"Please, sit," Athena says, pointing to a small divan. "Red or white?"

"What do you have?" I ask, taking my seat. The leather on the divan gives in to my weight with a little-too-audible fart.

Tomas snorts.

"I have a French merlot and a very crisp, floral almost, chardonnay from New Zealand."

"I'll have the white," I say.

Tomas snorts again and rolls his eyes.

"Good choice," Athena says. She reaches over and pours me a glass and the agitation inside Tomas grows.

We clink our glasses together while Tomas contents himself by staring at the ceiling.

"I don't want to make this too formal and announce this as a meeting," she says. She puts her legs down and slides her feet into a smart pair of burnished leather mules. "It is not a meeting."

"Absolutely not," Tomas says. He gulps down the remainder of his wine and reaches over to a side table and pours himself another glass.

"Your background interests me," Athena says. "Tomas told me about your clafouti argument."

"I wouldn't call it an argument," I say.

"It was close to one," Tomas says.

I cradle my wine. I probably shouldn't cradle white wine, I'm thinking. "I just had something to say. I don't know why I said it."

"Tomas said there was yelling," she says.

I look at him and he looks at his wine. "I don't think anyone raised their voice," I say.

Athena gives Tomas a look. "It doesn't matter," she says. She puts a hand through her hair. "I am interested in some of the things you said. Anyone who uses the word 'brand' in the correct manner is useful." She laughs at this. I manage a smile.

"It's a bad word," I say.

"It's just overused," she says. "But you used it correctly. And you were right about what you said."

Tomas sighs.

"It's a tasty clafouti," I say.

"You were the crazy guy that drove across the country, no?" she asks.

I don't say anything. Tomas laughs. "What guy?" he asks.

"Yes," I say, trying to appear unconcerned. "And you still hired me."

"I didn't hire you," she says.

"That wasn't even me," Tomas says, in a tone that suggests I should respect the hierarchy that the act in question has established. "Well, Carlos hired him."

"I don't care," Athena says. "We are the sum of our stories, right? So. Here is mine." She takes a sip of her wine. "I'm from Greece. I managed some very excellent hotels there. In Athens. But also in Thessaloniki. The city got hip somehow. I could see it coming, but when a city gets hip in Europe it means Germans and the English and the English drink too much and puke everywhere. I felt the need to get away. I was at that age. I worked in the Maldives. But I got claustrophobic there. There was nothing but sea. And I'm Greek!"

Tomas laughs at this. Perhaps trying too hard.

"And then I came here. Hotel GMs are a kind of nomad. We travel a lot. The good ones are like me. They work far from home. They feel rootless. And so they try to recreate a home out of the hotel. They work hard at this. They see guests and employees as family. That's what makes them good." She takes another sip of her wine. "We're like flight attendants, but not as severe. They can literally sleep in a different city every day. But the idea of it is the same. It is rare to find hotel GMs or even chefs here, like Tomas, who work in the same city they are from. To be honest, I wouldn't trust them."

For whatever reason, the idea of parking a car enters my thoughts.

"I came here because it was new," she continues. "I liked the challenge. It was so far from anything else. And it was also far from my reality. From what I knew. Because the land . . . I could not believe the size of this property. And I still love it here. I've run this property since it opened. I've found a special place."

I'm thinking about the theology of parking.

"That's a good point," Tomas says. "About trusting." He stands. "I'm going to raid the fridge."

"I want to make it better," Athena says. "And your argument with Tomas . . ."

"Discussion," I say.

". . . about clafouti, of all things, made me think. I looked up your file. I looked up the ad agency in New York. And then I realized you were the guy who made that crazy drive."

"It wasn't so crazy," I say.

"And I thought I need to exploit this talent."

"My craziness?"

"Your past. Your experience."

"How old is this duck breast?" Tomas calls from the kitchen.

"When did you make it?" Athena shouts.

A long silence. "It's too old," Tomas says.

Is the act of parking Catholic or Protestant? Or Buddhist? And does it depend on where one lives?

"I'm calling the kitchen," Tomas says.

"I have grapes," Athena says. "Some cheese, too." She turns to me. "What do you think?" She smiles. And it's possible I'm squinting.

"About what?"

"About what I've said."

"What have you said?"

"Exploitation. I want to pick your brains."

"What is there to pick?" I ask.

"I love that expression. Pick your brains. In Greece, we have a similar one but it has to do with octopus."

"Which shouldn't be on the menu here," I say.

"Fuck off!" Tomas yells.

"It sounds like I'm offering you a job," she says. "At least to me it sounds like I'm offering you one."

"What are you offering me then?"

She laughs again. "I have some Brie and old cheddar," she tells Tomas.

"A consultancy?"

"Perhaps," she says. "For now."

"I leave the room for a second and he's been promoted to consultant," Tomas says, sitting down.

"Nothing has been decided," Athena says.

"I see nothing wrong with having a nice clafouti on the menu," he says. "The guests love it. And more importantly, I love it."

You drive and drive around searching for a sign that gives you permission to park. One sign among countless signs, most of which are prohibitions. And when you find that spot . . .

"The clafouti question is interesting to me," Athena says, "and I'll tell you why." She puts her wine glass down and sits up. "In the Maldives, our hotel obviously had a lot of fish on the menu. Vegetables are expensive there. Everything has to be flown or shipped in. But the menu was fusion. It had a French base. The chef was from India but he'd studied in France. In Lyon. So the menu made sense to guests. They felt like they were enjoying refined local cuisine."

"Where is this going?" Tomas asks. Skeptically. He sits on the edge of the couch.

"This clafouti discussion, this mentioning of the brand, it made me realize I could not quite describe the brand here. What are we selling?"

I cleared my throat. I was still thinking about parking. Was I missing home? "Depends on who's buying," I say. Athena leans forward. This was an invitation to continue. "I'm guessing your PR and marketing has been focused on a handful of places, just from the guests I've seen. Japan is an obvious one. California. New York. Florida. All high-end. The economic situation has hurt. American security restrictions. Fewer Europeans are traveling. I know that. I heard we're getting more Canadians. That makes sense. It's so close. This is a very *Travel + Leisure* kind of place. It's made to look like it should be in the pages of an Australian travel magazine. The kitchen pumps out pretty food. Outside of the steak dishes, it's all very elegant. Tomas's brasserie background is evident. The food is pretty. And it's simple. I don't know how else to describe it."

Tomas shifts his weight. "This is going where exactly?"

"This is supposed to be a ranch," I say.

"With a spa," Athena says.

"And plunge pools, fuck!" Tomas says.

"I know, but it's still a ranch," I say. "You can still take a horse into the mountains. You can ride off into the sunset here. You can fancy it up as much as you want, but the idea of a ranch is simple."

"You can have a four-star fuckin' catered picnic up in those mountains with foie gras empanadas on an onion compote with a chilled St. Émilion," Tomas says.

"I love your empanadas," Athena says.

"I just think there could more unity to the offering," I say, my first real opinion of the night. "The clafouti, to me, sticks out. Maybe it's all the peeling I have to do. Or maybe it's just not simple. Apple pie is simple. It's easy to understand."

Tomas downs his wine. "I can't believe this fuckin' discussion."

"Tomas," Athena says.

Tomas squirms on the couch. "Fuck this and fuck you," he says.

"C'mon," I say dismissively.

"OK, a consultant," Athena says. "Officially."

"I'd like to continue working in the kitchen," I say, not quite believing I'm saying it.

"No," Athena says. "I don't want you to get too food-focused. You already are. This is an overall vision. I'm not looking at changing anything. But I also don't want to have to fly some consultant in from God knows where and deliver an obvious list of recommendations. You know this place. You've been here long enough. There's an extra office downstairs. You can start when Tomas finds someone to replace you."

He snorts, again. If we had snacked, would he have been happier? Athena stands up. The evening is over. Which is good; the wall clock reads midnight. She turns to Tomas. "This isn't about the clafouti," she says. She touches his shoulder, the first sign of any kind of affection all evening. "Even when this is over, when Joe has studied the situation, you can always have Mathilde's clafouti on the menu."

Tomas does not speak. He definitely can't look at me. He's offended. I stand and Athena offers her hand. We hold hands but don't really shake. "This is going to be fun," she says.

I'm still not sure what she wants from me, but as she closes the door behind me, I can see another door opening. A larger one. Something more important.

Parking a car in New York: Prohibition. Prohibition. Prohibition.

Prohibition. Fire hydrant. Prohibition. Prohibition. Prohibition. Salvation. Parking a car out here is something else. There's so much choice. Not a lot of thought. There's a New Age quality to it. But in New York when you find a spot, and it's on the street, the joy you feel at that moment is an intense, stupid kind of joy.

PEACOCK TAIL

The media sensed the traction Dan had described. And so they were fruitful and multiplied. Flies to shit, I told Dan. The sheer amount of hours and outlets and pages and bandwidth makes anonymity impossible. For anyone.

And so, a day later, television found me. Dan granted interviews all day. Television trucks joined the food trucks on the street. Reporters interviewed people in the crowd. Helicopters hovered overhead and I expected a blimp to show up soon. The television people descended like a swarm, there really is no other way to describe it, and the force of their numbers, meeting the crowd on the street, had the makings of a battle scene from a big budget epic. *Here we go*, the Man said. When he spoke, my heart would beat faster. Or something. I would take a deep breath. *Here we go*, he said again.

I wouldn't talk to the media. And Dan saw some value in my decision. If I was going to talk, if the interest built up to that level, I would talk to someone big and it would be exclusive. And possibly lucrative. And this repulsed me on a level I found surprising.

I dreamed of an amusement park. I saw myself, a child, on a roller coaster with my father. And behind us sat the Man. Ridiculously drinking coffee.

Because of the television coverage, the next morning saw the largest crowd yet. Barricades went up. The police deemed it best to close the street to traffic completely. Day and night. The food trucks had to leave, allowed in only with special permits. The barricades had the perverse effect of denying commerce. The established hierarchy of the crowd was now lost as old-timers were jostled out of the way by tourists. They were nothing more. Soon, there would be signs like "Sheila from Buffalo!" and "Rochester, MN Marching Band Loves U Joe!" like an outbreak of weeds after a fire. With television comes the carnival.

A cop told me the mayor had taken a keen interest in my story. He was following it closely, monitoring it. "For what?" I asked and the cop laughed. Dan told me I was the perfect diversion, that I would be built up by the mayor's office while he announced unpopular measures. "Politicians always seek diversions," Dan said. "And if they can't find one, they make them up."

With the addition of helicopters, the noise of the street reached something incredible, an endless commotion, a crowd noise that was the loudest murmur I'd ever heard: just talk, constant talk, and above that the police whistles and the noise of the security apparatus and above that the helicopters. The major networks lined up for interviews. The prime-time newsmagazines jostled for rights. The morning shows were demanding access. Dan mentioned money again.

"Ka-ching," he said, in the smarmy tone of a strip club announcer.

"I'm not talking to anyone," I said. "Not for cash. And not the stupid newsmagazines." The newsmagazines mixed stories about global warming with celebrity interviews and, somehow, I had always found it offensive. The blurring of news and entertainment is the saddest expression of media oversaturation. Because people still watch the news to believe. There are no disclaimers on news shows, on the screaming talking heads, the guys who will say anything for the sheer entertainment value of the string of words they put together. The cynicism used to be checked when the red light went on. But now it went into overdrive after the red light went on. It was the point. It was dangerous and irresponsible and making a lot of people very rich. Even as the country got poorer for it. The blurring of news and entertainment is base. It points to a media culture that no longer cares. About anything.

"This is a principle that surprises me," Dan said.

"It surprises me, too," I admitted.

"You can make money off this," he told me. "One day this is going to end and you'll have nothing to show for it. You live in a place that feels the need to reward people for being palatably freakish. For sharing their secrets. For exposing themselves. This is the new currency. Take advantage of it. Sell your story. This is easy money. People dream about falling into easy money. There's something remarkably and reassuringly American about all of this. It's like the lottery. Take away the hard work and it's a sped up version of the American Dream."

"I hated my job," I said, thinking about my career in the past tense for the first time.

"So what then?" he asked.

"Maybe after I've stopped being sideshow of the month, I'll make some decisions. Maybe I'll sell my story then." It saddened me to say this. I looked at Dan. "Maybe I'll let you write the whole damned thing."

Dan's eyes widened. "You're too kind," he said.

The thought had occurred to me as the words left my mouth. I wanted to feel bitter, just a little, but I couldn't rouse the passion. "Maybe," I said.

The TV news all had the same angle on the story. They presented me as another in a long line of New York eccentrics, another worm from the Big Apple. Look, America, look how weird this place is, lucky you don't have to live here. Since 9/11 that sort of line also included an ominous subtext: the place is just too dangerous. If it's not bombs, it's kooks. The threat of airplanes falling from the sky has replaced the more pedestrian gun battles, murder, and petty crime as the clear and present danger inherent in living here. And then we became the people that almost bankrupted the nation. We were greedy and self-important and too concerned with our own navels. The media are based here and they feed this to the nation. Because the media is the most self-important of all of us.

Spalding Gray called Manhattan "an island off the coast of America," implying a difference that clearly has more meaning for my fellow countrymen than for foreigners.

Various well-dressed, well-coiffed reporters stood ten feet from me, filed their reports, and left in a rush. Very few of them asked me to hold the pizza. They didn't care. And it probably made for a poor visual.

The *Post* decided to help me out by picking up the mortgage payments on my apartment. In exchange I allowed Dan access to write up his stories. My living room became his office. Two burly union men came and installed his computer and then two larger men from Verizon came to install an extra line and then Dan had a suitcase of clothes and toiletries sent over. "You've moved into my house," I said, flabbergasted.

Print journalists came by at all hours now, national, foreign. It seemed funny, if not incredible, that my face was being seen by millions of people around the world for no other reason than a strange and ill-conceived decision to do nothing, to listen to a voice in my head. If this indeed was in the Man's plans, I was willing to concede to him the brilliance of it all. Perhaps he would use me to attract media and disseminate the message. If so, I had to admire his sense of humor in choosing someone who wrote ads for a living. I could feel him laughing. His laughter came and went as well now.

One day, I told Dan I would speak to print journalists for five minutes each. Just to piss off the TV people. The foreign print journalists turned out to be very entertaining. A heavily accented blond woman from Finland asked, "Do you believe it is God who has spoken to you?" and followed that up by asking, "Did you know that the Finnish people don't really believe in God anymore?"

A well-dressed, extremely fit, middle-aged Brazilian man asked me, "What do you expect that your man will bring you?" His accent was vaguely British.

A fat but charming Irish reporter asked, "If you do not consider the Man to be of a divine nature, how do you explain his apparent omniscience?" I answered him by saying I would like to take him to my neighborhood bar for a pint when this was done. Flummoxed, he proceeded to ask questions of such an elevated theological bent I no longer understood him and I retracted the invitation.

A Japanese woman who had overdone the Chanel No. 5 but who had the most beautiful hands I had ever seen up close asked, "Do you think this man is an American or maybe he is from somewhere else?"

A reporter from India announced, "It is very possible that you are waiting for an incarnation of Vishnu. The white horse proves it. In time, I guarantee, there will be Hindus in India praying to you, sir. Not for you, but to you."

"But I'm waiting for an answer myself," I replied. "I don't have any to give."

The American reporters, especially, asked my opinion on all sorts of matters—on politics, world events, baseball. I complained about the Mets a lot. I deflected political questions. I tried to sell the idea that I was a simple guy doing a stupid thing, but that wasn't the story they were after.

And I felt the laughter some more.

Dan's role had shifted from reporter to press liaison to producer. "My brother's business is up three hundred percent," he told me. "Some of the newspeople file their stories from there. For authenticity's sake. He's getting tourists! Diane Sawyer stopped by! His front window is plastered with photos of you eating his pizza," he said. This was an individual delirious with the idea that his master plan was working. Because perhaps nothing in Dan's past had worked out the way he had hoped. And then I happened.

At night, the crowds thinned out, people going to the comfort of their beds. The children returned home. But then the hipsters showed up, the barflies, the cocktailians, the well-dressed girls in impossible heels on their way to a rooftop lounge. There was a lot more smoking at night. And people were bolder. They would come up to me. Some would speak. Others would ask for an autograph as if the cover of darkness allowed them to do what they had truly wanted to do all along. I signed everything I was asked to sign.

A pale thin man with huge hair and bigger glasses sat next to me and said he was the president of the local chapter of the Foreskin Restoration Club for Men. I wondered why the organization felt the need to add "for Men" to its name. He told me about using a system of weights to regain the semblance of a foreskin. "I've got them on right now," he whispered proudly. "I'm letting gravity restore what the medical establishment so callously lopped off." He told me his movement was attracting a lot of attention, that men everywhere were now questioning the validity of circumcision, that Europeans had, for the most part, abandoned the practice, and that the medical establishment was finally admitting that the procedure was a social one and not based on any health issues. I brought up the AIDS issue and what doctors were trying to do in Africa. He waved it off. That was the establishment's propaganda, he said. I looked for Dan but he was inside my apartment. The foreskin guy talked about himself for what felt like hours. I heard the word "foreskin" more times than anyone really needs to and then, finally, thankfully, he stood up, wiped the fake tears from his eyes, and thanked me for listening.

Women flashed their breasts at night. It was a thing. Flashes of skin at random moments, almost always in my direction. And then I closed my eyes and hoped the Man would appear and tell me what to do or where to go or what not to do. But he was silent. And when I opened my eyes, I saw a woman sitting beside me, staring at me, her gaze boring holes into me. "Hi," I said.

"Do you mind if I sit here with you?" she asked. She spoke with an accent I couldn't place. It wasn't American. Her voice verged on squeaky. Her eyes were the deep blue of cold water. She had the kind of mouth and full lips that make men think impure thoughts. There was something about her that made her seem like a really good-looking boy. And when I thought that, I realized I would never have admitted that to myself before this whole sordid thing started. I found her beautiful and attractive.

"You may," I said.

The Man was whistling. It was annoying.

"No one sits with you," she said. "I think that's weird."

"I think they're afraid of me," I said. "Except the kids. And the strange ones. Strange people will always talk to you."

"I'm so tired," she said, sitting beside me. "I just got off the bus."

"From where?" I asked.

"Montreal," she said. That explained the accent.

"And what are you doing here?" I asked dumbly. I knew the answer. How could I not?

"I saw you on TV," she said. "I saw you last night and I got on the bus this morning. And you know, here I am."

She smiled. Her teeth were a teeth-whitened white and I could smell the cigarette smoke on her. And the perfume she had sprayed to mask the smoke. But her smile sucked the life out of me. It was a smile so perfect it could have come out of an elaborately designed box. "You're kind of what I imagined French girls smelled like," I said.

"I'm Sophie," she said, offering her hand. "I feel a connection."

And so I felt stupidly defensive. "What kind of connection?" I asked, taking her hand.

"I saw what you were doing, on TV, and I heard your story. I got on the internet and I read more about you. And I had a feeling. I don't know. Like I needed to meet you. Like we're similar. You know?"

I decided to concentrate on her smell. I had a strong desire to touch her short hair.

"I'm sorry if I'm scaring you," she said.

"I'm just surprised," I said, waking up a bit. "I can't imagine what I'm doing would make sense to anyone." I said this despite the presence of thousands of strangers on my street every day, craving the moment when my understanding would be revealed.

"I saw you and something went poof! In my head," she said. She laughed. Her laugh was that of a girl's. It was vaguely innocent. Or free. "And last night I couldn't sleep. I turned and turned in my bed. So I went to the bus station and got the first bus to New York. None of my friends know I'm here." She reached into her bag and pulled out a blanket. "This is all I brought with me," she said. "Can you believe it?"

Sophie lit up a cigarette and spread the blanket across her lap and told me about her life in Montreal. She told me about her job in a department store in the suburbs, about how she worked a perfume counter and spent her days looking at her watch, about spraying samples onto the limp wrists of faceless women, about the intricacies of perfume and beauty and smelling beautiful. She told me she felt like a robot dispensing beauty tips to women who had no right to consider themselves beautiful, who had no idea what true beauty was. "They can be aggressive and rude and pushy and act like they know more about perfume than I do," she said. The ones who knew beauty didn't need her help. She felt dishonest.

"I'm Joe," I said.

Put your pants on, the Man said, oddly enough.

She laughed again. "I know who you are," she said. "You're on TV!"

The newspeople loved Sophie. Perhaps adore would be the correct word. She was a new angle. And she was far more attractive than I was. Dan wrote a long piece the next day and Dick's photo of us made the front of the *Post*. Sophie added a dose of sex appeal that had been lacking. It helped that her smile was gold, no doubt. She was photogenic and the camera guys ate her up.

Sophie started doing TV interviews. She did the morning show rounds. She left and toured all the morning show studios and returned three hours later. "Fun!" she squealed. Dan complained that he had become Sophie's press agent, which was a bit disingenuous of him. Her smoking became an issue with the parents of the kids who still hung out with me. They spoke of the example I should be setting, that Sophie was smoking too much, that she was always seen in the papers and on the television with a cigarette in her hand. They said she was making smoking seem cool.

Sophie said she would quit. "This is a good excuse," she said. So when the owner of the corner store came by with a carton of Camels, Sophie said no, reluctantly. "But I love Camels," she told the man as she begged off. Microphones picked that up.

The owner of the corner store returned with a case of Coke. A man who claimed to represent Coke wanted us to appear in an ad. Dan's brother, finally, stopped by for some photos. He shook my hand and thanked me until I had to tell him to leave. I told him his calzones were a disgrace and he promised to look into the recipe.

That night, Sophie put her head on my shoulder. And then,

ending an annoyingly powerful Paul Anka loop running through my head, she laid her head on my lap, adjusted her blanket, and fell asleep.

I didn't sleep that night. I was afraid to close my eyes. And so I stared at the sleeping beauty that was Sophie instead.

Something about Sophie's presence made me fear the world. I expected it to explode in front of me, the way it had when the sky fell and everyone channeled Chicken Little. Except on that day, no one was making anything up. I saw visions of the apocalypse, something a Bible thumper hanging out on the street was preaching, though I doubt his end of the world involved an endless basket of fruit, a herd of white horses, and the Man swatting it all away with a floppy hat the size of the sun. And with the reality of a beautiful woman lying here, on me, a strange thought occurred: profound regret. I looked at Sophie and regretted taking her from her depressing job in the suburbs of Montreal. I regretted leaving my job even, but more than that, I regretted starting something that had no finish. No end. The inanity of it. I would never have started it had I known where it might lead. I felt Sophie hold my hand. "This is a zoo!" she said.

"I know," I said. "And it's all my fault."

I saw society before me on the street and I was concerned and even ashamed. I saw society as a heavyset brute trying to balance itself on the head of a pin, threatening to tip over but always managing not to. "What do these people do?" Sophie asked, wrapping the blanket around her shoulders. I wasn't sure she was talking to me.

"They shop," I offered.

"I really need a cigarette," she said.

"It just gets bigger and bigger," I said. "I don't know how much longer the cops will allow this. I think they're getting mighty pissed off with me."

"Cops are always pissed off," Sophie said. "That's the same everywhere."

I put my arm around her. I heard a few cameras go off. The strobe of the flashes danced in my vision.

I leaned my head on Sophie's. Her hair smelled surprisingly clean, something I was definitely not. One of the morning shows must have given her a shampoo. I must have smelled something fierce. The deodorant companies would soon show up to sponsor this. Hadn't my agency handled a deodorant account? I wanted a beer. I wanted to watch a ball game. I wanted a bed. I wanted to stop being so afraid of everything surrounding me. I closed my eyes and took in a deep breath of Sophie's sweet smell.

UNDER PRESSURE

"I saw you on TV." This from one of the dishwashers, a Blackfoot named Keith. He's got that silent Indian thing happening, too, except he's quick with the smile. We're behind the kitchen, smoking. He's never spoken to me before. "You went on that made-for-TV vision quest special thing," he says.

That sounds about right. And whatever I did, it's landed me here, smoking a cigarette in the shadow of the Rockies. With an Indian named Keith. "That was me," I say. "Yes."

Keith takes a drag off his cigarette. "Well, you didn't end up in some totally lame-ass game show," he says. He smiles. "You know. Like *Hollywood Squares* or something."

"I didn't make it that far," I say. Instead, I'm here, and I'm peeling fruit and I'm about to become a consultant for this mixed-up place, where we serve steak and French patisserie to stockbrokers and Japanese executives and men who own mysterious businesses in far off lands. I'm in a place where even at the foot of the mountains the boundaries of infinity are unknowable.

I'm inside a world. A story. I'm inside a story, of me, standing beside it. A bystander. I'm in a place that permits freedom. Where the air is clear. Where the wind is pure and unbroken.

Keith puts out his smoke. "That was some vision quest," he says, before opening the door. "Usually, the TV doesn't care about things like that. It's too deep or something." He enters the kitchen.

Every religion and ideology has claimed my actions as their own. My actions were never, really, mine. I never owned them. In many ways, Dan can claim ownership of the whole thing. And being here, however I managed to find this place, I'm reclaiming my life, making things normal again, not feeling the world revolving around me. Making me dizzy.

Taking back control. Becoming me.

Sometimes at night, when I look out my window, I literally see nothing. And that's hard to imagine. Why close your eyes when everything around you is black? On cloudy nights, when the stars and the moon are extinguished by the weather's thick blanket, I'm not even sure the darkness can be called black anymore. It's more than black. It's nothing. And everything.

They've planted some trees around the property to act as wind-breaks. It's a conceit, the idea that we can harness the forces of nature to tame those same forces. We can't. We always hope to and we never can. Our homes tumble into the ocean. Rivers flood our farms. Our mightiest cities stop functioning because of a few inches of snow. Nature's afterthought.

The taller the trees grow, the more they bend away from the relentless wind off the mountains. The rocky tops of the mountains laugh at us from above. They can send snow our way in the middle of summer. They can change color depending on the sunlight. They can make you feel absolutely small or resolutely big. And they can't be tamed. Even by an invigorating Swiss steam followed by a hot rock massage.

Tomas makes slight alterations to the menu, perhaps as a result of our meeting. Mathilde bakes a stunningly complicated apple pie. Strawberry tarts. Raspberry molten chocolate cakes. And a whipped cream confection with nuts that hearkens back to her boss's Czech roots. And a clafouti. The clafouti will remain. Forever. I peel far more apples for the expected run on the pie.

LOVE LETTERS

My parents were somewhere between distraught and bemused by all this, a reflection of their personalities. I had not heard from them. I have to admit that I had not thought of them at all and it never occurred to me to warn them that Dan and his colleagues might appear. Because I underestimated, or refused to believe, the interest my situation might generate. It was possible, I realized then, that they had left messages for me. Inside my phone lay the digital remains of my parents' worry, the arc of their journey, from simple questions to valid concern for my sanity. And those digital bits would be mixing with other calls, dead-end questions that might never be answered, my response the simple act of sitting on the front steps while the world assembled around me.

I didn't think this story worth telling my family until it was too late to tell properly. We are not a family that speaks often nor do we feel we have to. They know where I am and what I do and are quite proud of me. And I know that they're in New Jersey, thinking about selling the house, but trying to somehow time a market no one understands, and they never do it. The house is too big, my father hates mowing the lawn, he calls lawn care an especially American form of tyranny, and my mother derides keeping a home clean when they don't use most of it.

We could go weeks without speaking to each other. This has always seemed abnormal to those around me but it is the way we are. Our level of communication does not point to a lack of love, or even warmth.

So when my mother showed up, it was a bit of a shock. Seeing her was a moment of two worlds colliding, of real life intruding on the abject folly of my situation. But that she had read about it in the paper, or seen my antics on TV, made me feel like a bad son. I was sixteen again, coming home stoned late on a Saturday night, my mother sitting in the living room, waiting patiently, a lioness stalking prey.

The Man laughed. And whistled. At the same time.

Before saying anything, she dropped a few boxes of food at my feet. Out tumbled apples and bananas and pears. She had prepared ham and cheese sandwiches, made her delicious creamy coleslaw, fried rice, chicken curry. She had picked up some shrimp dumplings because she knew how much I would have missed them. She smiled and kissed me and I gave her the warmest hug I had ever given her. "You smell," she whispered in my ear. And then she stepped back. And then she let me have it. "What's wrong with you?" she said. She was aware of the media presence, aware of Sophie, sitting to my left, aware of Dan, surveying the crowd from behind me. "Why didn't you warn us? I was about to book a flight to Houston to visit your aunt. But no, we have to read about this in the silly newspaper, we have to find out that our son has lost his mind, and then, the next day, there are strangers on my lawn, stepping all over my flowers, asking me silly questions about you. And I can't tell them, 'I don't know what he's doing, we haven't talked.' Because that makes us sound like a dysfunctional family. Your father is very upset. The neighbors are going on the news now because I'm not talking to anybody. I saw your old high school on TV. They went there and looked up your yearbook photos. They spoke to your old teachers. Remember Mr. Abelson? They spoke to him. I don't know why they always think high school teachers are so important. And you don't pick up the phone! But then you left your job. Your job was a good job. You worked so hard. You were doing important work. Why are you doing this?"

It was a sensible question. She was begging for insight, but more than that she was asking me to stop without asking. She thought that if she'd finally show up and say her piece I would somehow come to my senses and put an end to the circus. Are all mothers delusional about the power they think they have over their sons? Or does the trauma of birth addle something inside? She was being reasonable and unreasonable, meaning nothing had changed. This comforted me.

The Man continued to whistle. Without the laughter.

"I don't want any of this," I told her. I took her hand. I kissed it, as intimate a gesture as I had ever offered her. "I'm not doing this to hurt you. I'm sorry for that. I really am. I'm not doing this to hurt anyone. I'm just . . ." My voice trailed off. I wanted to smile.

"Oh, for God's sake," she said.

"I'm fine," I said, addressing her primary concern. "All I can say is don't watch the news. Don't read the paper. I haven't answered my phone since this began. I'm sorry for that, too. And we'll see if I can get the media to leave you alone."

"Don't watch the news? You're on CNN. Everyone in the world is watching this. I'm getting email from people I forgot we were related to. I even turned off the telephone, if you can imagine. So that makes two of us."

This startled me. My mother's home is a museum to the evolution of the telephone. Every kind of phone since the seventies is present, on display. There's even an old rotary phone in the basement. She has two lines for her personal use. She is an avid user of call-waiting, call-forwarding, ident-a-call, distinct ring services. She is a cell phone fanatic. Last Christmas, my father bought her a Bluetooth headset. She is intrigued by making calls on the internet. Her discovery of Skype was as momentous to her as Columbus seeing the New World. She wants her far-flung family to adopt the technology so they can all save on phone bills. She cannot hear one of her phones ring and not answer it. She is incapable of this. One time, after having lectured me about the sanctity of the family dinner, I watched her try to ignore the ringing phone. It was impossible. Like watching the thirsty ignore a glass of water. After four rings, she bolted from the table to answer it. It was dinnertime, she should have known it would be a useless call and it was. A poll. It was a poll. She had upended her entire argument because of a poll. "I told them I was for Clinton," she said and then we never heard about the sanctity of the family dinner again.

"How long did that last?" I asked, smiling finally. I had to. My mother was going for effect.

And because she could see the absurdity of all this as well, she also smiled. "Oh, maybe an hour. You know me."

Her smile did it. A deep pool of regret welled up inside of me. Looking into her eyes, I regretted the years I had spent being distant, aloof, even when I was sitting across the table from her. I saw in her all the disappointment I felt with my own life, the unfulfilled dreams, the hopeless banality of things, the way I had surrendered to events. Just like her. There must be a time when you realize you take your parents for granted, I thought. It's an awful feeling, more shame heaped upon the shame I felt by her being near me. That was all it took. I felt deflated. I felt like a naughty little boy. And shame being complete humiliation, I backed out. Why shouldn't she profit from this? I asked myself. She doesn't know these things. She doesn't know the commercial upside to having reporters trample the flowers in your garden. My arguments were not her arguments. They weren't valid. The context was different.

"Listen," I told her, my lips brushing the soft down of her ears, "make some money while you can. Enrich yourself. Do some talk shows. This won't last forever. It sounds crass but there's money in it. Maybe Dad retires or something. Sell your story to some tabloid. Find an agent. Dan here can help you. He knows more about this game than he's telling me. Everyone's making money off this but me. Jobs are being created around this. This has been commercialized already. Complete strangers are profiting. So why not you?"

"Your father keeps talking about this being a midlife crisis," she said.

"He might not be wrong," I said.

"They're killing my flowers," she said.

"Just think about it," I said.

She stroked my hair and made a face. "Take a shower," she said. She kissed me. "I brought you food." She stared into my eyes with a motherly reproach. I felt like I had just broken some plates in the kitchen. "How much money, do you think?" She smiled. "You are a very bad boy."

Her smile turned to laughter. "I love you," I said. "Just do it." The Man laughed and I took a deep breath. I put my hand to my chest.

She shrugged and walked into the crowd. Reporters chased after her. Cameras clicked furiously. "Let me through!" she yelled. My mother was besieged by questions, drowned by questions that didn't end, didn't begin, and she made her way through them, waddling, arms flailing. And then she stopped. "Where are the newspeople?" she yelled.

The commotion was immediate. The noise that rose in response to her question was the sound of the Age of the End of Media. Dan ran down to her then. And I saw my mother's head fall back with laughter. Dan reached her and put an arm around her and led her to the other side of the street. The media followed with their cameras and lights and booms and recorders. Dan set my mother up on the steps of a walk-up and held his hands high and then my mother whispered something into his ear and he laughed. The mess of media around them. Clamoring. Seeking attention. The need of a media scrum. My mother was its center.

"She's cool," Sophie said.

"I'd never have used that word to describe her," I said. My mother played the maelstrom around her with all the finesse of a toddler. She wanted everyone to know she was toying with them. She wanted to see who among the crowd was the most shameless. There was a perfection in it, a wit that was my mother's most admirable trait.

I leaned back and closed my eyes, surprised to have survived the encounter with my mother unscathed. I saw her in the garden, harvesting tomatoes. It's an image of her I've always retained. Her hands filthy, dirt on her knees, her black hair falling over her face, her smile as she worked her way through the tomato plants, her voice carrying through the breeze with song. She used to sing "Let Me Call You Sweetheart." She was the only person I knew who would sing the song not just with melancholy but with profound sadness. And her tomatoes would grow to be the largest on the block.

The Man appeared before me and flashed his big-mouthed smile. He really did have a tremendously large mouth. *Stay a little while*, he said. *And then you'll see.*

Where have you been? I asked. *Inside*, he said. *I've been inside, watching this with you.*

I opened my eyes. "Something's going to happen," I said, to no one, to everyone. I'd announced it to myself in the hopes that everyone would hear it. No one did.

My mother held court and then the Queen left. Dan told me he had made arrangements for her. An agent would handle my parents' appearances. For Dan, this was another rung on the ladder that he was sure would take him to the promised land.

"She's doing the right thing," he said.

"She always does," I said.

"You should, too," he said and he went inside.

He returned and placed a large plastic container filled with printed-out emails next to me. I glanced at it and looked up at him. "You don't have to if you don't want to," he said. I noticed then that he was wearing my pajamas. And he looked ridiculous in them. "I just figured this helps pass the time."

"What happened to the paperless office?" I said.

"And hardly any letters," he said. "Some. But mostly emails."

"To whom?" I asked.

"To you."

"No, I mean where are they sending these to?"

"We set up an email," he said. "Don't be stupid."

"It's a distraction," I said. It sounded ridiculous.

"And this isn't?" he asked, gesturing toward the controlled anarchy of the street. "You have a spectacle in front you. What's a little mail?"

"I hope you read English," I said to Sophie.

She pushed me gently. "I'm Quebecoise," she said. "Not stupid."

"And why are you wearing my pajamas?" I asked Dan, resigned to the mail, perhaps all of it.

Dan had moved in. He lived in my apartment, a situation that seemed to top the scale on the list of incredible things that had happened to me recently. "Mine aren't as comfortable," he said, beaming.

"So, what, you rummaged through my stuff and tried my pajamas on?" I asked.

"It wasn't like that," Dan said.

"They look stupid on you," I huffed. And they did. Dan was taller than I was. And the pajamas, something I hadn't worn in eons, were emblazoned with fire trucks. A client had given them to me after a semi successful campaign for an antacid product launch.

"I owe all this to you," Dan said. "I can file my stories from here, I can eat here, I can sleep here. It's almost a dream."

"You need to get a life," I said. "I'm serious. You're going to end up in worse shape than me."

Dan kneeled down. "I'm being honest here: I'm enjoying myself," he said. I could feel a tingle of something in his voice.

"You need a girlfriend," Sophie said.

Dan looked hurt. Or rather, he mocked the idea of looking hurt. "What makes you think I like women?" he said.

Sophie snorted. "You're not even metrosexual," she said. "I'm not sure you're even Italian."

Dan relaxed. "I'll admit something," he said. "My attention is on Angie. That's the truth." This touched me in places that were annoying at best. And where was Angie? She was obviously using the back entrance to come and go. And it occurred to me that everyone in the building must be doing the same. Except for Dan.

"Not the way you're dressed," Sophie said. "Women don't respect men in pajamas. Not even silk ones. Just so you know."

Dan sighed. "My inner Hugh," he said. He scanned the crowd for signs of change, a difference, a hook to help him write today's useless story. His search resulted in nothing. Again. There really was no story here. But now, now that he could spend his days in pajamas, my story was his lifestyle. And we all defend our lifestyles. He eyed the box of mail. "Maybe we can print some of the letters," he mused.

"Maybe not," I said.

"Do something," Dan said. "If you'd just get online, get a blog going, whatever. You need to be in touch with the world. There's interest in you. If the people out there don't convince you, think about Sophie. About why she's sitting here. Your Facebook page is huge. The Twitter feed has thousands and thousands of followers.

The website is generating big traffic. People are mashing up the video feed and posting on YouTube. Some of it's hilarious. I've heard of copycats in other places. They give up after a few days but still. The world is watching. They're plugged in. They're reading about you."

"Don't start again," I said.

"C'mon, Web 2.0, the conversation, it's what we're talking about," he said. "Media buzz words. Engagement. I mean, you know that word."

"Don't get me started on that," I said. I'd done a lot of thinking on the interactive web, back when I had a job, on its effects on the channels of communication and the changes it would bring. On return on engagement, on the metrics that might power the world forward and unleash new levels of money. The manner in which we could convince consumers we were selling the best thing ever.

"Everybody's a somebody," Dan said. "Imagine the popularity of a chat room even, something as old fashioned as a chat room, if you just showed up and held court."

"The web is just another part of our cult of entitlement," I said. "The web tells everyone that everything you say, every opinion you have, every action you take, has value. It's the logical conclusion to the entitlement that everyone feels. It's brought fifteen minutes down to one."

"Such harsh words," Dan mocked.

I reached for an apple. Sophie took one, too.

"So at least do the mail," he said. "Answer them or don't but even a photo of you looking over the mail will mean a lot, I'm guessing. We could run an entire page of your letters in the paper."

"No," I said. "It's not right. These are private. I don't know if I'll ever answer them, but you're not printing anything."

The idea of sending an email terrified me in an odd way. Not because I'm a Luddite, but because the immediacy of email would render this exercise untenable. Dan was proposing something that would result in me drowning.

"If I answer these letters . . ." I said.

The Man sat next to me. *This is interesting*, he said.

"You're going to answer the mail?" Dan asked.

"I can help," Sophie said. "Because I can write in English, too." She touched my arm and my insides warmed up.

"You can be an odd duck," Dan said. "I'm wearing your PJs and you're worried about privacy." He returned inside.

I reached into the box and pulled out a handful of emails. Sophie did the same. There were letters mixed in, something I hadn't noticed. Addressed to me. Stamps from England, South Africa, Japan, Indonesia, Canada, Ireland, France, Spain, Australia, Brazil, Thailand, Russia. Return addresses from across the country. Sophie held a letter from Liberia with a triangular stamp colored gold. "Aren't they shooting people here?" she asked.

The letters and emails were mostly religious in nature, more confirmation that all religions are the result of a single man's dream. My mother had once said that new religions were made impossible by the birth of psychiatry. How could we promote our visions if there were learned professionals willing to analyze our dreams for a few hundred bucks a session?

So what was I doing? I'm contradicting myself, I know. There's good reason for this and it covers the surprising aspect of the letters. One, I'm not religious. At all. A belief in God is too easy. It's necessary. I can understand that. But I also think the corruption of the idea of God with religion is all the proof any skeptic needs as to God's existence. To me, God is a good idea, a universal idea and desire brought out of Africa as a firm belief and then demeaned by human stupidity. Nothing new in that. It's what usually happens.

I also think psychiatry is a crutch for lonely people in a society that has forgotten the art of conversation. I argued about this with my father quite a bit. He was a believer in what he called "massaging the brain." He spoke of touching the right parts of it, that there was nothing ever wrong in exploring something we didn't understand. But we have replaced dialogue with nachos and *Monday Night Football*. The result is the water wall of noise that is talk radio. For example. Unless you're really insane, or seriously damaged, there is no need for a therapist. This is a line of thinking that always leads to great trouble with my friends and coworkers. So be it. This is what I believe. Life is hard. It's not meant to be easy. It is something we endure because we are born. My parents did not push their religion on me and my father wavered between bouts of skepticism and certainty. My mother did not suffer from doubt.

Sophie read an email from a rabbi in Australia who warned me against the lure of false prophets, bringing up Moses and the Golden Calf his followers had fashioned while he was hiking up Mount Sinai to pick up the commandments. I opened a letter from an Anglican minister in England. He also spoke of God's "infinite wisdom" and his "boundless love" and the "mysterious and frankly frightening manner in which He is revealed to His flock." The minister wrote that his congregation had been following my story closely and were prepared to send money so that I could "follow His word without fear, without reservation, and without the multitudinous headaches brought on by the mundane." He prayed for me constantly, he wrote, and wondered if I could not hear his prayers. He invited me to his church and said that I would find "comfort and a warm bed" should my travels ever take me his way. He ended the letter with the strange declaration that Paul McCartney lived close by.

Dan returned, his head brimming with more bad ideas. Looking into his eyes, I could see the excitement, the possibilities blowing through his mind like sheets of paper caught in a fierce wind. "You are an icon. You mean something. Don't you see it? People are going to start worshipping you! Literally."

"The Indian reporter said the same thing," I sighed.

"Should I call you Lord?" Sophie asked.

"No one's going to worship me," I said.

A woman from Sacramento wrote about her abortion. That's it. One long run-on sentence describing the abortion in gruesome clinical detail. Another woman from Seattle wrote of the guilt she felt for bedding her boss to ensure a promotion. A boy from Texas admitted to stealing money from his sister's piggy bank. A grandmother from Jamaica despaired over her grandson's recent conviction for murder. A man from Dublin wrote that he had been sleeping with two women, sometimes on the same day, and neither one was his wife. A man from Hong Kong wrote that he had walked out of a fish market without paying for his purchase. A teenager from Wichita wrote to say I was a fake, just another reason to believe that God could not be trusted. I was becoming the world's confessional. The individual isms that feed this world had found a release in me because, as one man from Holland put it, "You seem to have the ear of that which is mightier than we, which some will call God, but which I will call the cosmos." I read about crimes, infidelities, heartaches. Transgressions. Alcoholics who had returned to the bottle, junkies who could not end their habits, overeaters, undereaters, smokers, ex-smokers, the greedy, the flinty, the venal, the morose.

And, of course, from the religious communities, from all the communities I thought there were and then some. I heard from Moonies in Korea and from their Washington office, from small Christian sects in Idaho that built their crosses out of discarded rifles and semi-automatic firearms, from Christians of all sorts who were convinced the Man was Jesus. From Muslims. From Hindus. From Jews. From Jews for Jesus. From Buddhists. From Taoists. From a priest who said he was Farsi. From an Aboriginal elder in northern Australia. From a twelve-year-old boy in Orlando who said he was God and I was pissing him off.

FORCES AT WORK

The rain never comes as a surprise here. We can see the rain clouds forming over the mountains and then speeding toward the ranch. The majesty of the sky, the drama of it, acts as its own warning system.

Time to prepare.

The awnings come up over the dining patio, plastic sheets get pulled down, heaters come out if need be. The horses are brought in. Umbrellas are delivered to guests who have strayed too far from shelter. The Rainy Day Activity Plan is implemented. Guests are led to the indoor swimming pool or invited to the main salon for a lecture on "How to Create the Holistic Home." There are tours of the stables. A movie is announced for the theater, a western usually, *Stagecoach*, say, or to impress the guests, *Rashomon*. And then, usually within fifteen minutes, the clouds part and the sun breaks through and the sky returns to its swimming-pool blue. The wet grass sparkles with a vivid kind of joy. The earth heats up. Guests are encouraged to enjoy the outdoors again if they are so inclined.

The rains have been falling now off and on the entire day. Cycles of fifteen minutes. From wet to brilliant sunshine to a somber gray blanket to sun to wet. The kitchen staff spends days like these indoors—either in the kitchen or in the mess hall preparing the room for the next meal. In slow motion. If the night is rainy, or cool, or both like it is tonight, parties break out in the trailers, the halls become tightly squeezed dance clubs and everyone is on the lookout for a nighttime pull and poke.

There's a lot of sex here. For the workers, it's the only thing to do; booze and grass can only be so entertaining. People here need sex to connect to the world, I think, to take their place in a world where being rich doesn't matter, to feel the contact of skin, the feeling of being alive and wanted, where the size of the mountains doesn't diminish you, where the wind can remind you that you're nothing but dust. At least that's what the wind makes me feel like.

I sit in the employees' lounge, looking over the PR kit this place sends to media around the world. A small PR office in Los Angeles handles the account. There is one basic media kit for the entire world and it can be customized depending on the recipient.

Press clippings from sundry magazines and newspapers. A history of the property. The mission statement, which, like most mission statements, is banal, a generic mishmash of luxury and relaxation and empowerment. A dash of hokey western imagery, using a language that only PR people use. This language is arcane, empty, devoid of living. It speaks of nothing while promising everything. It is a hollow vessel, the air inside a crystal vase. No lies. Just omissions of truth. And always a smile, a breathlessness that manages to appeal to the reader, but only if they have already committed themselves to the idea of a vacation. This is not messaging for someone sitting down. It will only resonate with someone who has already stood up. And is thinking about planning something.

There are bios of the owners, of Athena, of Tomas. Beautiful shots of the rooms, the horses, a shot of the entire property with the mountains in the background. Probably taken from a barely hovering helicopter. The restaurant menu, the various offerings from

113

the spa, a checklist of outdoor activities. Dominant words include "active" and "stunning" and "holistic" and "pamper." The kit is done up in a white binder with silver, embossed lettering. It could be for any hotel from any city in the world. Or it could be for a bar of soap. Or a new brand of vodka.

But nowhere is the real quality of the ranch made obvious. Because it is impossible to understand the isolation of this place, the effect nature has on anyone who comes here, the quality of the sunlight, the bigness of the sky. All of that is primordial. It is what makes Tomas's food taste the way it does. It affects the quality of the sleep as much as the mattress or the elevated thread count of the Egyptian cotton sheets. It is what makes riding a horse here different from riding one anywhere else. It affects your mood and your sense of self. It changes you. This is the ultimate promise of any destination.

There is no admission of winter.

During the winter, half the staff is let go. Many head south, to Mexico. And live off their earnings. And then return in the spring.

There is no admission of winter because there is no plan for it. Like a lot of things around here.

Advertising, PR, whatever, has a way of rendering you inhuman. A transfusion of toxic blood. Or worse. Like having lite beer coursing through your veins. But it's also a way of telling the world you exist. It proves that you are. Advertising is the engine of our economy, of our way of life. It keeps everyone working. Because it's there to get us to consume. And without consumption, we have nothing. It is so central to our way of life that it is almost impossible to imagine a life devoid of it, of the message. How would we know what to buy or wear or eat or watch on TV without advertising? How would we know who to cheer for without advertising or marketing or PR? How would we consume the world's stories? How would we get out of bed?

I believe all of this even if the methods of getting the message out leave me cold. And unsatisfied.

But I believe it.

I also believe that when done properly, there is no more creative force in the world. And that belief, really, at its core, is what makes me sad. Not that I was good at it. But that our most creative endeavor is built around making you want stuff.

And I have thought that perhaps this whole thing came about as a form of apology.

I was a copywriter for an agency.

I often think about the power of the word. Or I used to. My job was to manipulate words in a way that would in turn manipulate someone else. To action. To modify behavior.

This is the true power of the word, or at least, this is the power of those who can assemble words in a manner that is at once understandable but not. I wrote words in which were embedded symbols and meanings that were easily accessible to the surface intellect of the listener or reader but that also penetrated the deeper neurons of the consumer. Meaning everyone. The danger of these words was the easy manipulation, the font of the delivery that could easily allow me to imagine a fellow human being as nothing more than a wallet with choices that needed limiting.

I was about limiting choices. People don't understand this. Advertisers aren't about choice at all. Advertisers are opposed to the principle that choice is the height of power and freedom. They don't want people to hear about or even want that power. They want to take that responsibility away. They want to make consumers children. They want to take care of consumers, nurture them, make their decisions for them, train away their instinct.

This is the story my boss told me: imagine a bird that simply knows where it must fly every autumn. One day, for no other reason than some deep-rooted itch, a bird will take off and fly thousands of miles just to avoid the cold. And then one day, it will do the same, only in reverse, just to lay eggs. And it will continue to embark on these journeys, year after year, until it is shot by a hunter or infected by a bug carrying some sort of imported trauma or it simply becomes old. It won't think about it. That bird will go about its business and never have to wonder if it did the wrong thing or not. This is what advertisers want for their public. Replace the bird's flight with the purchase of soap and you have something. Instinct. The freedom of not having to choose. The freedom to be.

And when I accepted this story as something true and beautiful, I knew I had become an ad guy. Which was a realization that didn't shame me as much as I thought it would. It still doesn't. I can defend all this even while I find it utterly distasteful. My father called it "being an adult." Perhaps.

But it is also an art, a black one surely, a kind of carnival magic that has a science behind it, that is taught in schools, that can be vastly rewarding if done properly.

And so this is what Athena has asked of me. To assess. To see if the words are correct. If they match the feelings this place wishes you to feel. To see if what has been manufactured builds a brand, tells a story. The right story. She wants this place to tell a story to the right people. To touch them. To touch them so deeply that they will reach into their pockets and pay impressive sums for the privilege of that touch. She needs someone to tell it.

WALK THIS WAY

Dan came out with more printed emails, more unopened letters, the next morning. He suggested a laptop for me again, and again I refused. "This is a dance you can't win," I said.

"You metaphor mingler," he said. "You are a phenomenon."

I protested meekly.

"A celebrity," Sophie said.

"You realize this, right?" Dan said.

"What is there to realize?" I said.

"When you become a celebrity, not just a news item, not just someone famous, but a celebrity, you become a kind of pet," Dan said. "Or, to put it in words you might understand, a brand. That's what's building here."

Sophie stroked my hair. As if I were a puppy.

"The public starts to care for you in a significant way," Dan said. "They project feelings and desires. And once someone invests feelings in you, you've passed from mere fame to celebrity."

I had not dreamed of the Man during the night and this caused me an odd kind of worry.

"Look, we could go through all the letters and print the most interesting ones," Dan said. "Publish them. That's a book. *Letters to Joe*. Bang. No names, nothing, just the letters. A title that pulls at the heartstrings a bit. With something interactive on the web. Or a TV special where we read them to the camera. Get stars to read them. I'm just saying." He shrugged and gave me a sympathetic look that I found discomforting. "It just seems easy right now," he said. He returned into my apartment.

Sophie continued stroking my hair. I looked at her and smiled. "Do I look like a celebrity to you?" I asked.

"You're cute today," she said. "On TV, you don't look so cute, but in real life, you have a nice smile. And soft hair."

"Soft and greasy," I said.

"You should take a shower," she said.

I knew I should do a lot of things. I should just do what Dan says because there's merit to it. I should control this story before I became an item in *US Weekly*, an obnoxious arrow pointing to my greasy hair. The text would read "Gross!!!!" I should go back to my office and beg for my job. I'll start over, I'd tell them. At the bottom. I leaned my head on Sophie's shoulder and closed my eyes. And the Man appeared on his horse, dressed liked a cowboy from the chorus line of *Oklahoma!* and said, *Go west. You know where to go.*

I opened my eyes and stood up. The cameras around me, the crowd, everything, fell silent. There was an air of expectation. As if everyone had heard what they were sure they could not hear. Life stopped. The world did not move. At that moment the city was as quiet as I'd ever heard it. The millions of cars and buses and subway cars and trains. The millions of people. Their cell phones. Everything appeared to stop. "What is it?" Sophie asked.

"I have to go," I said.

And then the sound returned, the cacophony of daily life, of New York, that sound that makes up the city. The cameramen sensed something and starting working. There was a storm. It sounded like hail, like millions of balls of ice hitting the sidewalks. Dan ran out. "What's this?" he asked. "What happened?"

"I don't know," I said. I turned to him. "I think I have to go." I looked down at Sophie and saw the concern on her face and the sadness and knew she would not be accompanying me. She wasn't crazy enough. And at that moment, I might have loved her. "I have to go," I told her.

She smiled. She stroked my leg. "I'm happy for you," she said.

I stood up. I looked at Dan. "I'm going to take a shower," I said.

And his face dropped. His wonder turned to concern. "You're going inside?" he asked. "That's the drama?"

I walked past him and into my apartment. For the first time since Dan had moved in I looked at it. I studied it. This place. These walls. This house. Mine. And now, it was a mess of cables. The junk that runs our world, the stuff we rely on to communicate. The couch had been moved closer to the TV. Dan had been sleeping on my couch. There was food on the coffee table, boxes of pizza and Chinese takeout. Dan had an open suitcase on the floor. The TV was turned on and on it a reporter I recognized from outside was delivering an account of the latest happenings. My latest happenings. She was trying to parse my words, what I might have meant by "I have to go," whether this meant a break or something more permanent.

"It's not like you haven't seen the place," Dan said.

I had once slept in here. This had once been my home.

Sophie stepped inside. "I want to take a shower, too," she said.

I turned to her.

"After you," she said.

And I deflated. And felt oddly comforted knowing she didn't want to have sex with me, or wouldn't, or possibly hadn't even considered it.

"I have to go," I repeated. Outside, the murmur was like the whistling of leaves in the wind. "Where the fuck am I supposed to go?" I asked.

PART FOUR

OUTSIDERS

The fancy dude ranch. It makes perfect sense to me. People need to feel that what they're doing is more exciting or exotic or dangerous or interesting than it really is so they can go home after a week here and say they went to a dude ranch in northern Montana. What they really should say is they went to a spa in northern Montana. Instead of busting broncos, they busted their guts on T-bone. They spent days in the whirlpool or experiencing the joy of shiatsu. They lounged around in the library drinking martinis. They watched movies in a theater sitting on fat couches covered in buttery leather. And sometimes, when they felt they really should see some of the countryside, they got on the horses. Or they went for a hike.

Which is what some of them are doing today. This takes me out of the kitchen on my days off sometimes. It allows me to see the area without much effort and planning. I'm driven to a ridge a half-mile up the mountains where I prepare a picnic lunch for the hikers before they arrive. Rare roast beef sandwiches served with stone ground mustard and wilted greens. Grilled vegetables. Polenta cakes smothered in creamed porcini mushrooms. An Oregon pinot noir, a cab from California, a Washington shiraz. All laid out on herringbone-patterned linens created by a small outfit in Idaho and served on designer china. This is the language this place speaks, the currency of its sale. The reward. Everything here is about the reward, the promise that effort brings.

Before the hikers arrive, I stumble up some rocks and sit on a perch overlooking the valley. I take out a cigarette and light it and spot the hikers edging their way up the gentle switchbacks that will lead them to their picnic. The size of the ranch is a constant surprise. It's a small country. And the ranch is just a small piece of what I can see. This place does a good job of making you feel like nothing. Down on the plains, the size you feel is dependent on your mood. The color of the sky. In the mountains, the only grandeur is the rocks. Not you. Never.

And here it is easy, perhaps, to acknowledge a collective failure of the human spirit to be soothed by this. People like John Muir shouldn't be exceptions. No one should have fought Teddy Roosevelt as he established the idea of the national park. We should not need to experience a feeling to know it is true. Too many of us are so far removed from the natural world that it has lost its reality. Its meaning. The natural world risks becoming a figment of the imagination, a good idea, maybe, but scary, too, a repository of old stories. Nightmares.

I suffered from those feelings, too. And it will never happen again.

A gust of wind blows the faint laughter of the hikers my way. One of them is singing. I see a group for a second before they switchback and are again hidden by the side of the mountain. I don't know if the guests who come here are happy in general but most of them seem to let loose at the ranch. It's hard to stay uptight in this place. This landscape touches something very basic in people. It should. The serenity is a given. It's obvious.

People come here to relax. If they can't, the vacation has failed.

It has served no purpose. It is the kind of failure that humbles and humiliates. The people who come here are not good at failure. Or at admitting to it. Failure is for sessions with the therapist. A secret. The awful shadow behind the sunshine of their smiles.

Six hikers reach the picnic spot, out of breath, exhilarated. They look over the valley and stare at the vista. They break out the cameras and snap photos. Video cameras scan the endlessness of it. They nestle up to the food and eat it and salute their achievement. They suck back the wine. I spend the next hour filling wine glasses, dishing out more polenta, more sandwiches. And then I call out, "I have one more thing to show you," and I take them to the Perch, a spot where the vista is especially fine, poetic even, and I'm asked to take photos. And then it's done. The food is gone and the hikers get themselves ready for the return and are gone. We load up the garbage and the dishes and the linens into the jeeps and drive back to the ranch. By the time I'm back in the trailer, the sun is low over the mountains, the day complete. I can open a beer and look at the sky. And fall asleep trying to count the stars and not feel overwhelmed by the sensation of unknowability. It's not in our nature not to know. It's what drives us. There's nothing left to discover. What drives us now?

STORM BEFORE THE CALM

And I took a shower. I stepped into the tub and unleashed the water and let it drown me. I stood in the current and closed my eyes and let the world vanish. It left me. The days and nights and weeks went down the drain. And I scrubbed myself with a bar of soap. I used up what was left of the soap and then I shampooed and rinsed and shampooed again. I rubbed the shampoo all over me. Into my armpits. And then I shampooed my head again. I turned the cold water low and lost myself in the warmth of what was around me. In the steam.

I turned the shower off. "I can hardly see you." It was Sophie. She was somewhere in the steam. I opened the curtains and I could barely make her out. She hovered, somewhere in the small room and I forgot about my nudity. My state seemed relative then; I had been naked before the world for so long already.

And I noticed she was naked. "I hope you didn't steal all the hot water," she said. And she stepped by me and into the tub.

"Should I stay?" I asked.

She laughed. So I stepped out.

"I'll find you a clean towel," I offered.

"Dan gave me one," she said and she turned the water on and closed the curtain.

I dried off and went to my bedroom. Dan had not touched it. Some part of him respected me enough to stay out of my bedroom and I found that odd. I toweled off, put on fresh underwear, a pair of jeans, a white T-shirt. My clothes still fit, the physics of the wait more meta than actual. I thought for a moment of making my bed, disheveled all this time, and so I did. I made my bed. I straightened the sheets and punched the pillows and all the while questioned why I was doing it. The Man sat in the corner of my room, a huge smile on his face.

Sophie walked into my room and toweled off and got into her clothes. She was extraordinary. "Why?" I asked.

"What are you talking about?" she said, smelling her bra and making a face.

I didn't answer. I didn't even know what I had wanted to ask. Perhaps everything. I left the room and stepped back outside, to a storm of lights and questions.

The news of my latest revelation spread through the media and then out to the world. In the following twenty-four hours, I was asked repeatedly about my destination, which I didn't know, and about what I expected to find once I got there, which was even more impossible to know, and how I would get there, which was the point at which the interviews became either redundant or funny, depending on one's point of view. I saw massive redundancy, Sophie saw great humor, and Dan saw a logistical nightmare.

The news was big. I understood this. And people needed to make sense of it. I didn't understand that part. Dan had not planned for this, of course. So he saw in my pronouncement an attempt to get out from under his yoke. As long as I remained on the steps, he could stage-manage things. My announcement made the situation more serious. It broadened the scope of the story. The inclusion of travel made his role, for the first time, potentially untenable.

I tried to make him understand the transcendent nature of the Man, something that seemed silly at this point. Like trying to teach a newborn the meaning of life.

"You need a car," Sophie said, perhaps the most logical thing anyone pointed out during this time. And this was true. Transport. I was headed west. Meaning what? New Jersey? Or California? I had no idea. Dan put out a press release and that evening a Honda dealer from Long Island announced that he was prepared to let me use a minivan as long as he could be the official sponsor.

"The official sponsor of what?" I asked Dan. "You say you're an official sponsor it has to be of something."

"Of this," Dan said, his arms sweeping across the circus before us.

"But I won't be here," I said. "I'll be driving. And I don't know where I'm going. So he's sponsoring what exactly?"

"You, I guess," Dan said. "Your adventure."

The Honda dealer was a short, spindly legged man with a thick head of white hair. He was obviously proud of this decision. He said with car sales the way they were, this was a great opportunity. For him and for Honda. He had no idea what to call his proposal either. "You're in advertising," he said. "Come up with something."

The calzone and pizza were mere prelude to the commerce my antics would generate. After all, the corner store had become my official supplier of Coke. A café supplied my coffee. A linen store in Soho had supplied me with blankets and pillows. I was media in and of itself. Even though I didn't say or do anything. And so having this short successful man standing before me, offering a minivan, a Honda Odyssey to be exact, comforted me in a way, because it made more sense than anything else that had happened. The logic was consistent with the factory of inanity my life had become. I was producing another reality now. There was a symmetry to the situation, I felt this, even though I couldn't understand it. Or perhaps I didn't want to. "I want a red vehicle," I told the dealer.

"I can arrange that," he said.

"I don't want rental colors. Green. White. Fuchsia. I don't want to be a sitting duck in Buttfuck, Ohio, in an obvious rental." I could imagine myself on the wrong side of the tracks in a small Rust Belt town, as a band of bored teenagers decide to rough up the deluded out-of-towner.

"So you're going to Ohio?" Dan asked.

"I'm going to be adamant about the red," I told the Honda dealer.

"I understand," he said. "I'm familiar with the color."

"A good red," I said. "Not feminine."

"Depends on the tone," he said. "Red can be virile. Like a punchy Italian wine."

"I guess I can't be choosy," I said. "You have me in a minivan."

"You've made a request. I can fulfill it," he said. "And you need a minivan. You need size. Who knows how long you'll be on the road? You'll need to pack. You'll need space. I'll make a call. We have good inventory right now. A macho red."

"How does this play in the media?" Dan wondered out loud.

"In Peoria?" I asked.

"Will you be driving though Peoria?" Dan said.

"I don't know where this is taking me," I said. Again. "I feel like a broken record saying this."

"And I would want to indicate my sponsorship on the side of the Odyssey," the Honda dealer said.

Sophie laughed.

"What would it say?" I asked.

"You think of anything yet?" he asked. "Official Sponsor of Joe Fields," he said slowly, conjuring. He smiled half-heartedly. It sounded idiotic to him as well.

Sophie's laughter had become a sustained giggle.

The Man was back inside of me now. And he was laughing, too.

"You're not really sponsoring me," I said. "If anything you're sponsoring the trip. You're providing the vehicle that makes it possible."

The Honda dealer scratched the white mane of hair that perfectly rounded the top of his round head. "How about just Official Sponsor, with my name and logo and the such," he suggested. "We'll keep it simple."

"That sounds reasonable," Dan said.

"It would be something," the dealer said. "I would be the official sponsor of something and that would be enough for me."

"Plus, it's an Odyssey," Dan said. "It writes itself."

"What a great way to get a car," Sophie said.

"It's a minivan," I said.

The dealer turned around and faced the masses. He raised his arm to ask for silence. Incredibly, he got it. The buzz quieted to a low hum. "Joe Fields, as you all know, has announced his intentions of driving west. And he will do so in a Honda Odyssey supplied by Rolston Honda of Uniondale, Long Island!"

The media descended upon him and he was lost inside a cluster of microphones. "What's the level of whelmed below under-whelmed?" I asked no one in particular.

Dan leaned over. "I'll make sure everything's done properly," he said ominously.

"This is all very tacky," I said.

"It's interesting," he said.

"There's a gulf between interesting and tacky," I said. "An ocean."

"I don't know that anyone makes that comparison," Dan said.

"I know what you mean," Sophie said.

"There's an odd classlessness to this," I said.

"Said the adman," Dan said.

And I shut up. And I understood finally what my father had called America's odd lack of shame. He claimed that the lack of order and dignity would one day be the county's undoing. The singular lack of shame kept breaking down barriers and soon there would be nothing worth breaking down anymore. I remember this conversation. I was being scolded for spitting on the sidewalk. I can see him in the silly purple sweatshirt that he'd purchased at a souvenir stand in Pompano Beach. I had always thought him wrong. American's strength was its shamelessness. Because this shamelessness was just another side of fearlessness. It's what the rest of the world doesn't understand.

The Japanese version of shamelessness had everything to do with humiliation, with the order of their society, its endless way of rendering one small. America's shamelessness was different. Yes, we don't care. It's too bad, but in the end, it's true. We don't care. And this allowed us the freedom to innovate, to aspire, to lead the world without fear of failure. He kept on about how this singular shamelessness allowed people to believe they could purchase class and that the worst type of person was the shameless who comes into money. Every time television hit a new low, he called me up to rejoice in his supposed triumph. I thought of this then, because this carnival was my doing. All of it. I may have felt powerless to stop it but I did possess that power. At some point. The fact that the tackiness of my situation was self-inflicted hit me with the force of a truck. Or a Honda Odyssey. And I was annoyed by a growing sense of something approaching self-importance.

I turned to Sophie. She was looking at me intently, studying me, thinking. I could see what was going on inside her head. Sophie was the kind of person whose face was simply a window into the mysteries of her being. And suddenly, I felt alone again. "Why aren't you coming?" I asked.

"I can't," she said, slowly shaking her head.

"You should," I said.

"I can't," she repeated. "I should go home. I've stayed longer than I thought I would." She kissed my cheek. "I'll stay here until you leave."

Through Dan I granted two interviews to the television people. To NBC because I felt sorry for the entire network. Because I used to like them and then they lost their way and then they lost it some more. And to PBS just to please my father. We did the interviews in my apartment. To both interviewers I repeated the fact that I had no idea how this would end up, how long it would take, where I was going, or that I would even recognize my destination once I'd reached it. And during the interviews the Man was inside of me, laughing. He couldn't stop laughing.

Later that night, sitting on the steps, Sophie leaned over and said, "I know you'll make it."

"Make it to what?" I asked.

"To something," she said.

Sophie had been doing interviews herself. A large contingent of media had come down from Canada. "I've been booked on some talk shows back home," she told me. "Maybe I can stop selling perfume."

I was glad that some good had come out of this. At least Sophie saw a brighter day. "You should go then," I told her. "Return to Montreal and become a local celebrity."

She held my hand.

Dan sat beside me. "I have to make arrangements."

"I don't doubt it," I said.

"You've thrown me a bit of a curve," he said.

"I'm here thinking about throwing you curves," I said.

"Don't get sarcastic," he replied.

His cell phone rang and he stood up and walked inside.

"You're angry," Sophie said, releasing my hand. She began stroking my back.

"I'm not angry," I said. I wasn't. I was annoyed and tired and fed up but I was not angry. Any anger I might have had was washed away in the shower.

"You're what then?" she asked. "I don't know the word in English. You don't know what foot you're dancing on. It's cute."

"I'm not cute," I said, like a fifth-grade boy trying to be a man.

"Disoriented," she said. "Is that a word?"

I sighed. I felt as if the world, or at least the picture I had of it, was melting. I felt that all the mysteries of life that had shot by me for so many years were crashing down suddenly, like a box of ball bearings released. I felt like letting the wind pick me up and drop me far away, to an island somewhere far removed from this city, another island, uninhabited. I closed my eyes and saw myself alone. I saw myself on this street, alone. And then I knew this was impossible. I faced a future where I could never be alone again. "Is there some place where they don't have television?" I asked.

"I once read that the Chinese don't allow television in parts of Tibet," she said.

"Television-free Tibet." I sighed.

Sophie reached for a slice of pizza. "I'm so tired of this stupid pizza," she said, picking a piece of pepperoni off her wedge. "When I go home, I'm eating a nice salad; I'll have some wine. Read. I like reading; did you know that?" she asked. "I'm going to light some scented candles and lie in my bathtub and read a good book."

This was an image I wished I could hold on to. Something that might keep me going. "Don't drown," I said. I felt as if I were speaking from authority on that at least.

EYES WITHOUT A FACE

Very few people recognize me here. By working in the back of the kitchen, by having the dumb luck of occupying the last room in the trailer, by being antisocial. I have remained relatively undetected. I think. I don't expect this to last. And when someone does recognize me, I can talk my way out of it. None of the guests have direct contact with me except on those hikes. I am a worker here, not a front-line employee, and so I am mostly invisible to them. I have added a beard. Even on the steps I managed to shave. I had an electric razor and I shaved every morning. I hate stubble. I was always clean-shaven, a pretension that made me feel presentable to the world. I was always the most clean-shaven guy at the office. I learned this from my father. Who had learned it from his. A long line of clean-shaven men.

My hair is long now. I usually wear a ball cap. I've put on weight. After all I went through, I put on weight here, eating a celebrity chef's rich food and his silly clafouti. Athena doesn't ask questions. Tomas wants to. Because he knows. I'm the reason he wishes he'd read more than the sports pages.

There is no manhunt for me. I expect this to change at some

point. Dan is either continuing his search or, sensing closure, has cashed in already. Am I worth more to him invisible? What if I showed up in Hollywood ready to sell my story? What if I walked into a newsroom right now? What if I granted an exclusive interview to a tabloid? To one of the networks? Would they laugh me out of the office? Or write me a check? And how would any of these actions interrupt Dan's planning? I see my story more as his. I was merely a subject. Dan was the storyteller, the driver of the thing. He ensured its momentum.

I almost miss him.

But as much as I do, I don't want him to find me. I enjoy being nobody. The act of being faceless is one of the most liberating things I've ever felt. Here, I have no past. Except for the parts I keep inside of me.

Last night, staring out the window, drinking a beer, I counted shooting stars. The wind blew through the trailer, creating a hum. Everyone was asleep. I was hypnotized by the sound of the wind. The tall grass swayed gently, lit up by the moon and the stars. The mountains the color of glow-in-the-dark stickers. And I realized I wanted to stay here. Not to revel in the anonymity of the place, or to hide from the world, or to turn my back on the life that led me here. But to work, to do the work that Athena had assigned me, to see what would happen. The mountains, the land, made me optimistic. Small. Insignificant. But optimistic.

Last night, suddenly, I stopped feeling like a failure. I can try to understand what happened to me or I can try to internalize the ordeal and move on. I think I have achieved some understanding of what happened, on some level, and this is letting me understand who I am. Even who I was. I have my talents and I have to accept them. I have come to accept them. The reality of life gets in the way of total happiness. Expectations need to be modified. Desires. Our ability to say yes and no and maybe. The pursuit of happiness just leads to an endless run, not even a marathon, because the finish line keeps fading from view. I do stuff. I can manufacture words. I'm about to do something like that again. And instead of lamenting the irony of it, I see it and know it, finally, for what it is. Acceptance. And I can use that to build something, something as big and as ambitious as I can dare to imagine. Or not. I've tempered my dreams, perhaps, but they remain limitless. Except now they may have form.

What is there to live for after 100% satisfaction is not just guaranteed but achieved?

And the thing I learned is the main idea behind every ad ever made.

Today, in the kitchen, Tomas walks up to me with a smirk on his face. "We're moving a lot of pie," he says.

"Everyone likes a good pie," I say.

"You'll have to do more peeling," he says, the winner of a contest I haven't even entered.

"I figured that."

"With the mechanical peelers, you get problems. Abrasions. Bruising. They're too rough on the fruit. Only hand-peeled apples taste good."

"I'm not arguing with you."

"I'm just telling you. So you don't think I'm trying to stick it to you or something. Because I'm not."

"Great," I say.

"Just so we're clear."

"Good."

"I'm following your plan."

"What plan?"

"Well, what you said."

"OK."

He taps me on the shoulder. "Teamwork," he says.

"Good."

He walks away and moments later four men, including Keith, walk in bearing crates of apples. "Maybe the game show circuit doesn't look so bad," Keith says.

"It does from here," I say.

"There's no shame in work," he says.

"Peeling apples or being on a game show?"

He puts the crates down to my left. "Both," he says.

"Right," I say. I reach into the first crate and begin my work.

ALL ALONE

Dan made arrangements. Many. He was like Mercury orbiting the sun. I felt a certain awe watching him work. I say that only because it is still hard for me to admit. The amount of work he performed was cutting away at my antipathy like an ice pick. Food had been donated. He had procured a media bus that would follow the Odyssey. The bus was equipped with satellites and modem hookups and a fridge—everything journalists would need to tell the world my demented story. The webmaster for the site was joining the trip. Bloggers had been invited. The social media team. The bus was being outfitted right now by a company near Providence that specialized in this sort of thing. Industry was being created. Blips to local growth projections. Jobs.

I tried to shut myself off. I saw myself alone, surrounded by thousands of people, misunderstood—and if not that, at least, unappreciated. I felt like the cheap punch line to an egregiously bad joke. Something perhaps told by a failed comic on a three-digit cable channel after midnight. The entire ordeal had come to this and had achieved a kind of light-speed momentum. I felt a bit off balance by the movement of the thing. "Don't leave,"

I told Sophie and she didn't respond. I was groveling and it was pathetic.

Ever since the television interviews, the Man had remained silent. I tried to will him into my thoughts and could not. I didn't feel him inside of me. He was probably out west already. Somewhere. Some place I was supposed to be and couldn't fathom. The mystery of this journey had already been compromised. There was no more journey. There was only an event now. A random chorus of atonal, unplanned things. A search for an ending. A bad show on late night cable. A movie. Dan's book. This was product. The creation of a brand. The media bus would follow me to see how the brand developed. The world waited to see whether or not my brand was positive. I was hoping that the media would highlight the tackiness of my station and the world would lose interest. Dan kept calling my journey "gold."

Because I had the sense that despite Dan's best efforts, this wasn't huge. It wasn't going viral. It was niche. I was just another bit of noise in the world. Some people listened in but many didn't. Dan was the media, after all. He needed this story to be big. And the bus and my journey were his last chance to make it into something bigger than just me. And a few thousand lost souls around the world went along for the ride.

That was my sense of things. I had no way of knowing whether I was right or not.

The night before the departure I awoke from a nap to see Sophie staring deeply into my eyes, into my head, it seemed, trying to understand the torrent inside. My blanket was slipping off and heading down the steps. "Hi," she said.

I opened my mouth to speak, but she put a finger to it, shaking her head. "Don't say anything," she said. "Don't say anything. I know you're unhappy. I know it. I understand. I would be, too. There's something inside of you that makes you unsatisfied with living this way. You are unhappy. You were. I should say that. And now you're getting away. You'll keep driving until you get tired of it. Or until something special happens. You're looking for magic. And I hope you find it. It's very noble what you're doing. And because it's noble and special, people will lose interest. It will happen at some point. You've created a complicated thing. It's not really good on TV. The less you speak the better."

"You're an optimist," I whispered.

"You are, too," she said. She stroked my hair and began rocking back and forth. "Keep your mysteries to yourself. Don't give them the satisfaction," she said, gesturing toward the media. "You feel out of control but you're not. They don't know you. That's when it finishes, when they think they know you. Then they take advantage."

"A very cynical optimist," I said, smiling.

"Just think, you'll be by yourself," she said. "When was the last time that happened?"

That was a truth that had yet to occur to me. "I don't know," I said. "I've felt alone the whole time here. Until you arrived."

She leaned over and kissed me. My lips parted and met hers and I wanted to write country music. "I have to go home now," she whispered.

"I wish you wouldn't," I said.

"I have to go home and start my life," she said and it sounded like such a sensible, wonderful thing to be able to admit and do that I sat up straight. It was an odd reaction.

She stood up. "I'll watch you on TV," she said, without a hint of irony, and walked off, ignoring the pack of media that surrounded her. Dan walked down the steps and caught up to Sophie. He said a few words to the reporters and camera guys and they fell back and the crowd parted before her, magically, as she walked down the street toward the barricades. A limo waited for her on the other side of the police cordon and she got in it and disappeared. I suppose Dan had arranged that as well.

The crowd rumbled. This was an episode that needed discussion, analysis. There was something to Sophie's last words. I was getting away. Getting in the Odyssey would be like exhaling. I might never see this place again, I thought. And even this didn't bother me. No matter where I found myself, this would always be home. No matter where the Man took me. No matter what happened.

PART FIVE

WILD IS THE WIND

I'd heard about this. That sometimes it snows in the middle of the summer. That sometimes the cold winds that come off the mountains don't warm up, don't hit some hot air, and a perfectly fine summer day can become winter in less than five minutes.

It snowed after breakfast. The morning had been cold but that only made it like other mornings here. By the time the breakfast shift ends and we're ready to ramp up for lunch, the ground is warm and the insects buzz and it's summer. Not today.

Today walking outside is a fight through blowing snow. Bits of ice blow into my face, my shoes crunching on the ground. It sounds like broken glass. From the kitchen window, the mountains look like giant snow sculptures. The tall grass bends under the weight of the ice and snow. They look like they're suffering. Even the plants don't like the weather.

It's beautiful.

In the movies, snow is almost always clean and beautiful and pure. It makes everything seem fresh. And even now, even though it's summer and snow is as welcome as a plague of locusts, there's still something about the whiteness of the landscape that makes everything look new.

The wind is messing with the horses. It's uprooting fences and small trees. The snow is ruining people's vacations. All outdoor activities have been canceled for the day. The beautiful snow is bringing misery to everything it touches. It's so windy it's even hard to say snow is falling. Can something fall sideways? The snow is falling parallel to the ground. Is this what usually happens? And if it's not quite falling, when does it touch the ground? Wouldn't it just keep blowing?

It's August.

Some of the old-timers are always prepared for winter. They've got their boots and fleece layers on and lean into the wind while going about their jobs. There's work to be done. Crews run around looking for something to fix, for someone to help, watching the mountains for signs of the end of the storm. It's hard to tell where the sky ends and ground begins. There's no horizon.

And it's wrong. Everyone can see through the beauty of the event. That's what it is, an event. Athena runs through the kitchen, swearing. The unexpected seasonal change requires new plans, contingencies. Realities alter. Expectations shift. Tomas wonders out loud if he should add a stew to the menu for lunch, though it's too late for that. I watch a wrangler run toward the stables, head down, one hand holding his hat to his head. He runs and runs on unsteady feet, unsupported by the wet and slick ground and his legs give out from under him, and he falls hard on his ass. He lies on the ground, not moving, a blue denim spot on the speckled earth. He gets up slowly, wiping the snow off his pants. He rubs his tailbone and limps around the corner of the fence and is gone.

In the distance, the mountains take shape and suddenly the sun is shining and the snow on them glitters like casino lights. And slowly, the snow stops blowing or falling or dive-bombing the ground, the clouds scatter, the wind travels someplace else, and then, like a gold medalist, there's the sun, and the day is changed and the window is warmed and the sun's rays shine their crazy life everywhere and things start to feel normal again. The snow melts. It retreats in the face of the power of the sun.

Athena finds me in the kitchen. "Are you thinking?" she asks, flashing her smile.

"I'm always thinking," I say. "That's the problem."

"Did you see the weather?" she asks.

"It frightens me," I say.

And then Athena feigns concern and comes over and gives me a light hug. She hugs without really touching me. "There there," she says. And she walks into Tomas's office. And shuts the door. I hear laughter. Very loud laughter. And I wonder who told the joke. And hope it wasn't me.

Athena exits the office quickly. "Let's have a meeting," she says.

I put down my peeler. "Now?"

"Later," she says. "Tonight. Come to my place."

And this is when I start to wonder whether I should keep peeling. Whether or not this part of my work is starting to become an affectation. I spend the day thinking of her, a new optimism that washes over me like warm water.

I walk to Athena's place. The winds have changed direction. They aren't coming off the mountain anymore. The winds have changed direction since the snow. They come from the north now, from somewhere beyond Alberta, where it's always cold and the ground is always covered in snow. Each gust is enough to make your nipples hard and is a reminder that the snow that fell as a fluke a few days ago will soon become normal. Soon our ground will be covered with something frozen for months and the ranch will become a giant blanket of white.

I knock on her door.

Athena motions for me to sit on the couch. She pours me a red wine. She's dressed in her uniform, or big sky casual: frayed bootcut jeans, white cotton shirt, a red scarf wrapped around her neck and falling over her shoulders. "Did you ever think you'd see snow in the middle of the summer?" she asks.

"We're not really going to talk about the weather, right?" I say. "I'd like to think we're beyond the weather discussion."

"Haven't you noticed?" she asks. "Everybody here talks about the weather. It's not rude. It doesn't show a lack of familiarity. I can imagine in families it is the first topic of discussion in the morning. It is a relevant topic here."

She's making conversation. "I wish I knew something about the sky," I say, doing the same. "I wish I knew the constellations. There's probably something, some app, that tells you everything you need to know about your bit of sky. Well, not here. A book. Some local amateur astronomer probably has a book about the stars above Montana. It's odd that all we really know is the land. Most of the earth is water. And all of space is the sky. And we're tied to the land. And even at that I don't know anything about it. I don't know rocks, for example. Geology. I wish I knew geology."

I'd felt this more and more. Out here, I want to go beyond remarking about the beauty of the rocks, of the landscape, to knowing more about it. Geology is the story of the stuff we're standing on and I don't know the story.

"In Greece, it's all about the sea," she says, taking a sip of her wine. "The land is just the place the sea isn't."

"I can't even imagine the sea here," I say.

"One time, it was sea," she says. "There's a good book on the physical history of Montana in the library. There was a sea here. And then land. And then the mountains came. After the west coast floated over and hit North America. It was the first book I read when I got here. The Rockies are still growing."

"What does that mean?" I ask.

"I mean they are still rising," she says. "They are young. Just like the Himalayas are young."

"You're a fountain of knowledge," I say.

"I read the book," she says. "That's all."

"You read the book," I say, laughing.

"Yes. I read the book. I don't pretend to understand what it means," she says. "Everything about the rocks that make up Montana. I looked at the mountains and I found this old book in the library. It was a good book."

"It's very useful," I say.

"Don't mock me," she says. And with this, I'm about certain she's flirting with me. Or I want her to. I want the thrust and parry of a good flirt. Does Tomas know of our meeting? "I'm an elitist."

"No, you're not," I say.

"Why not?" she asks.

"An elitist looks down on the world," I say. "An elitist expects you to see things his way because he knows he's always right."

"I am," she says.

"Not in the same way."

"What's the difference?" she asks.

"An elitist sets the standards," I say. "He tells you where to look and what to see. In ad terms, we call these people influencers. They're even more elite than Washington's 'media elite' bogeyman. When we look out and wonder what it is we're watching, the elitist tells you and expects that all is understood. It's an expectation. It says, 'I understand so you must as well and if you don't, you're stupid and unworthy.' It's a bit poisonous, I always thought. Because it means never staying in one place. Never being happy with what you know. So you are constantly seeking more. More knowledge. Because with knowledge comes your opinion. Your edge. And these people believe in their role. Their place. They believe in the patterns to knowing, patterns that are new and improved and clean and clear and bright and minty fresh. Because we all believe in the end that we should know things we have no right to know and suspect things we have no right to suspect so that now, when we drive past a suburban office-complex parking lot, and see the darkened cars sitting alone at midnight, side by side, we wonder whether these are totems of adultery. We think of the partner at home knowing and not wanting to know. We don't want to see two cars in a parking lot. We see an old man and a young woman enjoying a burger in the neon-washed window of a fast food restaurant and wonder how much he's worth without even once considering that perhaps he's an uncle or a grandfather or Tony Randall. We think these things not because we want to but because we feel it is our place in the greater culture to think these things. Because we're participants in it, too, even though we've elevated ourselves, and sometimes we resent this, because we want out, we want to find an out, so we search for meanings where perhaps none existed, we search for patterns and lines where there are none and we become more susceptible to the messages we think we can avoid."

"Isn't Tony Randall dead?" she asks.

What am I going on about? I'm trying to decide whether I believe this or not. These are the arguments I left behind. Am I trying to impress Athena? Realizing that I believed everything I've said, at one time in my life, causes a pit inside of me the size of . . . Montana. "That's not the point," I say.

"You're rambling," she says. "Making conversation. And you just did this marketing speak like someone might talk about the weather. And perhaps you hate yourself, too."

"I used to," I say. "I don't anymore. I know that now. That's a good feeling. I admit that much."

We change. This is something that took me a long time to figure out. Nothing stays the same. Thinking this now, I feel almost stupid because it's such an obvious truth. A simple idea. People who don't change get left behind. If we hadn't changed we'd still be stuck in caves, beating off the saber-toothed cats with big sticks.

146

"Your little trip was like therapy?" she asks.

I slouch into the couch. "Maybe." I just can't admit to it. No one ever said therapy was cheap.

"Are you comfortable?" she asks.

"How big is that question?"

"With yourself," she says. "Here. With your situation. Have you processed what you've done? We're all here, in this place, for a reason."

"Are you talking about the ranch?" I ask. I need to be sure.

"Maybe," she says, smiling, taking another sip of wine.

"Or am I comfortable here, in your apartment, having a meeting?"

Athena laughs. Her laugh is like something out of Hollywood. It's deep and resonant and sexy all at once. Forties Hollywood. "I do want to discuss matters," she says.

"Does Tomas know I'm here?" I ask.

"He doesn't hate you," she says. "And we are not an item."

This news is neither a relief nor an added burden. "I think he resents my little clafouti campaign," I say. "That our little discussion has been elevated."

"He's insecure," she says. "That just means he's a good chef."

She gets up and goes to her bedroom. What am I supposed to do now? She returns, her arms full of papers. She throws them down on the couch, filling the space between us. With this she has answered any dirty questions I may have been harboring. Because I was. "This is the job," she says.

I take a long drink of wine. I pour myself another glass. "The job." I sigh.

"I think you will do it well," she says. She sits on the couch again. Closer. Between us, papers, letters, brochures, the paraphernalia of the sell. "I think your being here is a kind of miracle," she says.

BEGIN THE BEGIN

The Odyssey arrived, red as blood, or Australian wine, as the dealer had promised. It wasn't quite virile, but that's not the term one would expect to apply to a minivan. In a minivan, the masculinity is confined to the size of the cup holder. And whether or not it can keep drinks warm or cold. Or the coolness of the DVD player. Or the electronics on the dash, the computerized wizardry that can make the driver forget for a moment what he's driving.

Or maybe it's just impossible. Maybe the emasculation of the male has everything to do with the fact that millions of them are driving around the country in minivans. The first company that can make a virile-looking minivan is going to win the war, is going to bring their left-for-dead company out of the ashes into the share-holders hall of fame. The ad would have a suburban dad walking slowly toward the minivan, buckling up the kids and getting in, turning the ignition, all the while the Spencer Davis Group's "I'm a Man" played in the background. Any campaign that could equate masculinity to this *shape* would alter the landscape of our economy. I suspect that company will be Asian. Perhaps even Chinese. Americans can't build cars anymore. No, that's not true. We can build them. We just can't sell them properly. We have passed the mantle of design to the Japanese, the Koreans. The Europeans have always had it.

Two things we used to be good at: cars and skyscrapers and now we don't do either of them well. We can't make anything that takes your breath away. Look at all the starchitects: Europeans. Since the birth of the skyscraper, new buildings anywhere in the world have made a city look American. Now, even here in New York, all the new towers look like they're from Shanghai. I'm not sure when this happened but like everything else, I'm willing to concede 9/11 as some kind of dividing line. We don't want to admit it, but that trauma is still with us. Not in the stupid punch-drunk-with-rage wars we're fighting overseas, but something deep within us died that day and it's still dead. And it will stay dead forever. And a lot of Americans are still angry about it. Because they *know*.

Dan and I packed the Odyssey with sponsored goods. A giant cooler courtesy of Rubbermaid. Inside an assortment of Kraft cheeses. Fruits and pre-cut vegetables courtesy of Costco. Sandwiches courtesy of Dean & DeLuca. A dozen cans of tuna courtesy of StarKist. From the corner store an assortment of chocolate bars, fruit bars, granola bars, two bags of lemon cream cookies, a carton of orange juice, two bottles of Coke, two Sara Lee pound cakes, bags of Doritos, two jars of salsa, and a case of bottled water. A small portable microwave provided by Best Buy. Two more pillows, blankets, and a terrycloth robe courtesy of the new boutique hotel up the street. Three loaves of semi-frozen microwavable bread from a commercial bakery in Brooklyn. Two large pizzas from Dan's brother. A French cosmetics company provided me with a box of spray-on dry shampoo, which I wished they'd done sooner. I'd never heard of spray-on dry shampoo before. Outerwear from North Face. It was summer but they made a big deal of supplying us with outerwear. This took up the morning. Many photos were taken.

Someone from Popeye's came by with a bucket of fried chicken and a video crew and when they left they'd taken the fried chicken with them. Which was just as well.

Dan had also packed a duffel bag of clothes. And all the while, the media crowded around us peppering us with asinine questions. "Is that salsa?" "Dan, is that salsa hot or mild?" "How long will the subs keep?" "Were Dean & DeLuca not prepared to provide salad?" "Dan, what do you say to nutritionists worried about a balanced diet?" "Joe, are you worried by the lack of anything here?" And on and on it went. I missed Sophie. More than I thought I might. I didn't know how to find her if I wanted to. I didn't even know her last name. Dan had hired security to keep a clear area around the minivan but boom mics were still breaking the line and slamming me in the face, grazing the top of the Odyssey, reaching into spaces they shouldn't have been reaching.

What seemed like the entire sales team from Rolston Honda were on hand. The company logo was affixed to each of the front doors with a white store-bought "Official Sponsor" sticker beside them, along with a "Made with Pride in Lincoln, Alabama, USA" decal. The media bus was late in arriving and Dan would not allow me to leave without it. "There's no show with no show," he said.

Throughout all of this, I felt a kind of otherworldliness; a silence had surrounded me and shielded me from the chaos. My life had dissolved into a kind of surrealism and my only defense was autism.

Dan begged me to release a statement. He had spent the night composing press releases to ensure that every sponsor was mentioned and thanked. And now, he said, the media was thirsty for something. "The fine line between media and PR," I said.

"You need to say something," he said, ignoring me. "You're leaving these people."

We retreated to the steps and behind a line of failed linebacker types, we composed a press release. In it, I said, to my eternal shame:

It is with a sense of hope that I embark on this voyage. I don't know where the road will take me or for how long, but it's something I feel I must do. Your patience with me has been striking. I want to apologize to my neighbors for the inconvenience I've caused.

The journey to this point has been one of small surprises and discoveries. I have been honored to have shared it with my city, my country, and the world. I would like to thank all those who have aided me in New York, especially with food. I want to thank the NYPD for tolerating this. And I would also like to acknowledge the support of my many sponsors. Thank you again. We're going on a road trip!

I read it over and felt the makings of nausea. " I don't believe a word of it," I told Dan. "Except the apology. I don't talk like that or think like that or write like that. That's not me. The whole thing sounds like it's been written up by a big PR firm. Let me rephrase that. By a bad PR firm."

"We should have a PR firm," Dan mumbled. "In case this whole thing goes pear-shaped. Marketing people. I should have some PR chick on the bus."

"You're not listening," I said. Dan had stopped listening to me a long time ago. There was no point in listening to me. I was the least important part of the story in many ways. I wasn't to be listened to. Merely tolerated.

"Do you have any idea which way you're going?" he asked.

"I'm not sure anymore," I said.

"Because the bus driver would like to know at least your route out of Manhattan." He opened up his laptop and started typing out my statement.

"Do you have a book deal yet?" I asked.

"The bus driver's union," he said, not looking up from the keyboard. "You don't want to fuck with the unions."

"How much did you get?" I was sure he had lined up a book deal. Maybe he wasn't even typing the statement into the laptop.

"What are you talking about?" he asked. "And, send." He punched the enter key and opened the van's window. "Statement's out, boys," he told the press corps. He closed the window and turned to me. "What book deal?"

"About this. Don't play dumb," I said. I wasn't sure whether or not to jump into the front seat and drive off or sink to the floor in despair. Or laugh. Ever since packing the Sara Lee cakes I had been on the verge of laughter. I used to love Sara Lee pound cakes growing up. Perhaps autism was best.

He smiled a crooked smile. "You have the story," he said.

"I can smell smoke emanating from your pants," I said. I locked him in a stare. He looked at the floor.

"No," he said. "I have an agent, that's it. I've had offers. But until this thing plays itself out, there's no story. I'm small fry. My agent asked me to talk you into selling your story when all this is done. She sees books and a movie." He tried to smile now but I was being too serious.

"A movie about a man driving around America in a minivan?" I asked.

"Are we going to drive around America?" Dan said. He opened up his laptop again. "Good movies have started with less. Albert Brooks drove around in an RV. What was that movie called?"

"And if I don't?" I asked, crossing my arms.

"And if you don't what?" he asked.

"If I don't want to sell."

"I don't understand why you wouldn't," he said. "Fine. You don't see the theatrics of this or the opportunity, which, frankly, is surprising coming from an adman. So think of it from the financial perspective. There is a great tradition in this country of cashing in on life's adventures. You're going to end up God knows where and then what? Do you have a job right now? Perfectly rational people are willing to throw money at you. They are eager. Everyone in the world is allowed to be remunerated massively for a great idea. It's what unites people across income and geography and religion. One good idea. This one is yours. The money's on the table. Who would pass that up?"

I resented his use of the word "idea." "What if I do?" I said. Dan's question had the advantages of both logic and common sense. But I didn't care.

"And you know as well as I do this won't last. You know this even better than I do probably," he said. He put his hand on my shoulder. His eyes fixed on mine. "Look, stop shooting the messenger. I'm just saying. It's an escape from writing witty slogans for dog food. For foisting Irish-style beer with German slogans on society. I mean, that was brilliant but it didn't make you feel any better about yourself. If you deny it, you're a liar, too. This thing is the same for me. I admit that. I've used you. I admit it. Just as you've used me. If the end result is our mutual happiness, I don't see anything wrong in that. Do you?"

His question hung in the air like the effluent from a smoke stack. I was confronting something, I understood that, but I had no idea what that something was. I felt stupid, finally. But Dan was looking something worse. Almost desperate, I thought. And that made me feel if not better, superior. Purer. "I haven't had any notions here, Dan," I said. "And even if I had, I'm sure they wouldn't have sounded half as complicated as yours."

He let go of my shoulder. "What do you want from me?" he asked.

I wanted to watch him squirm. "Nothing," I said. "I want you to keep the people away from this minivan. Every night—or whenever we stop—I'll grant one interview. When I feel like it, let's say that. If I have anything else to add to the conversation, I'll approach you. I won't turn on the cell phone unless there's an emergency. Maybe we'll talk when I have to stop for gas. And that's that. Now go."

He stared at me, stunned. "Joe," he said, his voice trailing off. He rubbed his face in his hands. And then he turned around, slid open the door, and stepped out. "Departure in five minutes!" he called out. "Endless stories shortly thereafter."

I crawled over to the driver's seat and began adjusting the seat and mirrors and steering wheel. The key was already in the ignition. It appeared to glisten. I turned it and the Odyssey hummed into power. The dash lit up with that soothing cobalt car companies use. I lowered my window and stuck my arm out and struck a pose. One-millionth van sold! An onslaught of shutters were pressed down, creating a sound that I remembered from childhood. It was the sound of tap shoes. Of hundreds of tap shoes tapping the wooden gymnasium floor. Tap is like the soccer of the dance world: no one cares about it after the age of twelve.

I waved to the cameras. I even gave them a thumb's up. I wanted to wink but held back. I looked for Dan and he had to smile at the shamelessness of the gesture. I was angry with him but also relieved to be leaving. I wanted my neighbors to return to their normal lives—fighting off excessive gentrification and obnoxiously aggressive architecture, marveling at the new restaurants and boutiques opening up, wondering where the drugs had gone, complaining about the audacity of the new people moving in. Lamenting the loss of those who could no longer afford the area.

Normal life.

The media saw something. I turned around and saw the bus. It was large and black and ominous. On the roof an array of antennae and satellites gave it the look of a military command vehicle. A line of tired-looking men and women loaded it up with bags and cameras. Dan switched into the kind of organizational mode I associate only with the remarkable efficiency one sees in the third act of disaster movies.

I shifted into drive and the Odyssey slowly moved forward. The crowd parted, hesitating to let me leave without the bus. I was ruining the sense of event. Dan's expression leapt to terrified. He ran over to the minivan, knocking frantically on the window. I stopped and rolled the window down. "Very funny," he said.

"You're not laughing," I said.

"We'll be ready in two minutes," he said, looking back at his bus. Because it was his. There was no doubting that.

"Then you shouldn't have any problems finding me," I said. I was behaving like a child. I turned my baseball cap around. "It's a big country. What's two minutes?"

"Stop it," he said.

"This thing has GPS," I said. "And I'm sure you have some kind of tractor beam on me."

"Your van doesn't have GPS," Dan said. "I was worried how you'd take that. So they took it out. I also asked them to dismantle the tractor beam."

He was telling jokes again.

"Holland Tunnel," I said, just realizing my direction. It was the only road that made sense to me. It was also the only road I was sure about. It was the way to New Jersey, to my parents' home, west. New Jersey was west of Manhattan.

"You're taking the tunnel," he confirmed, composing himself. "And then the, what, the 78?"

I nodded. "Don't tell anyone," I said. "I don't want crowds along the highway."

"I won't announce your intended route," he said.

I smiled. I was ready. "Thanks." I closed the window and watched

Dan run back to the bus, his arms flailing wildly, the calmness he had exhibited now overtaken by fear. Inching the Odyssey forward was the confirmation that the story indeed wasn't his. I was controlling it. He had reminded me. And now I had reminded him.

What am I doing? I asked myself.

The bus was loaded and the media embarked. The police had cordoned off the street and at the end of my block I stopped the van and rolled down a window. A cop greeted me. He was a big man, with a belly that looked a bit ridiculous scrunched into his uniform. "Son, we're going to escort you out of town," he said.

"I appreciate that," I said.

"So if you told me what kind of route you had in mind . . ." he said.

"Holland Tunnel," I said.

"And then you're on your own, unless they have plans for you in New Jersey," he said.

"We'll see on the other side," I said.

He smiled then. "Good luck to you."

And I smiled back and extended my hand and we shook. He walked away and said something into his shoulder radio. I closed the window and moved forward and I was suddenly in the traffic of a regular workday in Manhattan. The police escort consisted of two cars ahead of me, two motorcycles on either side of me and two cars behind. Small crowds of people gathered on the sidewalk to watch me pass by. Various digital devices were held in my direction. I noticed a new cocktail lounge where once there had been a pet shop. And next to it, a school that taught "kinky belly dancing." I'm sure that had been a dusty carpet store earlier. And I noticed that the traffic lights had been synchronized so that I wouldn't hit a red. It was a nice touch.

I waved to people. I did some smiling. I passed my favorite lunch place, a small Asian diner with pork buns I wanted desperately to taste again. And then the entrance to the tunnel loomed before me like the open mouth of a hungry dragon. Without the traffic and the lights, I again realized how small Manhattan really is. We had driven there in less than five minutes. I entered the tunnel. The world felt better somehow, a feeling I've never really had on the way to New Jersey. I felt a kind of freedom. Everything seemed dark for a second and then my eyes adjusted to the sad jaundice-colored light. I may have smiled then. A genuine smile. An indication of happiness.

I passed the endless suburbs of New Jersey, the communities of winding streets and Little League strip malls, of half-finished developments and neighborhood associations and backyards and weather stripping and lawncare and barbecues, the kind of place I grew up in, somewhere out there, where the high school meets the liquor store and shares a parking lot with a McDonald's and a dry cleaner, just behind the corporate parks overrun with Canada geese, next to the Hiltons and HoJos, just across the six lane highways from the old-fashioned diner with the fattiest, tastiest bacon and the wide-hipped waitress who knows you by name.

A caravan grew. It remained behind the bus mostly but every so often a small sporty car would come speeding by me and a girl would flash her breasts. It became a strangely common thing to see and it started to make me feel old.

Looking into the rearview mirror, I could see a parade of cars that stretched back toward the towers of Manhattan. Each exit produced more cars, people who just wanted to get in line so they could say they did it, more trying to get in on an event before they'd turn around and go home in time to settle down on their couch and catch the opening pitch from Yankee Stadium. Above me, two helicopters hovered, a camera leaning out the side like a suction pump. The journey looked like the funeral procession of a semi-famous philosopher. Or meteorologist.

I turned on the cell phone and called Dan. "I love a parade," he said, with some obvious joy.

"Helicopters make me nervous," I said. And they did. There was no reason for it, just a fear that I'd picked up somewhere and never let go. There was a touch of menace in the sound of the helicopter, the unnatural way they hovered. I don't like dragonflies either.

"They're New York," Dan said. "It shouldn't last long."

"First it's New York, and then it's the next city, and then the next. It won't stop," I said.

"I'll see what I can do," I heard Dan say. The reception rendered his voice barely above a whisper. American cell phone reception used to be a big topic at the office whenever someone returned from a trip overseas. "But not all news channels have access to choppers. Just so you know. You need a good-sized market. This won't be a problem in, say, Louisville."

"Am I going to Louisville?" I asked.

"We're going wherever you lead us," Dan said. "This whole thing is like follow the leader."

The little boy in me wanted to start changing lanes indiscriminately to see what would happen. "I'm going to leave the phone on. Please don't abuse it." I put the phone down. I considered turning the radio on and resisted. I hadn't broken bread with the media since the beginning of the wait and starting at this juncture seemed like bad karma, another reason for the Man to stay away. I drove in silence, my head barren, as if thinking about anything would interfere with the instruction I was sure was coming. I had nothing to do. We've mythologized driving without once admitting how boring it really is.

I crested the hills of New Jersey and drove toward the Pennsylvania border. I crossed the Delaware and was met by the sedans of two state troopers. One of them drove ahead of me, slowly, clearing the way, the other got behind the bus and stopped.

Out the rearview mirror, I saw the trooper attempt to discourage anyone from following me. Quickly, two more troopers appeared and a roadblock was set up. The convoy was over. I was still in the Eastern time zone.

And then I noted the absence of helicopters. And then I realized I was about to ram the backside of the police car ahead of me and I slowed to forty, unsure of whether or not it was good form to overtake it. I called Dan. A familiar voice answered. "Angie?"

"Hi Joe," she said. "Surprise, surprise."

"Did I call your home?" I asked, flummoxed. I slowed down again to avoid hitting the trooper.

"Don't be silly," she said. "Dan kind of hired me."

This put a smile on my face. "As what?" I asked.

"Secretary, personal assistant, organizer, whatever," she replied. "I was helping him with the press releases and stuff at home. And, of course, he wants to fuck me."

"Is he making you do real work?" I asked.

"It's all legit," she said. "I think he knows he doesn't stand a chance."

"Is he paying you well?" I asked.

"Well enough but not well enough to fuck me," she said.

"No, really," I said.

"He's overpaying me," she said. "Why else would I come? Plus, it's like an adventure. I needed a break."

That Angie had somehow profited from this brought me a perverse kind of pleasure. She was the kind of good person you think only exists on TV until you meet them. As long as she didn't sleep with Dan, this was a good development, I thought. Though I don't know why a Dan-Angie coupling bothered me so much. "I need to speak to Dan," I said.

"*Ciao bello*," she said, and I heard her hand the phone to Dan.

"What did she say?" he asked.

"Don't get high school on me," I said.

"No," he said. "She's a champ. She's an organizational genius. I really need her."

"Fine," I said. "I called because this state trooper is breaking his own laws. I'm not going through this state driving forty."

"Are we going right through the state?" Dan asked quickly.

"Stop it," I said.

"Yes. It's getting old," he said. "The troopers. Seems they don't want you on the interstate, the turnpike, or any other major road. They also said they would prefer it if you stayed away from major cities. Harrisburg. Hershey. Pittsburgh. Places like that."

"They think those are major cities?" I said.

"They're not joking," Dan said.

"Of course they are," I said. Where was I supposed to go? How was I supposed to drive west without the use of the interstate system? I wasn't even sure that was possible. Had all those small towns that the system bypassed died in vain? "I should be allowed to drive anywhere. If the authorities have a problem it's with the bus and the caravan. They seem to have stopped the latter. As to the former . . ."

"And *that's* not funny anymore," Dan said.

"I'm not taking a detour for anyone. I'm not doing anything illegal. As long as I'm not instructed otherwise, I'm staying on this road. And you know what I mean by instruction," I said. And at that I wanted to feel the Man again. I wanted him in this minivan. Sitting next to me.

"I understand," he said.

"You've dealt with cops before," I said.

Dan sighed. "I'll see what I can do," he said and hung up.

I swerved out of the lane and passed the trooper and he sped up and started pursuing me. I drove by Allentown and Bethlehem chased by a trooper, a large black bus, and another trooper. I would have laughed but something about Pennsylvania had always frightened me. The entire road unfolded itself before me like a bad circus act, the Odyssey the lead vehicle in a parade of elephants wearing tutus, a nice commingling of the news, entertainment, and law enforcement industries. Which just about covers everything, doesn't it? This was a variation of the O.J. picture. I was the white Bronco. I saw a day when every car in America was behind us, tailing the Odyssey, not knowing why, just doing it because, living another slice of the American experience. I could see tour operators leading picnic buses that would hitch up with the convoy as we passed through their area, just long enough to let clients experience the thrill of the chase before turning back.

For the first time, I understood that I was throwing a flower on my old life. I was different now. New York's gravity no longer exerted itself on me. I was going somewhere. I was being followed by state troopers in a slow motion chase through woods in Pennsylvania. I had never pictured the state to be so lush. I pulled the brim of my baseball cap tightly over my forehead until it about covered my eyes. I could barely see the road.

Just outside Allentown, where the sprawl thinned out and the countryside asserted itself again, the troopers ended their pursuit and pulled off the highway. And that was that. No troopers. Dan was responsible, I was sure of it. All those killings and rapes and cop beats for the *Post* had given him the skills needed to negotiate this journey effectively. I would thank him later. Finally, the hills got steeper, they had dynamited the road through, you could tell, and I relaxed again, adjusting to my new reality, not only to the journey but to the person I was becoming.

Without the troopers the caravan formed again though not with the immensity it had grown to in New Jersey. I thought that at some point I would drive through the boundary of my notoriety and would be able to continue my craziness with my own silent desperation. I called Dan. "I'm hungry," I announced.

"Food isn't a problem," he said.

"When I eat the food, do I have to hold it in any special way?" I asked. "Meaning, do I have to eat food with product placement in mind? Hold things toward the camera in that unnatural way actors hold things in commercials? Do I need to ensure that labels are visible? Do I chew gum holding the package just so? When I drink some water, should the label face the camera? And should I show pleasure? Should I smile after every sip? Should I wet my hair so I can shake in slow motion?"

"Please," Dan said. "Get over yourself."

"So I'm going to stop," I said. "I thought you should know."

I heard Dan ask for something. I heard Angie's voice. "There's a rest stop two miles away," he said.

"That's impressive, Captain," I said.

"It has restrooms and candy machines but no restaurant," he said.

"I don't need a restaurant," I said and hung up.

And sure enough, there was a rest stop with "no service facilities" two miles ahead. And though we were surrounded by trees, we could smell farmers' fields newly sprayed with fertilizer. The air was redolent, brown almost. I could almost see the smell. Surely this kind of pollution was bad for the planet as well. Crap was natural. What these farm animals ate most definitely wasn't. And natural or not, we were breathing it in, swimming in it. The smell was inside every bit of me. The air was thick. And sweet. But mostly sour.

I parked the Odyssey and got out. I opened the back door, took the cooler out, and opened it. And suddenly I wasn't hungry at all. The odor from the farmlands combined with the smell of the food commingling in the giant cooler made the idea of eating impossible. Like going out for a burger after you've visited a slaughterhouse and then fallen into a vat of the still-steaming entrails of the thing you are about to eat. You smell this smell and you know you're very close to seeing someone make sausage.

The bus pulled into the rest area and stopped. It did not park. Cars from the caravan pulled in and parked around us. People got out with cameras around their necks. They stood at their cars and started snapping photos. I waved meekly.

No one exited the bus. I could see cables run from its roof and down the side, disappearing into the baggage compartments. A smaller satellite dish has been welded to its back. The thing looked absolutely like something the Pentagon might develop for a quarter of a billion dollars. Its dark windows hid the media from me, from the world. I had no idea how many people were on it. That's Darth Bus, I thought.

A car pulled into the rest area and stopped beside the Odyssey. Two teenage girls ran out, screaming, little groupies. I expected to see their breasts soon enough. They were dressed identically, with lowcut jeans displaying pink thong underwear, powder blue tank tops, their equally blond hair done up in pigtails. They approached me with a terrifying swiftness. And now I was besieged. The girls' approach was a green light. Others came to shake my hand, or kiss me, or take photos, or get autographs. I stood up on the cooler and stared in the direction of the bus. The girls, especially, were reaching for my shirt, begging for kisses, pressing themselves upon me. But their breasts remained hidden. Cameras buzzed.

Dan emerged from the bus and slowly the media descended. Here was a photo op, for sure. Angie followed Dan and they walked toward me. Dan gently but firmly pulled the girls away. I noticed that each held one of the back pockets of my pants. I felt around my seat for gaps in the fabric. One of the girls was crying with joy. Dan and two large men from the bus pulled the crowd away and created a sort of barrier. The big guys were surely cameramen. Someone must have found the scene ironic. I came to Pennsylvania and became a Beatle.

Angie handed Dan a piece of paper. She gave me a wink. "People," Dan said, holding a hand up for silence. "I understand all of you want to follow Joe and see what happens. To experience this event and tell your friends that you played a role in it. You want to be able to say you were witness to something that is consuming the nation. The world even. It's an event we have here. Something huge. I know. But I can tell you this. Nothing is going to happen if you continue to follow him on his travels." The news cameras were now aimed at Dan. Microphones were being thrust in his face. The media formed an inner circle around Dan and me. The followers, the people from the caravan, were craning their necks to get a glimpse of the proceedings. "Now, this isn't a normal event. It's extraordinary. But we need some rules. I'm not ordering anyone to stop because I can't. It's not in my power and this is a free country. That's why we love it. But please, listen. No one is going to miss a thing. I promise you. Because my colleagues and I are committed to providing around-the-clock coverage of this journey. We'll be interviewing people close to Joe. We have a website for instant news, a map of the journey, analysis. We have interactive features and a timeline. We have a place for the public to chat, talk about the meaning of this, upload photos. We're doing this so as not to slow down the incredible voyage that Joe is taking. So what I'm asking, in the most respectful manner I know, is please go home. You won't miss a thing."

Dan's public applauded. I wish I knew why. Maybe they appreciated the performance. Because it was, in many ways, masterful.

I felt sick almost. It was probably the air. I was sure this was some kind of speech Dan would have delivered in New York had I not left so suddenly. The two girls ran to the Odyssey and began touching it. News cameras followed them. The Honda people from Uniondale were already getting their money's worth. I could see them in the dealership hailing the boss for his vision. Some Japanese executive was going to visit Uniondale and there was going to be an ad. The crowd stood around wondering what to do next. I stepped off the cooler and reached in and took out a bottle of Tropicana apple juice. I couldn't drink it. The smell of the land around us was tremendous.

I walked back to the driver's seat. An elderly gentleman reached his hand out and I shook it. "Good luck," he said. Some of the reporters took notes. People in the crowd were being interviewed. The media left me alone. I felt awkward and quietly relieved. I was no longer the story; the events surrounding me were. This had probably happened in New York but I had failed to notice. And perhaps at that moment a bit of my resentment faded.

I decided I had to piss. I made my way toward the washrooms. Inside I stood at a urinal next to a short man with an impressive beer belly. He smiled. The awkward silence of two men trying to commit a private act in a public space. "That's quite a scene," he said finally.

"You're telling me," I said.

He shook himself dry and zipped up. "I hope you find what you're looking for," he said and washed his hands and opened the door to leave. I heard cameras click.

I finished and went to the sink and splashed water on my face. I pulled a paper towel out of the dispenser and dried myself. And then I felt a presence. I turned around and standing at the door was a Chinese guy. Or maybe he was Japanese. With sunglasses too big for his face and the kind of hipster wear the Japanese can pull off without looking stupid. I decided he was Japanese. He had a small brushed-aluminum digital camera in his hand, a Canon. "Hello," he said nervously.

"Hi," I said. I stuck my hand out and he looked at it and then shook it.

"Takeshi," he said. He wore a big chunky Fossil watch on his left wrist.

"Joe," I said.

"I'm from Japan," he said.

"You didn't come all the way from Japan just for this," I said. Takeshi looked confused. "Just to see me."

165

Takeshi managed a smile. "No, no," he said. "I'm a tourist. I read your story online. I'm hitchhiking. Someone following you picked me up."

"Where you headed?" I asked.

He shrugged. "Like you," he said and smiled again. He had a nice smile. I think I knew he was a nice guy right away. "I'm starting a big job this fall. My first real job. Until then, I'm traveling."

"Anywhere special?" I asked.

He shrugged. "I'm flying out of L.A.," he said.

"Are you enjoying yourself?" I asked. What do foreigners see when they come here? How do they picture us? Are their expectations met or does our country disappoint them? America is so embedded in the world's psyche that our reality must be distorted.

"I've seen the Grand Canyon and Dallas and New Orleans. I took a bus to Memphis and then New York. Now I'm hitchhiking."

He'd seen more of the country than I ever had. "You're going west?" I asked, surprising myself with the question. I was going to get a companion.

Takeshi's eyes lit up. He knew as well. "Yes," he said.

"Want a lift?"

"I'll get my bag," he said quickly. "I'll meet you." He ran out and I followed him. Dan was at the door, ensuring my privacy. I'm not sure how Takeshi had made it inside.

"I've got company," I said.

"Who?" he asked skeptically.

"Some Japanese kid," I said. "He's hitching around the country."

"Is that safe?" Dan asked. He showed genuine concern.

"I'm getting a good vibe."

"He's really Japanese? From Japan?"

I could see the spin he was ready to put on this. He was concocting story lines, preparing for the invasion and interest of the Japanese media, going over the logistics, of international media, all the while dollar signs in his sights grew larger. Now they included Yen.

"Stop drooling," I said.

"Oh, shut up," he said.

"Also, your speech was quite something. Insincere is a good word for it. But I also want you to know I appreciate whatever it was you did to get the troopers to heel." I didn't want to come off as spoiled or pampered. I didn't want to ever do anything that would allow Dan to call me a diva.

"You're being nice to me now," he said. "I'm touched."

"I'm being civil," I said.

We walked back to the Odyssey and I got inside. I closed my eyes and the Man was nowhere. I was worried. I had to admit that. If he was gone, how would I know where to go?

A cordon of state troopers had shown up to keep the public at bay. Takeshi came running toward me, a huge electric blue backpack in his arms. The parking lot had lost about half its cars. The caravan had thinned. Dan's pronouncement had worked to a certain extent. And the presence of police always thins a herd.

Takeshi got in and threw his backpack onto the seat behind us. The media took this in with a frenzy of camera work. Questions were being directed toward Dan. There was shouting and shrugging and confusion. Arms were raised. Pencils to paper. Voices to recorders. I pulled out. In the rearview mirror I could see the media running to their bus. I began to laugh. I pulled onto the highway unable to contain my laughter. I had no idea what I found so funny.

We drove through the Pennsylvania countryside in silence. I think Takeshi was busy assimilating what he'd gotten himself into. "You need gas," he said finally.

The needle was pointing toward empty. I called Dan. "I need gas," I said.

Silence. "Should be about five miles," he told me.

I pulled into a gas station and Takeshi agreed to fill the tank. The bus pulled into the station as did the caravan, now trimmed to about a dozen vehicles. A gas jockey came by and asked if he could take my photo and I rolled down the window. He held a disposable camera and snapped off four before he turned to Takeshi and did the same. Then he asked Takeshi if he would take a photo and the jockey stood next to the window and Takeshi snapped one. Then Takeshi asked me for his camera and I reached over and threw it to him. He took a photo of me and the gas jockey.

Dan walked over and gave the gas jockey a credit card. "That's the deal," he told me.

"This must violate some sort of journalistic code," I said.

"Maybe ten years ago," he said and returned to the bus.

We drove by Harrisburg and deeper into the mountains. We got on the turnpike and that decimated the caravan. I called Dan. "The entourage has left the building," I said.

"Why pay when you can get this for free?" he said.

Takeshi crawled over the seats to the cooler and came back with a bag of Doritos. I watched him open it and he caught me looking at him.

"Can I?" he asked.

"Of course," I said. I reached into the bag and then decided not to eat. I wasn't hungry.

"America doesn't have enough chip flavors," Takeshi said, crunching into a Dorito. "In Japan, we have your flavors and then we have our flavors and we already have more kinds of chips than you to begin with."

"I'm not eating shrimp-flavored chips," I said.

"Americans are both open-minded and suspicious of foreign things," he said.

"And the Japanese aren't?" I asked.

"We like foreign things," he said. "But don't like foreign people."

The minivan was taken over by the sounds of Takeshi's eating. Chips are incredibly noisy. Beyond the crunch, the bag. If someone could invent a silent chip bag, I thought. "So different," he said.

"What is?" I asked.

"America," he said. "It's so empty. There's so much of it."

"Wouldn't you rather experience it?" I asked. "Instead of driving through?"

"I don't have time!" he said, shaking his head. "I came over for a quick look. I saw the Grand Canyon and Hollywood. I saw The Rock at House of Blues!"

We passed through a tunnel that took us deep inside the mountains. In the darkness, I half-expected to hear from the Man but heard nothing. I was driving through places I'd never seen, through country I thought I knew, and I saw none of it except the mysteriousness of what lay ahead. I drove blindly in many ways. Meaning I shouldn't have been driving at all.

We exited the tunnel and within a few miles were in another one. And then another. And after each tunnel I was expecting the land to change somehow, for something miraculous to happen, but nothing did; it was just the road ahead of us, the endless road and the land was always the same, with the sharply sloping mountains rising from the highway like dark green shower curtains and behind us, always, the hulking black media bus. Maybe the Man had never left New York.

Takeshi looked out the window, transfixed by this giant country, by the immensity of the land. We passed a sign for a place called Breezewood. Takeshi whispered the name, as if studying for an exam.

"Are you tired?" Takeshi asked.

I wasn't. Not a cell in my body wanted to stop driving until we had arrived somewhere, until something was resolved. "I'm fine," I said. "Thanks for asking."

GUEST ROOM

Athena has given me an office. Of sorts. It's in the basement of the main building, beneath the lobby. It is a large windowless room, square, unfurnished save for a desk and chair. In the darkest corner is a stuffed mountain goat that has been violated, sporting a maroon baseball cap of the University of Montana. Its fur is mottled by age and neglect, a lonely thing in a lonely place. The phone hasn't been hooked up yet and that might take a few weeks. This makes my evolution official. I'm out of the kitchen. Athena has also hinted at an apartment upstairs, next to hers possibly, but for now, I'm stuck in the trailer. And perhaps that's not a bad thing. If I live and work in this building, I may never get outside again.

Scattered about me on the floor are reams of papers. I have printouts from marketing campaigns and branding initiatives Athena admires. And the one thing that unites all of these efforts is . . . everything. It is all the same. A hotel is a hotel, whether it is in Bangkok or Boston. All of these hotels, at this level, are after the same clientele in the same demographic, sharing similar psychographic profiles, all being chased by the same pitch, employing the same tools. Every property, every brand, promising the same thing, the same luxury, the same service. Every room looks the same. Every website follows the same basic architecture of information. The same hierarchy of services. Every beach view, no matter what body of water one sees beyond the white curtains, looks the same. Every palm tree. Every hotel, whether it labels itself an inn, a ranch, a spa, a chateau, a hideaway, a lodge, a resort, whatever, announces its exclusivity and uniqueness by drawing from the same phrase book. The vocabulary at this end of the hospitality industry is remarkable for its poverty. I am staggered by the whole thing.

I walk into Athena's office.

"I need to study this place," I tell her.

"Be my guest," she says, laughing. Does she laugh every time she says this?

"You're going to see me walking around a lot. It might seem like I'm doing nothing."

"Then I appreciate the warning."

"I also want to collect guest data."

"I've given you everything we have," she says. "I've found all the statistics and numbers I'm going to find. I've also ordered shelves for you. And a computer." She smiles. Her eyes are a lake in sunshine. She's naturally flirtatious. She has no interest in me. "I'm happy you're doing this."

She's thrown money at me. I'm surprised by what she's willing to pay. Especially since I have nothing to spend it on. And this kind of analysis is not, strictly, what I'm good at. My experience lies elsewhere. "Are there expansion plans?" I ask. There must be a reason for all of this interest in my supposed skills.

"Not here, no," she says, hinting at something broader.

"I'm just a copywriter," I say. "We just write."

"That writing is a message," she says. "We need to stay on message. I think you are capable of helping us craft it."

"Content is just the base. Floorboards."

"I believe content is everything. It's the soul. It's where the meaning comes from. The story. And with the story you have connection. And then you have something to market."

"When I really get going, I get very insecure," I say. "I need validation." I take a step back. "I'm just warning."

"That could be charming," she says.

"I've always thought it annoying," I say. Why, exactly, I'm saying this is a question I can't begin to ask. "It's a sign of weakness."

"Or it's a sign of your creativity," she says.

"You're being nice," I say. Is it possible that I'm flirting as well? When you know you don't stand a chance, flirtation is like a gift certificate to your favorite boutique.

I walk through the lobby. It is quiet and even here I can see some problems. The furniture is nice but it's too angular, too European, to match the bits of rustic here, like the lasso that snakes along the wall behind the check-in desk, candles set around it, each one set atop a spur. The carpet. The marble floor with wood trim. Even the staff, in their western chic, look odd in this room, like interlopers. This whole lobby is like a pair of gorgeous pants that are tight in the wrong places.

I step outside. I drink in the sun as it warms my face. The sun feels warmer here, as if it were closer to the ground. The light is brighter. There's a purity to this place that marketing can't touch. And it's why it should be central to any marketing effort. The quality of light is a promise that a brochure can keep. The taste of the sunshine. The majesty of the mountains. The feeling of the wind.

I walk through the grounds toward the stables. Two guests watch as the stable hands prepare the horses for an excursion. The guests are Japanese. They wear chaps over their jeans. The Japanese, especially, want a Wild West kind of thing. They want to experience an America they have seen in their dreams. Though their getup is proof of the limitations of that dream. The bars here are stocked with fine single malts and cognacs. The Japanese are very fond of the steam baths, the saunas, the Thai pressure point massage. They want an America that conforms to their desires. Here, finally, they can bend America to their will. And they will pay handsomely to do so.

SMOKE AND MIRRORS

Pennsylvania is an odd kind of police state. Every few miles, a bend on the turnpike revealed a state trooper waiting in predatory ambush, drooling over the prospect of a chase and the public humiliation of being pulled over. We were like some clubfooted antelope to them, the poor animal the camera zooms in on when the big cats begin the hunt. I could hear Marlin Perkins's nasally underwater voice: "On the turnpikes of Pennsylvania, the dangerous state troopers are for-ever on the lookout for the publicity-seeking simpleton from New York encroaching on their territory."

We exited the turnpike where it veered north to Pittsburgh and headed toward Ohio. Night fell and I continued to drive, not at all feeling the effects of a full day of concentration, of steering, of looking out for the dreaded state troopers. Takeshi kept asking if I was OK, wanting desperately to be able to return home and report that he had driven the highways here, but I refused to give up the wheel. I was going to drive, even to the point of exhaustion, because each mile felt like another mile closer to something, closer to a meeting, closer to the one thing that could change my life forever.

Where was the Man? I would speak to him, think about him,

expect to see him by the side of the road but he was nowhere, aloof, a memory.

"When does it end?" Takeshi asked.

I didn't know. What could I tell anyone about the Man? As if this absence would allow me to forget him. As if I could forget why I was in this minivan to begin with. He was all I could think about. I was consumed by the thought of my promised meeting, by the promise itself, by the idea that my life would somehow improve, that it might actually mean something, something I could understand, and that this new meaning would enable me to live the rest of my life with some kind purpose. Direction. I wanted to be happy. Each mile was a mile away from home, a mile away from a life that meant less and less to me and seemed more and more foreign and bizarre. I realized the meaning of the words turmoil and chaos finally and understood the basic facts of my life.

"I don't know," I told Takeshi.

"Pennsylvania is very big," he said.

And then he was asleep and I was witness to Takeshi's horrific snoring. Driving that night this is what I thought: nothing. I had lived a life that meant nothing. I had drifted about, had been paid to be clever, had been paid well, and it had all meant nothing to me. And I thought this while driving to a destiny that was incomprehensible. My life had no meaning. And it was still meaningless, still out of my control, but at least, I felt it had a purpose. A direction. Literally. And though I didn't understand that purpose, it was there. I could taste it and that was good enough for me.

And I realized I had never thought these things through. I still had not fully understood any of what was happening but I was projecting meaning onto all of my remembered conversations with the Man, creatively wanting things to come of all of this, and it made me feel good in a way. Passing over the hills of West Virginia, I thought, OK, I've made some rationalizations here, and that's fine, it's fine to make a few rationalizations out of chaos, out of the surreal nature of my life right now. I'm in West Virginia, for fuck's sake!

And then we weren't in West Virginia. Just like that. How could a state be that small? This was the only time during the trip I wanted to consult a map.

I pulled into a service station in Ohio and the black bus pulled in behind us. From it I saw the media run to the Burger King, eager to fill their stomachs with food, or a close approximation of it. Some of them looked at me and mouthed thank-yous. I got out of the Odyssey quietly, careful not to wake Takeshi. I walked to a small island of grass set amidst the concrete parking lot, a deserted, eerie place in the dark of night. I lay down and asked the Man for a sign. Somewhere overnight in Pennsylvania, the convoy had petered out to two cars. I was thrilled.

Dan walked over and sat next to me. "That was quite a stretch," he said. "I think our drivers are trying to figure out what they've gotten themselves into."

"You have two drivers?" I asked.

"Three," Dan said. "Union regulations. Or something. I asked for a driver and he came in triplicate."

"I'm not even tired," I said. "I think I could drive around the world right now."

"That would be a feat," Dan laughed. I only understood his joke much later. He stretched his arms and craned his neck back and forth. He straightened his legs and touched his toes. He straightened up and leaned back on his elbows. He sighed, looking forward to when this would all end, I think. He wanted the hint of a conclusion. Maybe even more than I did.

"I don't feel like stopping," I said, closing my eyes, trying to summon the Man, pleading for help, a sign, direction. "It's like it's not even me when I drive."

"You're possessed," Dan clarified.

"I'm possessed," I mumbled. I mulled these words over, turning them around in my head until they didn't mean a thing. "I'm not possessed," I said.

"You're on a mission," Dan said.

"Maybe," I replied.

Dan lit a cigarette and I took it. "Since when do you smoke?" I asked. I took a deep drag and held the smoke in my lungs and felt lightheaded. "Wow."

I smoked my first cigarette in high school. I can remember sitting underneath the stairs that led to the front door of my high school with Louie Jones, a hyper-sized black kid who played linebacker on the JV football team. We were thirteen, and we figured it was time. The episode ended with a fit of coughing, with Louie throwing up on his new Astroturf cleats, and with both of us wondering where the glamour was. And now this cigarette felt good. Transformative. I stared at it, the glowing tip, the long white body of paper, the orange filter, and the cigarette seemed somehow sexy. I'd smoked off and on since that first silly cigarette, but never really considered the art, or the object. I just smoked. Sometimes. Not even often enough to consider myself a smoker. I was a non-smoker who smoked. I looked at my hand holding the cigarette and it looked cool, sophisticated. Everything I knew about cigarettes, about how inane it was to smoke, about the values imprinted on smoking by the ad industry, evaporated like so much smoke.

"Where do you think this is going?" Dan asked.

"Addiction. Medical bills. Premature death," I said.

"The trip," Dan said.

"The trip," I repeated. "I don't know." I took another deep drag and felt the heat of the smoke in my lungs. I exhaled. "I wish I did. I really do. We're only in Ohio. Maybe it'll end right here. In this parking lot. Maybe it'll end on a beach in California. I have no idea. Every mile is new to me. I'm starting to really wish I knew where this was headed. I'm with you on that. I'd like to know. A sense of direction."

"Some of the reporters are already losing interest," Dan said, news that made me delirious with happiness. "I keep saying it's only been twenty-four hours. Look what's happened in one day. There's great drama here. I've started to get inquiries from Japan. The web hits from Japan are through the roof. Doesn't seem to matter. Some of the newspaper guys are going to get called back soon. They didn't really think through their involvement. The broadcast guys can be easily replaced with the news. You're fighting for space. For interest. Freshness. With the world. With the White House. The longer this goes on, the less it interests people. The convoy is almost gone."

"And you think this bothers me?" I asked, smiling broadly.

"This event has lost its eventness," Dan said. "One day out and we're losing momentum. The news cycle is a vicious, nasty bitch."

I inhaled more smoke and tried blowing it out my nose. I wanted to do all the cool things you could do with smoke.

"I know it doesn't bother you," Dan said. He punched my arm, which I found strange. "It's going to kill me, though."

"I'd say I'm sorry if I felt I had anything to apologize for," I said.

Takeshi got out of the Odyssey and walked over to us, bleary eyed, taking in the parking lot, trying to place himself. "No McDonald's?" he asked.

"We have food," I told him. "Just open the back. There's even some healthy food back there. Fruit." For Takeshi, of course, this wasn't good enough. Neither was Burger King. He was on the road in America and he wanted to consume the totems of our culture.

"We are where?" he asked, sitting down, rubbing his eyes.

"Ohio," I said. "We're in Ohio."

"Ohio," he said slowly, rolling the word around his mouth a few times. Saying the word silently, he looked like he was imitating a goldfish.

"Where?" he asked again.

"Buttfuck, Ohio," Dan said, laughing.

"This is Dan," I said. "He's the press guy."

Dan put out his hand and Takeshi looked at it and then took it and shook it quickly. "Takeshi," he said.

"You should talk to Takeshi," I told Dan. "His story's as interesting as mine. It must be." I knew this was, to Dan, completely untrue.

"You still don't get it. No offense," he said, looking at Takeshi, "but no one is interested in you. I mean, they will be. NHK called. I'm sure the Japanese media is going to be all over this. I've seen how crazy they can be."

"NHK?" Takeshi asked, his bleary eyes suddenly awake. "They're interested in me?"

"I can set up an interview if you want," Dan said.

Takeshi thought about this. He put his hand to his chin and stroked the few strands of hair growing there. "No," he said finally. "No interviews. My father would be very upset if he found out I was hitchhiking."

"I'm sure he already knows," I said.

Takeshi considered this. "I'm not here to be on the news in Japan," he said.

"I can't stop them," Dan said. "No one can stop a story from getting out. Or from people getting interested in it. We don't have that right."

Members of the media started to file out of the restaurant, stretching, yawning, checking their watches. They walked back to the bus in twos and threes, looking like a bunch of drunks kicked out of the bar after last call. They eyed us, the tiny assemblage on this island of grass. They entered the bus ready to sleep again. I had no idea what time it was and I wasn't interested. Time didn't matter anymore and this idea gave me a profound sense of freedom. A cameraman toted his camera on his shoulder, a hulking video apparatus that looked a lot heavier than it needed to be. He aimed it as us. Three guys talking under a tree. To be beamed to an uninterested world.

Wasn't that signal, the absolute uselessness of it, a kind of pollution?

Angie walked slowly toward the bus and waved. I waved back, embarrassed for some reason. "How's Angie?" I asked.

Dan shrugged. "She's a big help. I couldn't manage this thing without her. I'm doing phone-in shows every few hours with radio stations all over the place. She handles everything. She's a natural. She's handling some of the video feed, too. The vlog. Stuff like that. Still can't get her interested in me, though. And now some young intern from AP has his eyes on her. He's good looking. He looks like the kind of guy who's going to get posted in Europe some day, some nice place like Paris."

"But how is she?" I asked again.

"She's being a bit too professional about everything," Dan said.

"I'm ready to go," I announced. I stood up and stretched. My legs were stiff and this was the only physical indication my body offered that I had just driven nonstop to Ohio.

"Wait a bit," Dan said. "Let the boys get back on the bus."

"Ohio," Takeshi said. "It's a fun word."

"If you look at it long enough, it starts to look strange," Dan said.

"Arizona," Takeshi said. "Another good word. And Ellay. Not Los Angeles. It doesn't sound like the name of a big city. But Ellay is a good word."

"I want to say something about L.A.," Dan said, for no reason.

"El Paso is also a good word," Takeshi said.

I walked back to the Odyssey slowly, staring at the stars, thinking of nothing, thinking of the Man. "You filling up?" Dan called out.

"I'm filling up," I said.

I opened the door to the minivan and climbed in. Takeshi got in as well. "What's in Ohio?" he asked.

"It doesn't matter," I said. And I guess it didn't. Only one place mattered and I didn't know where it was.

BORDERLINE

The winds are definitely changing. They aren't warm anymore. They threaten frost and ice and snow. They threaten dislocation, a change in the chemistry of things. It feels sinister, like waiting for a punch you know is coming. You need sweaters and jackets at night now. Sweatshirts. Layers. Nothing heavy but enough to ward off the chill. Feet get cold faster. Our rooms are getting colder. The fireplace concierge is a busy man. Locals are saying it's a sign, that the warmth of the days doesn't mean anything anymore. Heat evaporates, they keep saying. It rises. It goes away.

Athena has put a carpet on my floor. It's a brown and white irregularly shaped faux-cowhide thing. There are shelves along one wall. She put up a nicely twisted piece of wood on the opposite wall. The light bulb has a shade over it. My desk now comes equipped with a small halogen lamp. The stuffed goat remains in the corner. I have taken to calling it Jacques. The thing just seems French.

The air in here is awful.

Tomas has put clafouti back on the menu. The ranch is full now, probably for the last time this summer. Japanese cowboys and Canadian oil men and women with obvious enhancements.

A couple from England. A minor German celebrity. I can only imagine what one must be to attain the height of minor celebrity from Germany.

As nights get colder, activities move indoors. The restaurant stays open later, as does the bar. Movie nights include double features. For whatever reason, they showed *Gigi* and *A Touch of Evil* last night, an oddball combination that I'm sure worked. A bartender in the movie room dispenses cocktails. Tomas serves what he calls tandoori chicken nuggets. Mathilde has made some caramel popcorn dusted with Spanish paprika.

There's an odd feeling of emptiness inside me I can't shake. This is the feeling of autumn. Anything that is empty can only bring disappointment. The symbol of that windswept whiteout is easy to understand here. We refer to winter as bleak but we're really describing ourselves. Our inner world. It was emptiness that got me into my situation. I needed something. Someone perhaps. And I went out in search of it. My need was so strong I was willing to follow its dictates, despite the risks. Which is brave. I can see that. This is something I've learned. I am here through a combination of boredom and bravery. Restlessness.

I'm sitting in the employee lounge, nursing a beer, and Keith walks in and sits beside me. "You mind?" he asks.

"Why would I?" I say.

Keith shrugs. "You're management now. Or something," he says. "Whatever you're doing. That's some kind of slick promotion."

He orders a beer and sits back.

What is his story? The lower end of the kitchen staff is mostly Latino. The chambermaids are all Latino. The guys who pick up the horse shit are Latino. How did Keith get here? "You're Indian, right?" I ask.

"Blackfoot," he says, pulling on his beer. "Me and Ben come from the same place."

"And that's from around here?" I ask, ashamed by my ignorance. The reminder of the Native loss is everywhere around them. Especially when anyone opens their mouth.

"This is our land," he says. "Here. On the Canadian side, too."

This is a kind of permanent displacement I can't quite grasp. I might be feeling that here, but that's just loneliness. How long can you feel like a refugee before getting on with your life? When is it time to move on? "So what are you doing here?"

Keith sighs and puts his elbows on the bar. "I had to get away," he whispers.

"From what?"

"The reserve. I lost my status. I'm not a Native anymore. According to the fuckin' government. But I had to leave. Everyone knows everything about everyone else. It's a small world on the reserve and I want something bigger." He downs his beer. "Don't tell anyone."

"Who would I tell?"

He shrugs. Again. He doesn't look Latino. Why wouldn't someone be curious about him? Or me, for that matter. Has the curiosity been sucked out of everyone? We are a nation of passive voyeurs. Perhaps that voyeurism ends when we are asked to participate directly.

I order another beer. I look around this room and I could be anywhere. But I'm not. My journey to this very spot, my voyage, has meaning. It must. All our lives must. They do. Everything is burdened with meaning. Every step. Every gesture. Every breath.

"I keep thinking of going up to Canada," he says. "That might be a good place for me to end up. That or south somewhere. Up in Canada, I'd go to the oil fields. Make some money."

"I know a place where there are no border guards," I say. "You'd think with Homeland Security and all, the border would be secure, but there's this place where it's just a lonely dirt road. No sign of anyone. You just drive through. You're on a road and all of a sudden you're in a different country. When you think about the state of the world, it's actually a little surreal. Or it should be. Changing countries should be more dramatic. If it's not, what's the point of having a different country?"

"The border's not a problem for me," Keith says. "I'm Blackfoot. We come and go, it's not a problem."

"So the border's not there for you?"

"We were here first."

I take a pull of my beer. "I can't argue with that."

"We have treaty rights."

Whatever that means. I know nothing about Indians except a lot of them died. "Really? You don't need to sneak around?"

Keith smiles at this. "Away from the family maybe. Old girlfriends. But not across the border."

"The white man's border," I say and immediately I feel like the kid in school who tries just a bit too hard to fit in.

"We don't really call it that," he says. "I think that's a Hollywood thing." He gets up. He finishes the last of his beer. "I'm guessing that's how you got here," he says. "I know the place you're talking about. How you found that dirt road is kind of weird."

I shrug. "I have no idea," I say.

"And then you walked here?" he says. And laughs. "Fuck, man." He pushes his beer bottle away. And he leaves.

I return to my office and do a little more research. It's what I do now. I want to learn about this place. This land. Rocks. Indians. History. And luxury beddings. It's who I am here. I'm fine with it.

THE GHOST INSIDE

The hills gave way to ground as level as a bowling alley. The sun came up behind us, just as the surprisingly excessive sprawl around Columbus gave way to farms and small towns and industry. We hit Indiana and the highway became a straight needle through its heart. The line of cars behind the bus grew as the sun rose higher. At every exit cars got in line and got out, too. There were obviously those in each community who wanted a part of me, of the event, and so they drove to the next exit before returning home with a story to tell. On overpasses, crowds gathered, some holding signs, encouraging me. There was something communal about it.

And still no Man. I was happy for Takeshi's presence. In many ways. But I was still driving blind. The Man had been with me for so long. Inside of me. And now, just as quickly and suddenly as he had appeared, he was gone. And if he was gone, why was I still driving? What compelled me forward? I had no desire to stop.

We drove through Indianapolis. Takeshi wanted to see the Speedway. I told him if he wanted to he could get out and find a ride with someone else and he seemed unwilling to do this. "No stopping, OK," he said quietly. "No exit." He continued to beg me to let him drive and I wasn't willing to do this either. The act of driving was important to me. It kept me focused. It gave me a sense of control.

The cornfields of Indiana buzzed with crop dusters and huge circular sprinklers and I thought that we take better care of our food than we do ourselves. There was very little else to see. Or that I noticed. We see what we want. And there was nothing I wanted to see here. Unless I was told to. The flattened earth was all around us, the farms that fed the nation, and I found the lack of distraction a great comfort, as if the road had been made tedious to light the path to my destination, like the little blue beacons that light airport runways at night.

"Are you hungry?" Takeshi asked.

"Not at all," I said. "I should be."

"You need food," he said. "You need strength."

"Just having the cooler is comforting," I said.

Takeshi looked toward the back of the van. "But you don't eat," he said.

And this was true. It was as if my body had stopped functioning properly. "Are you hungry?" I asked.

Takeshi nodded. I pulled into the next service station on the road, just outside Terre Haute, and parked in another lot and for a moment I thought we were back in Ohio. The parking lot was a gallery of cars bearing the license plates of travelers and tourists. The trucks at the end of the lot belched fumes and farts. Trucks pulled in and out, station wagons, minivans, buses, RVs. Families and seniors, young couples, inordinately large truck drivers, small children delighting in the purchase of another Happy Meal. This is why we have such fond memories of family vacations: the endless supply of fast food, meals as candy every day, the joy of eating things our parents don't normally encourage us to eat. And eating them all the time.

The media bus had to park in another section of the lot with the other buses. I lost sight of it as it turned the corner and disappeared behind the McDonald's and I felt a smile creep across my lips. I had the notion of leaving immediately but then Takeshi got out of the Odyssey and raced toward his date with a Big Mac. And then the notion hit me again.

I couldn't do it and didn't. I would have felt lost. Or more lost. I waited for him. I should be in there, too, I thought. I could not recall the last time I felt hungry. I opened the back of the Odyssey and looked inside the cooler and took a bottle of Tropicana. I forced myself to drink it. The juice tasted rancid. I bit into a Pepperidge Farm cookie. It was the texture of sawdust. And then I looked into the cooler again and the thought of food made me ill. I felt nausea cling to me like plastic wrap. I needed to purge myself. Sooner than what would be comfortable. I ran to the washroom to see what I would bring up.

I found an empty stall. I closed the door and found a foul shit-laced toilet. Piss surrounded the bowl and I raised my shoes to see that I was standing in vile brownish water. And then I threw up. I just opened my mouth and out it came, the memories of pasta and calzone, the fried chicken eaten out of pink and lime green Tupperware, the hot dogs, the Cokes, the stale coffee Dan bought me in the mornings. I threw up more than I knew I had in my body and I threw up some more. I threw up the days and weeks of sitting on my front steps, the groupies and crowds, the priests and rabbis, the photographers, the reporters, the helicopters hovering over-head, where sleep became impossible and I feared I'd lost the Man. I threw up the hills of New Jersey, the mountains of Pennsylvania, the farms of Ohio, Dan's cell phone, the black bus. I threw up Dan. I leaned back against the door, light-headed to the point of dizziness. I had trouble breathing. Spittle hung from my chin and stretched back toward the awful liquid on the floor. I felt empty, a shell. I felt like crying.

Someone knocked on my door. "You all right in there, son?" a deep Southern accented voice asked.

I realized where I was. "I'm fine," I stammered between breaths.

"You sure now?" the voice asked.

"Yes," I said. "Thank you for asking."

The washroom was silent. Everyone had obviously heard me throw up. "I'm all right," I announced. "Everything's OK." I paused to catch my breath. "Honest."

And slowly the sounds of the washroom returned. Flies being undone and redone, streams of piss hitting porcelain, taps being turned, hands being washed and dried under the mechanical hot air, farts, heavy turds hitting the water, sighs of gratitude.

I wiped my chin, extricated my feet, flushed, and opened the door. The men in the room granted me a wide berth. I walked to a sink and turned on the taps and cupped my hands in the cool water. I splashed the water on my face and put some of it in my mouth. I rinsed my mouth. I did it again. My mouth tasted of metal and I could not wash the taste out. I wiped my face with a paper towel and studied my reflection in the mirror. There were bags under my eyes but otherwise I looked the same. What's going on inside, I asked myself. I dried my hands under the blower. I exhaled, trying to release the stench of decay, but I could not. I needed some gum. Maybe brush my teeth.

I walked into the lobby of the service station. The media were waiting for me. A multitude of cameras and microphones and digital recorders were pointed in my direction. Fuzzy boom mics hovered like blow-dried vultures above my head. A crowd had gathered around the reporters, curious, overjoyed by this sudden and surprising vacation event in the middle of Indiana. A wall of noise greeted me, the questions being hurled all at once, enough to make it seem as if I were being attacked. A deadly clamor. Why now? I thought. The reporters had been so civil to this point. I looked for Dan and Takeshi but could not find them. The questions kept coming. I shielded my eyes from the glare of the cameras. I thought about retreating to the washroom but already there were people between me and the door. I felt helpless. I raised my arms to plead for calm. I yelled for Dan. I closed my eyes.

Strength, the Man said.

I opened my eyes, surprised, bewildered. I looked around and there he was, with the reporters. Smiling. A toothpick in his mouth. The reporters and vacationers and cameramen and the sound technicians went silent. I could hear the beating of my heart.

I smiled.

Slowly, the noise grew back into a roar. Dan pushed some reporters aside and appeared, self-important, like an explorer successfully conquering the jungles of Africa, and made his way toward me. I had questions, too, but not for the reporters. The Man stood there. He drank a Coke. "I need some gum," I told Dan. He reached into his pocket and handed me a pack of Trident.

He raised his arms. The crowds were silenced. I felt grateful, finally, genuinely grateful for Dan. "Let's do this in an orderly fashion," he insisted. "This wasn't in the plan. So do it properly or you get nothing." He looked at me for approval and I nodded.

"This is your turf," I told him.

He stepped away from me. He pointed to someone I could not see and this person asked, "Is it true you were just sick in the washroom?"

I was stunned by the immediacy of the question. By the speed of the transmission of this news, by the poisonous feeling from the stall, and now, I realized, it would be on the news. I shouldn't have been surprised and wondered if I was surprised by my own sense of surprise in the first place. I could still taste the bile. I popped a piece of gum into my mouth. And then I popped another one.

Dan looked at me sympathetically. "Go on," he said. "I'm afraid we have to do this."

I cleared my throat. The Man had asked for strength. I looked at him and he raised his Coke and winked. "Yes," I replied. "I was sick. I threw up. I feel a lot better now. We had a purging." I paused. "I upchucked. But I'm ready to hit the road."

Laughter. The boom above my head inched closer. Dan pointed to another reporter. "Will you have to abandon your journey?" was the question.

"No," I said. "Not for something like this."

Dan pointed to someone else. "This is a two part question," the faceless reporter said, another male voice, and it suddenly hit me that Angie was the only woman on the bus. "Did you just hear the Man's voice? You seemed to have a moment there. And if so, what did he say?"

"I did hear the Man," I confirmed. A buzz came up from the crowd. "I haven't heard from him in a while and I was getting nervous. But I heard from him. Just now. And I'm not telling you what he said."

Dan laughed. He laughed at the presidential nature of the whole affair, I think. He pointed to another reporter. "Where is this heading?" a high-pitched voice asked.

I shrugged. I didn't know. We were holding a press conference outside a service station washroom in Indiana! The question was stupid and I fought a deep urge to say so. "Your guess is as good as mine," I said.

The reporters laughed again, though I noticed some of them checking their watches, worried, never having intended to participate in an open-ended news story. "If he knew, you'd have received a detailed itinerary," Dan said to more laughter.

"Maybe T-shirts at least," I added.

The laughter died down. The press wanted something tangible to justify their continued presence. They wanted to know they were riding the black bus for a reason. They wanted to know their stories would air that night, get printed in tomorrow's papers. They wanted to know the years of journalism school weren't completely in vain. "I'm just going," I said. "I don't know where. Obviously. But I'll drive into the Pacific Ocean if that's what's expected of me. Right now I'm driving west, like I was told to. And until he instructs me otherwise, I'll keep going. I'm sorry to have to put you through this. Honestly, I am. I'm sure all of you have something better to do, families to go home to. But none of this was planned. None of it."

Dan was beaming. Every time I cooperated, it was a complete surprise to him. A sign that the world works sometimes. He put his hand gently on my back. He was orchestrating a news conference. He pointed to another reporter. "I'd just like to get back to your recent bout with nausea?" a flat Midwestern-tinged accent said. "Are you worried that perhaps your food supply's going bad?"

I smiled. Though my mouth still tasted of my insides, I could feel the lights coming on in the world. I saw Takeshi standing anonymously, lost amidst the forest of media, and I found it funny, silly, but in a good way, in a stupid harmless way. For the first time since the journey began, I felt maybe I was enjoying myself. I must have thrown up a lot of the anger I had been feeling. Or perhaps I was just light-headed from the lack of food. "I love your accent," I told the reporter. "I've always liked the way Midwesterners talk." I didn't even know if this was true but I said it.

That's good, the Man said. *Now keep going.* And I took that to mean to keep going west.

Dan exploded. He broke into a great, big laugh and the media joined in. Some of the public broke into applause, strangely, and the cameras recorded the event, this love-in, the point where the entire ordeal ceased to be a chore. "It's a good thing we're in Indiana!" Dan bellowed. The Man disappeared. He was gone again. But he was here. With me. And that was good enough.

I made my way through the crowd and found Takeshi. "I could use a smoke," I whispered in his ear.

We left the building and walked through the parking lot to the Odyssey. "You're some rock star!" Takeshi said, finally, perhaps fully understanding the circus of my existence and appreciating his new-found surroundings, the story he was going to tell his friends back home getting better and better.

"Let's take a picture," I said.

Takeshi opened the door and searched through his backpack and produced his camera. He placed the camera on the roof of the minivan. He craned his neck to look into the display. "Self-timer!" he said, barely controlling his enthusiasm.

"Why haven't we been doing more of this?" I asked.

"I thought maybe you didn't want pictures," he said.

"You're right," I said. "But this is your vacation. Take all the photos you want."

"I have cigarettes, too," he announced. He pressed a button and ran toward me. He put his arm around me. "Say something funny!" he ordered.

"Mozzarella!" I shouted.

Takeshi hunched over with laughter. The camera took the photo.

"Mozzarella!" He screamed. I wasn't sure he knew what mozzarella was and it didn't matter. Things had taken a turn. I could feel it. The Man had delivered a one-word message that was enough to let me know he was still watching. It was all I needed.

We got into the minivan. Takeshi fished a pack of cigarettes out of his backpack and threw one to me. He lit mine with a heavy silver lighter decorated with a picture of John Wayne. "I bought this in Arizona," he said.

I took a deep drag. I was energized, again, and figured I really could drive into the ocean, that I could do anything that was asked because I was starting to think everything meant something, even though I didn't know what it was. Not yet. And I guess that is why I was doing what I was doing. To figure things out. To understand. To go someplace perhaps I was meant to go. To see things. To find an answer to a question I hadn't known to ask. To look around at things and think, finally, Hey, that makes perfect sense.

PART SIX

STAY WHERE YOU ARE

Athena has summoned the PR person. She wants us to meet. I protest this plan. I'm not ready. I don't possess the knowledge that can drive intelligent conversation. Not yet. "Then don't," Athena says. "Just meet her. She's nice."

"Why now? Why not give me a little more time?"

"Just a little chat. Your work will affect hers."

"Not any time soon."

"Next week," Athena says. "She's coming up for two days."

The meeting. At the agency, I'd flown across the country for a two-hour meeting. Eight hours in the air for two hours' face time. The need to meet face to face, given the technology that surrounds us, given the speed with which we can communicate, is testament to something resilient, to some primal need we share. The video conference will never become the go-to. The images that travel thousands of miles, by satellite, in cables, constantly hovering above us, have yet to overcome the power of a simple handshake. Chat has yet to replace the conversation. Social media has nothing on lunch. Our need to see someone, up close, to read their gestures, their facial ticks, remains. The idea of the meeting hasn't changed in thousands of years. It is why young girls will still scream at the sight of their heartthrob. Athena wants us to meet in person, which is the simple fact that all the hypemasters forgot when promoting video conferencing. You watch science fiction, with its vision of the future, of utopia, of dystopia, and people still sit around tables discussing things, making plans, shaking hands. Touching. Our technology has done much, but it has yet to replace human touch. Even a sour economy hasn't completely killed the face to face. "This makes it serious," I say.

Athena dismisses me. "You should just meet," she says.

"This place is full," I say. "No vacancy. Even with the world's problems. If the Big K Ranch and Spa had a neon sign out front, some of the letters would have burned out by now. You've had a great summer as far as I can tell."

Athena leans back in her chair. "Why are you so worried?"

I'm not worried. I'm simply unprepared. I have nothing to say to this person. She seems to be doing her job. "I'm not," I say.

"Good," Athena says. "She's nice. You'll like her."

I am worried. I'm worried about meeting PR people. Their job is to tell people things. They can only keep secrets for so long. I can imagine how much indiscretion a PR person from L.A. can muster.

And then I'm thinking about how I haven't considered Dan's next move. I don't know if he has one. But the more people I meet, the greater the chance of my past returning, right here, to this place. This sanctuary.

"Do I need to prepare anything?" I ask.

"That's very professional of you." Athena laughs.

Later that evening, after a staff dinner of mac 'n' cheese with a side of creamed spinach and bison sausages, back in my room in the trailer, the background awash in the noise of the employees' nocturnal bacchanalia, I think of the map I've created, the psycho-geography of my days. I have composed simple emails to my parents, imploring them to stay silent, to not let anyone know I was fine, doing well, happy even. I promised them more detail soon, at a time when I was sure I was safe from scrutiny. I could not press send. I don't know when that time will come. I don't even bother with the fake addresses anymore.

This place is not a sanctuary. Simply an odd career choice.

Our choices are made for many reasons, few of them conscious. And all of our choices take us somewhere, inevitably, as they must. Choices create their own momentum. Their own trajectories.

I'm agitated. For whatever reason. I head out and walk to the employee lounge. I order a beer and a shot of whiskey. I down the whiskey and I order another. I down it and order another. The bartender gives me a look. "Just do it," I tell him. He shrugs and pours the shot. I tilt my head back and down it. I take a long, thirsty gulp of my beer.

"You OK?" the bartender asks.

I nod. I feel out of breath, the whiskey burning my throat. I put my head in my hands and try to breathe normally. In this place, under the large, impossibly eternal sky, the world suddenly feels small. Again. I take my beer and shuffle off to a table in the corner of the room.

I'm feeling, what, paranoid? Is that possible? Of what? I am in a situation that is surprising, surely, but pleasant. The meandering course of my life, its strange trajectory, finding myself here. And now I have an actual job. At a luxury guest ranch with a ridiculous name. In northern Montana. There is nothing wrong with the picture.

Never assume you know how your life will turn out.

Without assumptions, disappointments can't haunt you. Everything is a surprise.

There's a lot to be said for mystery.

I finish my beer. "Another one, please!"

"Come and get it," the bartender says. "I'm not your fuckin' waiter!"

I take my empty glass to the bar and pick up a full mug. "Sorry," I mutter. Now that I'm management, my interactions have become complicated, bound by codes I never meant to write.

I return to my seat. I start to laugh. My life *is* funny. It has been. If I can't see the humor in it, if I don't see its arc as nothing less than funny, what am I left with? I take a big gulp of my beer. I'm a branding consultant for a high-end guest ranch in northern Montana. It's the punch line to a convoluted joke.

Or the beginning of the rest of my life.

GOIN' OUT WEST

We entered Illinois and I felt, for the first time, West. Growing up, this is where I figured the West began, when I thought of the West at all. Terms such as Midwest didn't enter my vocabulary until much later. All Midwest ever said to me was not east. The east stopped a few miles from the coast, somewhere in New Jersey. Everything between where I grew up and the Pacific was something else.

The flatness of the land was like a plate. And it didn't stop. Miles and miles of farmland surrounded us and on it, we saw farmers working, driving plows and combines and tractors, we saw the land being irrigated and sprayed and tilled. It was being worked. I needed to see these things to know that outside the Odyssey the world continued, people had jobs, things to do, vegetables to grow. Farming is the first rung on the ladder of a functioning world. I needed these things because ever since the crowd grew around my front steps and the media made me into a news item, my life had become a kind of reality TV, a permanent webcast, a diversion from what the world was. I caught glimpses but I could never be sure that perhaps I was not the center of the world's attention. Driving past the farms, seeing people live, I understood how easy it was to be fooled by your surroundings, how the presence of a few reporters made it easy to think the world cared about what you did, or that somehow your story, the story that the media claimed to be beaming to everyone, was nothing more than the story of someone living their life, and because it was different, it was news. I understood that the media had to make celebrities feel their fishbowl existences so that they knew they were special and worthy of the millions of dollars they commanded. That kind of money needs validation.

The farmers were going about feeding the world and no one much cared about them. Except at election time.

Every once in a while the Man sat in the backseat. This made me euphoric, and then he would disappear again. Sometimes, I would see him sleeping back there, or rummaging through the cooler. But he was there. Even when he wasn't. He didn't talk to me, not anymore. He wasn't inside like he had been on the steps. But he was there. On the roof of the minivan for all I knew.

Takeshi was mesmerized by the endlessness of the fields, by the amount of food he had already seen and had continued to see. Something about the world was making sense to him, I thought, something very basic. The realities of the economics of the world were careening by his window. He took picture after picture. "You make food, we make cameras," he said.

"We make food that feeds the people making movies with your cameras," I said. "And then you watch the movies and become more and more American."

"And you drive our cars," he said. "Like this one."

"And you eat our burgers," I said. "I know from my job, you guys love American food." I used to have a job.

"You watch your movies at home on our TVs," he said. "You eat sushi. You eat ramen."

"Movies by Sony," I said. "On Sony TVs and DVD players and home theater systems."

"It's all connected," he said.

The road was straight for the most part and we passed towns with silly names as we aimed for St. Louis. If my being in Illinois gave me some sense of being west, getting to St. Louis would be the confirmation. I remembered the Gateway Arch from watching the Mets play the Cardinals, the big white arch that looks like the canniest piece of product placement McDonald's had ever placed, right by the Mississippi, the monument you had to pass, or at least see, to know you were west. The Mets would get smoked in the shadow of the Arch by Ozzie Smith, starting one more impossible double play, or later, by Mark McGwire clubbing another moonshot.

You see the Arch from a great distance because the land around it is so flat. It appeared on the horizon like a shining white hill until I noticed it was an arch and that I could see right through it. There's something hallucinatory about it. Takeshi kept saying, "Cool."

The cell phone rang, and it startled me. Dan hadn't called me yet. I answered it. "The media want us to stop in St. Louis," he said.

"I have no intention of stopping," I told him, accelerating the Odyssey.

"Some of my colleagues want to get off," he said.

"Good for them," I replied. "They have real lives to lead."

"If you don't stop, the bus won't," Dan said in a tone that sounded like a threat.

"I'm not worried, Dan," I said. "I can only stop when I need to."

"Some of the national outlets have people waiting there. Replacements. There's also some local media that are interested in interviewing you," he said. "And the mayor's office called. He'd like to see you, too."

"You're not giving me a good reason to stop," I said. I had figured the press conference in Terre Haute would have been enough for a little while. I kept forgetting the incredible appetite of the media for news, for content, things to fill the channels we zoom by while sitting on our plush La-Z-Boys in darkened homes. We are insatiable, after all. We eat our Pringles and drink our Cokes and when it's all gone we want more. The news guys know their careers are a distracted viewer away from the toilet. It's a tough way to live.

"I'm a bit surprised," Dan said. "I was under the impression things would be different."

"Because of Terre Haute," I said.

"And I thank you for that," he said.

"I puked and the whole world knows about it," I reminded him.

Dan laughed. "That was unfortunate," he said. "But you're OK now, right? That's the most important thing." He didn't sound sincere.

"We'll stop when I need gas," I said. "I'm in a good mood for once. Don't ruin it."

Ahead of me, at a large interchange, I saw signs for Kansas City and I followed them. "Where are you going?" Dan asked.

"West," I said, bored. How many times did I have to tell him this?

Dan was thinking. I could hear him think. Behind him, I could hear the voices of the media. Some sang "Kansas City." I heard complaints about not stopping in St. Louis. "The Gateway Arch is supposed to be something," he said. "You can go to the top, you know, in these noisy, archaic pods. I can't believe they let people in them, but there you have it. I went a few years ago. It's worth a stop."

"We're not tourists," I told him.

"I'm not suggesting you are," Dan said defensively.

"You're thinking of a photo op," I said. Dan was using my opening in Terre Haute to see how nice I could be. I may have felt better about things, but that didn't mean I was feeling nice. "I'll stop when I need gas," I said, closing the door on him. I surprised myself with my tone, by how quickly I could take my feelings of peace and happiness for granted.

I hung up. Though I don't think that's what you do with a cell phone. The vocabulary can't keep up with the technology. Did I turn it off? I pushed a button.

The land around us became wooded and we hit some hills. But the road was razor straight and that damned "Kansas City" song got caught up in my head. I had images of smoky honky-tonks and large cattle lots and the George Brett Pine Tar Incident.

We had long passed over the Mississippi and were now, officially, West. No one could deny this. The river cut the nation in two and I expected to see the Man on the side of the road with a sign. I expected to find him standing in the middle of the interstate, his hand up commanding the Odyssey to stop. Something dramatic. I tried to picture the meeting and I couldn't because my expectations were so inflated as to render my imagination mute.

We entered a service station and it had just occurred to me that the perfect location for a service station was some anonymous nowhere people chose not to settle. I felt silly thinking this, realizing how long it had taken for me to figure this fact out. It was not a salient observation.

Takeshi was thrilled to see a McDonald's and ran from the Odyssey as soon as I had parked it. I got out and waited for Dan to walk over and try to convince me of something else. The black bus rolled to a stop in that part of the parking lot reserved for large vehicles and Dan exited and ran toward me.

We're not done, the Man said. And I looked for him but could not see him.

"We're losing at least a quarter of the bus," Dan said with alarm, his undone shirt flapping by his sides.

"You got a cigarette?" I asked. I had the urge to smoke constantly and was thinking of going inside the station to buy a pack.

Dan tossed a pack of Marlboro Lights my way. "We're losing some very important media," he said.

I held out my hand for a lighter and Dan reached into his pocket and gave me one. "Keep it," he said. "Keep the cigarettes, too."

I lit my cigarette and felt instantly, infinitely, better. "It was going to happen," I said, exhaling. "You knew that. You can't be that optimistic."

Dan began to pace. He radiated an awesome nervous energy. He took another pack of Marlboro Lights out of his breast pocket and tapped out a cigarette. I lit it for him. He stopped pacing. "I'm not trying to be optimistic," he said and he took another drag of his cigarette, "but what I'm worried about is coming this far and losing everything. There's a story here and the people leaving now aren't telling the whole thing."

This was, in a different way, the same fear I had, a fear that was tempered by a kind of hope that felt boundless. Dan had nothing to hold back his fear. Everything he had perhaps feared before the journey was about to come true. "I'll speak to them again," I said. "I don't care if they leave but I can't stand your desperation." I was angry at Dan for making me feel this way but his eyes were pools of loss, and he hit my sympathy button. He meant to do this, just as he had when he called me outside of St. Louis. Dan was too smart to chance anything. And like me, he was a guy a long way from home with nothing to show for it. "But no questions," I said.

We walked to a small patch of grass next to the parking lot and I sat on a picnic bench. Takeshi found us and joined me. He opened a paper bag to produce a Big Mac, a large fries, and a Coke. Behind us, a map of Missouri with a convenient arrow pointed to our exact location made for nice visuals for the TV guys. Dan assembled the media. He told his colleagues not to expect the news conference to become regular but that he had requested I make a statement, now that we were beyond the Mississippi.

Dan stepped away. I looked into the tired, unscrubbed faces of the media and felt sorry for them. "You guys are a mess," I said.

Nothing. No reaction. They wanted me to provide the sound bite they needed to file their stories. I cleared my throat. Takeshi ground his face into his burger. "We've been on the road for a while now," I started. And I realized that I had no idea how long it had been. Nights and days had lost their meaning for me. I could not recall the time of day we passed St. Louis or Terre Haute or Indianapolis. I had no idea what time of day it was. The clouds obliterated the sun and any hint I might have had. "I appreciate what you have all had to go through to get here. Honestly, I do. We could all use a shower about now." There were murmurs of agreement from the media. "However, I really believe we're getting close to our goal. We've crossed the Mississippi. That's the West in anyone's book. And though the Man was not very specific about where he would reveal himself, he did tell me to go west. And so here we are. And he's back. The Man's back and once in a while he tells me to keep going. Honestly. And that's what I'm doing." I paused. I wanted to reach into my pockets and pull out a cigarette but I was worried about my mother seeing me smoke on television. I smiled thinking this. "I just want you to know I'm looking. We're moving forward. I'm not trying to pull anyone's chain here," and decided to do exactly that. Something about the look on the reporters' faces made me want to lay it on thick. "Something profound is happening. Something amazing is going to happen. Something of a transcendent nature. I just don't know what that something is."

There was a sound bite. "Thanks, guys," I said. I got up quickly and ran toward the Odyssey. The reporters ran after me, throwing questions. I wasn't in the mood to play catch. I got in and waited for Takeshi. He got in, Big Mac in one hand, Coke in the other, and I turned the ignition. The Man was in the back, smiling. And then he yawned. "You should be taking pictures of this," I told Takeshi and pulled out. The reporters stood in the middle of the parking lot, stunned.

I drove to the gas pumps. Dan ran after me. I got out to fill the tank.

"Oh please," Dan said under his breath.

I ignored him. I picked up the nozzle and pushed a button to choose my gas. I put the nozzle into the tank. "If we lose interest, you definitely lose as well," he said.

"You lose!" I shouted. I took a breath. The smell of fumes. The beeps of the gas pump as the tank filled up. The energy that would move us.

I watched the numbers on the pump climb and climb. "We were just friends," Dan said, confused.

"We still are," I said. "I mean that."

Dan put his hands in his pockets and waited for me to fill the Odyssey. When I pulled the nozzle out, he checked the tally on the pump and went to pay the bill. I waited for him. "I was just hoping you'd show some consideration," he said upon returning.

"That's an interesting word," I said.

"These are my colleagues," he said. "I feel a sense of responsibility toward them. I made them a promise. The same thing you promised me, by the way." Dan was breathing so heavily I thought he would explode.

"I'm doing my best," I said. "Sometimes I don't know if I'm lying or not when the camera's on me. I don't like the idea that I might be performing. I resent that I've lost my compass for sincerity."

"That's rich coming from a man who used to write ads," he said. He looked toward the reporters who were still huddled together in a group looking like lost dogs. He sighed. "They're just tired."

"We're all tired," I said.

"Kansas City?"

I nodded. "Unless I'm told otherwise."

"Unless you're told otherwise," Dan repeated.

He turned and walked slowly to his bus. The reporters and

cameramen and technicians awaited his news with an awful kind of desperation. I watched Dan as he spoke to these people and their disappointment in what he had to say was obvious, even from a distance. Shoulders drooped. Shouting. There was a lot of shouting. Dan looked my way for help but I had none to offer. What help could I have possibly given Dan and his band of tired journalists? They chose to follow us, or they were told to. Someone had made the decision to get on the bus. Paymasters. Editors. Producers. Executives. To accompany me on my search. I could look at Dan standing with his lost tribe and not feel a bit of guilt. They had brought themselves here.

Dan went into the bus. Angie came out. He had woken her up. She walked toward me, her hair tied in a ponytail. She wore a T-shirt and khakis. She looked undeniably suburban. "Hi," I said.

"Mutiny on the bus," she said.

I had nothing to say about it. "Did he send you to, what?" I said.

"I'm an emissary," she said.

"Tell him we're still friends," I said.

"He wants something in Kansas City," she said.

"I'll take that into consideration," I said.

"You look like shit," she said, smiling.

"And you have this den-mother thing happening," I said.

"Stop flirting," she said and returned to the bus.

I got back in the Odyssey and pulled away. Takeshi was asleep, still clutching his Coke. The inside smelled like a Big Mac. It wasn't a bad smell. But it was a smell that seemed manufactured to warn you it wasn't healthy. There's something in the smell of fast food that repels. It's in the chemical makeup. The repellant notes just aren't as powerful as the parts that entice us. *Where do you want to go?* the Man asked and there he was in the backseat, studying a map. Where do you want me to go? I asked him. I'm following you. I'm doing what you're asking me to do, I said. And the Man turned the map upside down. *I mean, where do you want to go?* he said. Tell me, I replied. I had a hard time driving. And then he was gone. And I felt suddenly alone. And less hopeful. I felt as if I were failing a test, even though I was in the middle of the country, doing what I had been asked.

Missouri rolled past our window. Takeshi woke up, took in the surroundings, and then reached back for something in his backpack. He pulled out a map. "My God," I said, alarmed, puzzled by the symmetry of this. I felt, deeply, that the insinuation of direction, of knowing, would torpedo the whole thing. A map would deny the meeting with the Man of its magic. "No maps," I said. "Put it away. Bury it in your backpack." To his credit, Takeshi didn't understand my concern. Had he understood, I think, I would have let him off right there.

"It's just a map," he said, zipping up the backpack. "You have maps in your phone, too."

"Don't get me started," I said. I wanted to smoke again. I rolled my window down and lit a Marlboro. Takeshi did the same.

"Who is the Man?" he asked.

I shrugged. "If I knew . . ." And I stopped. There was no way I could answer the question. It was an impossibility. There was nothing in my past that would have prepared me for any of this. I had listened to the Man because it was outside the realm of my normal life. It wasn't a voice I could ignore. "I really don't know," I said.

"You'll find out," he said. He took a picture of the passing scenery.

In the distance, I could see the faint outline of the skyscrapers of Kansas City. The trees and farms had given way to plains. We were in a different geography now. The tall grass and wheat bent in the wind off the highway. The land was gold and yellow and green. Behind me, I noticed for the first time the absence of the black bus. The highway behind was a straight line and I felt I could see all the way to St. Louis but I could not see the bus. And I thought this would please me. But I was worried.

I was surprised by this. I could see myself alone, somewhere in the Rockies, without the Odyssey, searching, my clothes ragged, hungry, thirsty, my quest for the Man consuming my life like a fire. I kept looking in the rearview mirror but the bus was nowhere. I asked Takeshi for the phone. Sensing why, perhaps, he looked behind. "Where are they?" he asked.

I called Dan. After ten rings, he answered. "Where are you?" he asked frantically.

"I can't see you either," I said. "You had me worried."

"I'm touched," Dan said.

"We're nearing Kansas City," I told him. "We must be. I can see the buildings in the distance."

"We had a situation," he said. "We lost a reporter from the *Times*. Though we still have a web guy. And we lost one of the cameramen. Fox. That surprised me."

"Who needs them?" I said, sounding tough.

"It would have been preferable to keep the *Times* on board," Dan said. "They're the paper of record, right?"

"They're self-important," I said. I realized I felt hungry. For the first time since we'd left New York, I felt hungry. My stomach presented itself as the empty chamber it was and made an enormous, bear-like growl. "I hear they have great ribs in Kansas City."

"Really?" Dan asked.

"How can you not know that?" I said.

"No, I mean, really, you're stopping to eat?" he clarified.

"I'm hungry," I said. "Finally."

"So we're stopping?" he asked.

"I thought I could do without you," I said. "I thought I could do without that stupid bus trailing us. But I got worried. Honest."

"The times they are a-changin'," Dan sang.

"You know any rib joints in Kansas City?" I asked.

"It's eight in the morning," Dan said.

And that brought me to the ground with a thud. I was flattened. "Are you sure?" I said. I had completely lost track of time. I did not even notice the night anymore, or the sun. I felt as if I was not of this world and then suddenly I was. "Really?" I said.

"And now it's one past eight," he said. "A.M."

The earth closed in on me. My eyelids grew heavy. Gravity. My back ached. My right knee was throbbing. I wanted to stop the Odyssey. "I'm stopping at the next stop I see," I told Dan.

I hung up the phone. I felt lost. I felt unattached to the world. I did not know where I was, finally, and the prairie outside the van looked like the plains of Mars. The next stop appeared and it was much like the stop in Pennsylvania. Nothing surrounded by more of the same. I pulled in and braked hard in a parking spot. The minivan shuddered to a halt and Takeshi was thrown forward. I could feel my heart pounding through my shirt. I undid my seatbelt, crawled into the backseat, and lay down. I was probably asleep before I closed my eyes. I was probably asleep a long time ago and didn't even realize it.

TAKE ME TO THE RIVER

Tomas comes down to my office. He has no reason to be in the basement so I'm assuming he wants to talk. "Sorry to bother you," he says. He's also being polite. "Later, I'm going down to the Gulley, make a fire. Maybe pop back a few beers."

"Aren't you working?" I ask.

"It's my day off," he says.

"OK," I say. "Which gulley?"

"*The* Gulley," he says, in a way that means I haven't learned anything yet. The employees' geography of this place is foreign to me and it shouldn't be. "I'm inviting you to join me."

"You're not going to kill me, are you?"

He smiles. "Don't flatter yourself."

Arrangements are made. Tomas will bring beer. At the appointed hour, he meets me by the trailer. The night's chill is awesome. The wind descends from the north. It's Canadian. "Let's go," Tomas says, and we walk off in the direction of the stables.

We walk past them, past the horses and their braying, past the earthy, musty smell, to one of the minor trails that takes hikers toward the mountains. He's almost jogging. We reach a gulley, formed by the streams that come down from the mountains, and he leads us down a rough trail until he's at water's edge. He puts the beer down in the stream and starts collecting sticks and branches. "There's a fire pit here somewhere," he says.

"This is the Gulley?" I ask.

"People come here for privacy," he says. "You know."

"Meaning you want to fuck me?" I ask.

Tomas dumps some branches on the pit and starts looking for more. "I don't play for that team," he says.

I follow him to help gather wood. He climbs out of the small ravine and goes off into a grove of trees. He's more nimble and agile than I would've guessed. Tomas has the body of man who tastes too much of his cooking. He's not fat but he's soft in a lot of places. I pick up some kindling and dump it on the fire pit. Tomas returns with three small logs, perfectly chopped. "Look what I found," he says.

He stands over the kindling. He reaches into his pockets and pulls out some newspaper. "In the spring, this is full of water, with the snowmelt. The stream becomes a river. It's torrential." He tears the newspaper up and bends down and places it beneath the kindling. He puts more twigs on the pile. He reaches into the pocket of his windbreaker and pulls out a box of matches. He lights the paper and soon the kindling is cracking in the heat of the small fire. Tomas walks over to the stream and fishes out a beer. He twists the cap off and puts it in his pocket.

"'Give a hoot,'" I say. "Now there was a campaign." I study the fire as it grows and put two of the logs on top of it. They catch quickly. Sparks fly off into the night.

"And there's more logs," Tomas says.

He sits down finally and we both get lost in the dance of the flames. I don't know anyone who can watch a fire and not stare. It's an attraction that makes no sense. We're supposed to run from danger, aren't we? "So what's this about?" I ask when I've broken free from the fire's spell.

"Last year, a woman came here with her cat. We don't allow pets normally but she was a rich lady. She'd rented two of the tents. Her husband, two kids. And the cat. They were staying for a week. Height of the season. She and her husband owned some software company. From San Francisco. So she has her cat. Calico, I think. And then two days later, it's gone. And she's worried sick naturally, and Athena has three guys looking for this thing full-time. The lady is beside herself. And it affected me. I became worried about her cat. I kept thinking of the wolves around here. It affected my work. I couldn't think about anything but her cat."

There is no way he brought me here to tell me this story. "So what happened?" I ask.

"We found it two days later. It was hiding behind the kitchen. It had made its way to the Dumpster and I found it underneath. I heard it and there it was."

"So a happy ending."

"She was irate."

"But you found it."

Tomas takes a pull of his beer. The wind blows past us. The trees rustle. "I've been thinking a lot," he says. "I've been thinking about this place. About my place in it."

I sit back, leaning on my elbows. "And you want to talk about this?"

His face glows orange in the fire. "I thought so, yes," he says. "You have no history here. You have history, I know that, but not here. I came here two years ago. I was excited. This place has been a constant source of excitement and inspiration for me. And now I'm feeling maybe the thrill is gone."

There is a long silence between us. The sounds of the crackling fire, the rushing of water on its downward journey toward the sea.

Why is Tomas unloading this on me? He finishes his beer quickly and stands to get a new one. "I have a general worry," he says. He returns with a beer and sits back down. He pokes the fire and adds a log. The fire flares up and sparks rise before disappearing. There is no wind tonight. The glow of the fire is a zone of warmth. "Maybe I worry about stupid things."

"Like what?" I ask.

"I left Chicago for a reason," he says. "I saw what was happening. I was becoming famous. Stories were being written about me, articles. First in local newspapers. Then in local magazines. Then the big food magazines. The national ones. And then the critics turned. There was talk of television. Cookbooks. I saw what was happening and I looked into the future and I didn't want it. I didn't want to become a celebrity chef. I didn't want to become more important than my food. Or my restaurant. I didn't want the hassle. I didn't want to write cookbooks or have a cooking show or a line of spices and sauces. I didn't want to endorse knives or Crock-Pots. I didn't want any of it."

This sounds eminently reasonable. Tomas didn't want to become a product. What sane person does? I've never understood anyone who wants to become a brand. How odd it must be to walk into a store and see your face plastered on everything. Why does anyone ever want to be a movie star? What's the point? "I don't blame you," I say. I knew something about how he felt.

"That's why I left," he says. "It has nothing to do with lack of ambition. I'm just simple. I went overseas. But I missed America. That sounds odd to some people. But I missed the feeling of comfort. Home. I missed being in a place where I understood things. And then I heard about this place. I called and we had meetings. They hadn't started construction yet." He pauses and drinks some beer. He burps. "I wanted simplicity," he says. "To be a chef and cook good food. Nothing makes me happier. I like running a kitchen.

I enjoy this. I wanted my life to be simple. And, yes, I've done a cookbook. But I'm not here to become famous. I'm here to cook. Simplicity. That's what I found."

I throw some small sticks into the fire.

"This is my future," he says.

"Your dream."

"Yes."

He's found the sum of the difference between what can be and could be. What we could be is the stuff of dreams, sure. It's the path. It's where we want to end up. The lucky ones do. Intelligence has little to do with it. "Most people are happy being what we are and letting things happen," I say. "Hardly anyone is their own boss."

"I believe that," he says.

"But they stop to study their lives and realize, suddenly, it's not good enough. And then you need the courage to follow the path. And luck. We all need some luck."

The fire sparks up and an ember is sent hurtling toward the stream.

"So this is the problem," Tomas says.

"What is?"

"The worry I have. With what you're doing. What Athena has asked you to do. What you could unleash."

What is he getting at? The clearest path to understanding should never involve a hop, skip, and a jump.

"This branding business," he continues. "It has a lot of people worried."

I poke at the fire. "Please," I say.

"A lot of people are here for the same reason as me. To get away. From something. To escape. Some of it is bad. There are people with very interesting histories here. More interesting than yours." He pulls a stalk of grass and puts it into his mouth. "But they all ended up here. For the simplicity of the place."

"That sounds like the making of a brand." And it is. Simplicity implies a lot of things. Mostly positive.

"Even at that, I worry," he says. "A brand is like a blanket. A big, wet blanket. Everything gets buried under it. I've seen some restaurants that got branded and suddenly the chef loses his personality. He must be the brand, too. And he is no longer himself. When he speaks, who is doing the talking? Him? Or the brand? It's a dangerous thing. I've seen chefs become very successful and lose their way all at once because of the power of branding people like you."

"Everything has a brand," I say.

"All this personal branding is like a form of mental illness."

"Forget the word. It's overused. Think about its meaning though. What does a ranch, a spa in northern Montana, mean to people? Should people come here and expect to eat, say, Chinese food? Should all the managers be Oriental? Would that make sense?"

Tomas doesn't answer. "You're not listening."

I sit up. "I am listening. I've heard every word you've said. I understand."

"I brought you here to say don't fuck this place up," he says. "Don't make it into something it's not. It's doing well. People are still finding this place and spending time here. All this without a master plan. I know the owners need a plan moving forward. I respect that. Just don't fuck up a good thing."

"What 'moving forward'?"

Tomas lies down. He sighs. "I'm not supposed to say."

"It would help."

Why Athena hasn't told me the whole story is impossible to understand. She has asked me to help map this place out, its future, but she's not telling me everything. I don't know if she's doing it on purpose or if communication isn't her strength.

"They want to maybe open a few more properties," he says. "Athena wants to bring in investors, put some money in, partner with the owners, open a few more. All around the Rockies. All the same idea. That's what she told me. And that's why she wants the plan. She needs to make this place into something before they expand."

"This place needs personality."

"Yes."

"A brand."

"A brand."

"This place needs to be some kind of flagship," I say.

"I don't know," he says. "I don't know that they're going to become Holiday Inn. Just a few properties. Make it into some international hotel group. One of those associations. I know the owners are all over the world studying small hotels. They have some acreage up in Canada. And also somewhere in Idaho."

"This is interesting," I say.

"I was sure she would have told you," he says.

"Probably not," I say. I stand up. "But I hear you, I just want you to know that."

"About what?" he asks.

"Why you're here. I think I'm here for the same reason. I got here through sheer luck but I'm here now." I pick a beer out of the stream. "And I like it here." I've just decided this. I'm surprised. Mostly at myself. Until now, I'd seen myself as a New Yorker. A person who found everything west of the Hudson demeaning, silly, unsubstantial. Irrelevant. A typical New Yorker.

"There are people who are threatened by you," Tomas says.

"Are you?"

"I know your past. I saw it. The thing was hard to avoid. For a while. I got bored with it, frankly. But when I put you in the kitchen, I figured you were just hiding out for a bit and then you'd leave."

"So you knew?"

"I knew part of the story. Like I said, I got bored with it. I turned it off. And I didn't recognize you at first. And then one of the guys mentioned it in passing. One Google search and there you are."

"I didn't have a plan."

"I was your boss and I wasn't afraid."

I gulp down my beer. It's gone. "No one has ever had reason to be afraid of me."

"And now you're staying and you have the power to influence change. I wouldn't have hired you if I'd known, even slightly, what was going to happen."

"And I would have kept walking."

"So that's the luck part," he says.

"It's something," I say.

"It's something," he says. He burps again. The sound of the night, of the world, surrounds us. I can hear my own breathing.

"Thanks for the beer," I say, turning to leave.

"Should I be worried?"

"No," I say. "I wish I could say something convincing. Something that would tame this fear of yours. We're on the same page." I don't bother turning around. I find the path in the darkness and struggle through it. And then I'm in the clearing, and the stables come into view and the lights from the buildings create a glow that is a hearth in the middle of the wilderness.

WHY WORRY

I slept the deep sleep of the dead. I did not dream. I was told later that I had slept throughout the day and the night and into the next morning. A day. I had slept an entire day to make up for the sleep I had lost. My body was trying to find the equilibrium my mind had taken away from it.

I awoke to see Takeshi and Dan in the front seat sleeping, leaning against each other, their heads resting together like blissfully contented Siamese twins from a multicultural union. The black bus was parked next to the minivan, creating the illusion of night. To my right, however, just inches away behind the side door window, were the cameras. Cameramen jostled to get their shots, filming my awakening for that afternoon's news. My sleep was probably being streamed live to anyone with nothing better to do. Everything I did was someone else's pleasure.

I sat up. The reporters, stuck behind the cameramen, started barking questions. Their shouts were muffled by the fact of the Odyssey. Dan snorted and was soon awake as well. I heard him stretch and turned around. Takeshi's forehead had been imprinted in his. He checked his watch and his eyes widened. "Did we have a good sleep?" he asked.

"I don't know," I said. And I didn't. I wasn't sure if the sleep had done anything for me. I sensed that my body ached.

Takeshi woke and rubbed his eyes. He opened the door, allowing the questions being hurled at me to enter the cocoon of the minivan, and he stepped out. He walked into the crowd and was gone.

"Any dreams?" Dan asked.

I thought about it. I could not even recall sleeping. It was as if I hadn't existed for, what. "How long?" I asked.

"Twenty-three hours," Dan said. "I think I won the pool."

"I slept," I said, as if saying this would allow my body to relax, to feel as if it had been at repose. I said it to convince myself it was true. "I slept a whole day?"

"No visitors?" he asked.

I opened the door and made my way through the throng. All the questions related to my dreams, or to my lack of them. I did a lot of shrugging. I walked to a small grove of trees and found a spot hidden from the cameras. I leaned against a tree. And I thought.

Where are you? I asked the Man. I heard my own desperation. Standing there, I was overwhelmed by doubt, by the idiocy of this, not just the journey, but the very nature of the voice itself. I had slept a day and yet I was exhausted.

Takeshi emerged from behind a thicket of hedges, doing up his pants. "I've peed all across America," he said, smiling.

"I'm so proud," I said.

He walked over to me and put his hand on my shoulder. He flashed concern. "My ass is sore," he said.

I laughed. I hugged him and laughed. "You smell," I told him.

He pulled away and sniffed his underarm. "There are no showers in your Honda," he said, smiling again.

I turned around and unzipped myself and pissed against a tree.

"Did I really sleep for an entire day?" I asked. I watched myself water the tree. I couldn't stop.

"We took your pulse last night," Takeshi said. "Everyone was starting to get a little worried."

I finally stopped. I had flooded the soil around the tree. I was afraid I might have killed it. I shook and zipped up and turned to face my Japanese friend. "Really?" I asked. "You took my pulse?"

"Angie's idea," he said. "She was making everyone nervous. We ate ribs and then Angie told Dan to call a doctor."

"You had ribs?" I thundered. Dan had found us and he shot Takeshi an angry look. Did he think they could keep something like this a secret from me?

"There's a rib joint not far from here," Dan said. "Sorry, very, really, but we were all getting hungry. They'd heard you wanted ribs so they brought out a slaughterhouse-worth of ribs. Fed everybody, even the reporters. Takeshi ate four racks. He made the news last night."

"The fact that we were sleeping, the ribs, or because Takeshi ate four racks?" I asked.

"Um, yes," Dan said.

Takeshi licked his lips. "We tried," he said. "Really. I punched your arm. Dan shouted. We turned on the radio, loud, loud, loud. That's why Angie got worried. We took your pulse. A doctor came and did a checkup and said everything was all right. You were just tired. Exhaustion, he said."

"Doctors?" I asked. "I was examined?"

Dan lit a cigarette.

"Did you at least save some for me?" I asked.

"No one wanted to," Dan said. "I said you didn't deserve it. I held a bowl of BBQ sauce under your nose and you didn't move. It was thick and smoky. Redolent. What a good word. This whole area smelled like BBQ. The bus still does, I'm sure. You were undeserving.

A sentient being should not be able to withstand a smell like that. I was about to auction the last rack off and then Angie interceded and there you are. She held off the guys. They were like vultures around carrion. I called her Wonder Woman."

I had an image of Angie in Lynda Carter's getup. It was at once ridiculous and vaguely erotic.

We walked back to the Odyssey. Angie was in the passenger seat, a broad smile on her face. Her hair was tied back in a ponytail. She was wearing a Yankees T-shirt. At that moment I could not fathom my neglect of her. Walking toward the minivan, the world seemed to slow down and Angie looked like some ideal of womanhood. I made my way past the media and opened the door. On Angie's lap, a Styrofoam container. "Hi, sleepy head," she said. I got in. She stroked my cheek and I felt it down to my toes. She opened the container to reveal a small mountain of baby back ribs and a small Styrofoam cup of dark, congealed sauce.

"My God!" I said.

She handed me the container. "The things I do for you," she sang.

I took a rib. "I'm so hungry," I said. I looked to her, seeking permission, I think, though I don't know why.

"Normally, I'd say your food's getting cold," she said.

"Thanks," I said and I bit into the rib. It was cold and had toughened up but I could imagine it warm, the meat falling off the bone and melting on the tongue as the smoke and seasoning danced around my mouth. I dipped the rib into the sauce and bit it again. My tongue sang hallelujah. In the sauce and the rub I could taste the history of BBQ, of the Midwest, I could taste the history of BBQ all the way back to Mexico. I tasted America. I tasted our country in this simple lump of meat and fat and bone. More so than hamburgers and hot dogs and cotton candy and fried chicken, ribs are America. Ribs. Pork, beef, it doesn't matter. I wanted to sing. The word "ecstasy" boomed around my head. I was so happy I wanted to sing some-thing trite and corny and awful. I rolled down my window. "Tell the people who made these ribs they are gods," I announced. "And tell them they can quote me. Wait. Let me phrase it in a manner they can use. These are the best ribs in the world," I said. "Hell, they're the best ribs in Kansas City."

The media laughed knowingly. They knew a good slogan when they heard one. I rolled up the window. I devoured the ribs and stuck my fingers into the sauce and licked them clean. Angie produced a can of Coke from a paper bag at her feet and I drank it down with the greediest of gulps. I saw Dan and Takeshi by the trees, smoking. I wanted a cigarette, too. "Thank you so much," I said to Angie. I leaned over and kissed her.

I sat back up. She smiled and wiped her hair off her forehead. And then she wiped my BBQ sauce off her face. "You're welcome," she said. Wonder Woman.

I got out of the Odyssey and walked to Dan and Takeshi. "Let's go into the grove again," I said. I still didn't want my mother to see me smoking.

Dan and Takeshi followed me. I leaned against a tree and took out a pack of cigarettes from my pocket. Takeshi produced his lighter. I took a deep drag. "For the first time, I feel almost good," I exhaled.

"About the journey?" Dan asked.

"No," I admitted. "I'm at wit's end about this whole thing. I'll admit that to you. I'm talking physically. I can actually feel my body. I'm aware of my physical self. I can feel my hair. Until now I've felt disembodied in a way. I've been this antenna set up to receive signals. Now I feel human."

"This is good," Dan said.

"I don't know if it's good or bad. But it feels different," I said.

I finished my cigarette. I stubbed it out against the tree and handed the butt to Takeshi, who threw it into the direction of the shrubs. "The foreigner comes and pollutes our land," Dan said.

I returned to the minivan. Angie had retreated to the bus. I had stopped on an extra wide shoulder on the side of the interstate, not a rest area. I could see now that on the other side of the grove of trees lay fields of corn. I could make out an enormous silo in the distance. Around us were other cars and trucks and minivans, their occupants craning their necks for a look. And around the perimeter were state troopers. They had closed off a lane of highway and were directing traffic away from it. Others formed a barrier between the public, and the bus and my Odyssey. Cars on the highway honked as they passed. I had noticed none of this until I was ready to leave. And then I saw the Man. On the highway. He looked like he was meditating. He did not look at me.

We hit rush hour traffic on the outskirts of Kansas City. The uneven skyline lay before me like a grade school class picture. It took us an hour to get through the city and out the other side, on the Kansas side, when we hit a turnpike and the world was flat and golden and rolled westward like a sun-dappled sea. The driving was easier here, on the flat, straight roads, and we passed Topeka before we had time to consider it. And once we passed Topeka I couldn't get *The Wizard of Oz* out of my head. Every once in a while I would say "Dorothy's home!" and point to a farm near the highway and it was not until the fourth time that Takeshi caught on and I once again realized the sheer sweep of Hollywood.

We stopped for gas near Salina and Takeshi bought another Big Mac and I ate a rapidly browning banana from the cooler. There was a foul odor emanating from something inside and Takeshi helped me throw it into the garbage bin. A cameraman recorded the toss. "Thanks to all my culinary sponsors," I said, "and thanks to Rubbermaid for the cooler. Rubbermaid coolers are cool." The camera was sure to relay my slogan and gratitude.

The highway through Kansas cut through some incredibly empty plains. We drove for miles without seeing much of anything. The evening sun lay directly before us. We were driving into the sun. The landscape changed. Rocks appeared. And then we spotted some more towers of rock jutting above the plain like skyscrapers that had lost their way. The road was so straight, so obviously west in its orientation, I kept expecting the Man to appear. To end this thing. For the payoff. A windswept, desolate western place where the world was the same in all directions seemed like the perfect locale for our final meeting. I drove through Kansas thinking it had to be the middle of something because this is what I imagined the middle of everything to look like: featureless and plain, a place where one could lose oneself in the curve of the horizon, in the stillness of the tall grass, in the play of light and shadow across the land. Night fell and the strength to continue driving returned to me. It again felt like a purpose, not a chore. Hunger evaporated. The daylong sleep had meant something, surely. I had slept once on this trip and I was hoping I wouldn't have to sleep again.

We passed into Colorado. "We're going to hit the mountains soon," I said. Takeshi was asleep. I checked the backseat and the Man was not there.

I awaited the mountains. I was surprised by how flat this part of the state was. It was just like Kansas. But there was a noticeable upward slant to the road. We were rising. We would hit the mountains, go over them, and head to the ocean. Perhaps I would deliver Takeshi to the airport myself.

And the thought of this, the thought that perhaps all I was doing was helping Takeshi get home, filled me with something. Not worry. Not dread. A precursor of defeat. In a sense, the mountains could signal some sort of awesome inevitability. With the bus still behind, I started to feel the futility of this again, and I wondered finally about the public's perception of it. I was going to suffer a public and far-reaching humiliation. It would be international in scope. I found myself caring about something I had refused to care about.

The euphoria of the ribs had worn off.

If the Man wasn't going to appear, my sadness and disappointment would be played out before more people than I could count. I was worried about not meeting the Man and feeling like a fool for believing in him. I was worried about the Man knowing I was feeling these things. I was worried that my doubts were perverting the process, the lines of communication, were being projected onto a giant screen for him to see and realize I had been the wrong one, that my beliefs were scattered randomly like cards on a table. I was worried that my doubts would become nothing more than a signpost of fear. A billboard.

I was worried about what the world would say when they saw me cry.

I drove on, west, toward the mountains, the Great Plains behind us. The entire country behind us.

COME AND GET IT

This is my hunch. The public has forgotten. The media criticizes the public for their lack of an attention span but it is the media that feels the need to move, to create a new narrative environment, because they feel stale otherwise. The media can't stay on a story for long, no matter how important. And then someone who wants to stay with a story is called obsessive. Politicians used that word expertly. As an expletive. If politicians are good at something, it's changing the dynamics of our attention. When they fail, the scent of scandal pollutes the air.

I'm thinking Dan is writing his book without a valid ending. Or at least he'll leave it vaguely open-ended. I'm off the radar. The country has moved on. I didn't deliver what I'd promised and there's nothing the country likes less than someone who doesn't deliver. I led the population to a barren place. I was a false prophet. Except I'd never promised anything in the first place.

In this sense, really, I was a celebrity. And in this sense, Dan was right. And that is another reason to find comfort here. I want a kind of anonymity that I'm not sure exists in the world.

In an odd way, this place, this blip of land beneath the mountains,

is becoming a tonic. Or is already. Every time I realize this, the surprise registers with the force of dynamite. I feel new. Even this direction I've taken, Athena's project, a role I could not have conceived
even under the threat of torture, has my body feeling lighter. I feel
nimble. I don't resent what I'm doing. This job, this new life, has
energized me.

I'm walking around the restaurant watching people eat dinner.
I've never done this. I've never spent a meal on this side of the
building. I've never seen what the waitstaff has to put up with, the
daily humiliations they must endure, all for the chance to win that
one extravagant tip.

This is what I've learned. There is talk of treating the Germans
as badly as they treat the staff. Or there was but there are hardly
any Germans here anymore. Not enough to generalize. The English
are fun until they've hit the bottle. The Italians dress too well, even
when mounting a horse. Especially when mounting a horse. To
them this activity is equivalent to a night at La Scala. The Canadians
are polite, don't tip well, and look like they shop exclusively at the
Gap. Except they have a tremendous amount of money. To be
honest, we kind of resent it. The Texans come here with a "this ain't
a ranch" swagger but are pleasant about it. And tip like champions.
New Yorkers always worry about the lack of cell phone reception.
The fact this place doesn't have it confirms all their perceptions of
places that aren't New York. Californians enjoy the mud baths and
drink more wine than the Italians but they don't ever seem to enjoy
themselves. They seem serious, which is something I would never
have thought to accuse Californians of being. There is a lot of talk
about real estate.

Everyone loves the Japanese. Especially when they get on a
horse for the first time. The Japanese are not afraid of humiliation.
This makes sense to anyone who has watched their TV shows. They
laugh at everything. They love getting dressed up western. The men

really love the chaps. They drink hard and they drink expensive and they leave good tips. The noise a group of Japanese men will make after a bottle of scotch is something to behold. It is as if their normal reserve is just a way of saving up for the drunken firestorm that always, inevitably, must come. The Japanese are just as sloppy as the English when drunk, only nice and nonviolent about it.

Inside the main dining room, the rustic wood tables gleam with layers of varnish and polishing. The walls harbor authentic Remingtons. The silverware shines. The china is the kind of white that teeth whiteners promise. The waitstaff have a uniform: bootcut jeans, rattlesnake-skin cowboy boots, a soft cotton flannel shirt. The women wear bandanas around their necks and replace the jeans with denim pencil skirts. The real cowboys around here, the wranglers, for example, find the outfit the stupidest thing since *City Slickers*. It took me a while to understand why everyone on the waitstaff is from somewhere else, from California, New York, Ohio, Florida, places where the only cowboys are on television, where the West is a punch line for a lame joke, *Stagecoach*, John Wayne, Clint Eastwood, cowboys and Indians.

The restaurant's GM, Sandy, is also the room's hostess and she dresses in western-inspired evening wear and makes sure to show off her too-good-to-be-true cleavage and the men all think she loves them. She's very good at what she does. She makes good money. She just bought a home half an hour away. There are rumors she's a lesbian.

Tomas has made something he hasn't offered in ages. Grits are on the menu, paired with the porterhouse or a pecan-chipotle-crusted chicken. Each waiter works five tables, each seating four people. The tables are large, round chunks of wood. Sandy places the featured wines on each table, the house brand merlot from Sonoma and a pinot gris from Oregon.

I stand around with some of the waiters as we wait for Sandy to open the room. I go out back for a quick smoke. Some of the dishwashers stand around smoking, and we say hi to each other, and not much else. Coming back here, I can sense I've broken some code. I'm no longer kitchen staff. They must think I'm management and smoking with them breaks every rule of caste that has been elaborately built up here. For example, waitstaff spend most of their downtime with the wranglers. The kitchen mostly keep to themselves except when they need sex and then they hang out with housekeeping. I've often wondered how these codes evolved, or if there's actually some bizarre book that forbids, say, administrators from keeping company with the kitchen. The different jobs aren't racially defined, and the rules aren't about money either (if it were, the waiters might hang with housekeeping). It's based on what you do. It's as rigid a system—caste, clan, whatever it's based on—as I've ever seen. The commingling of the groups is treated with suspicion. Even hostility.

I throw my cigarette to the ground and stamp it out and walk back into the dining room. The waiters stand around, bored, with empty looks on their faces. We all wait for Sandy to announce the kitchen's ready and then Tomas will go to the terrace in front of the restaurant and ring the triangle. The guests love the triangle. An authentic touch to herald the West, a touchstone. A totem.

I hear Tomas yell "OK" from the kitchen. Sandy comes out and claps and this is the waitstaff's real signal to get moving. Tomas walks out of the kitchen through the dining room and onto the terrace. He rings the triangle. And the guests start marching in. Or barging in. The bankers and lawyers and accountants and oilmen and minor celebrities share stories about the glories of their day. I overhear laments about the economy, government intervention, about the direction of the stock market. Complaints about corporate tax structures. I hear a Japanese banker apologize to a group of American executives for his country's economic problems. I don't hear the Americans offer a similar apology. I hear a tanned trophy wife discussing the best plastic surgeon in Argentina with another tanned trophy wife. Or escort. I hear admissions of past infidelities and failed marriages. I hear men debate the pluses of high colonics and the best resort in the South Pacific. Waiters have struck it rich in the past, just by talking to the right person, overhearing the right conversation. There is a local legend about the chambermaid who is now the vice-president of sales for a successful dot com in Seattle.

On the board by the bar, I notice orders for two bottles of the house red, a glass of the pinot gris, four beers, two scotch, a Sidecar, three bourbon, two gin and tonics, a Moscow Mule, three diet colas, and two martinis, one vodka.

A table of four Japanese men all order steaks. They can't pronounce grits but they take it. They all order salads with ranch dressing. The Japanese love ranch dressing and the Americans order a Japanese-style sesame dressing. Almost always. A couple from Arizona that has been here a week order the filet mignon with the Belgian frites and lemon aioli and the grilled Tuscan chicken breast with succotash, beets, and a potato galette.

Another table, two couples from the East Coast, all order the specials, the men the steaks, the women the chicken.

At another table, English, the men already drunk on bourbon, all order steaks. Frites. More bourbon.

In a little more than three hours, the rush is over. The room is just this side of empty. Couples holding hands. The drunk English. A table of new friends, two couples, one from Canada, the other from Ohio. The plates and glasses are attacked by the bussers. They take everything to bins that are carried to the dish pigs by another set of bussers, people who haven't graduated to the dining room yet.

In the employee lounge I eat two baked potatoes and a green salad covered with the Japanese dressing chased by a beer. Tomorrow I'm going to watch breakfast. And lunch. I have plans to sit in on a yoga class and get on the horses. Maybe get a massage. There is already so much here. This business is successful on its own terms, whatever those terms are. The Big K Ranch and Spa delivers on a promise, whatever that promise is. What happens when you over-promise *and* overdeliver? Do you lose everything? Am I going to be the one responsible?

After eating, I ask Athena, "Why isn't there a golf course here?"

"I don't know," she says.

"Was it ever discussed?"

"Not in my time."

"Have you studied if it's feasible?"

"Is it necessary?" she asks. "Or does a golf course mean we would need to expand this property?"

"It's a feeling."

"Will that be a part of your report?" she asks. She smiles. I can't help but stop for a moment every time she smiles. "Yes?"

"I don't know," I say. And this makes Athena laugh.

"Are you OK?" she asks.

"Tomas told me about the cat episode," I say.

Athena rolls her eyes. "That stupid cat. He was this mess for two whole days."

"But he found it."

She grabs my arms and pulls me closer. "Is that what he said?" she whispers. "He didn't find the cat. One of the dishwashers did. On a cigarette break. And he brought it to Tomas and Tomas acted like a hero. Meanwhile he wouldn't work. He was so worried by that cat. He sat in his office and sulked. I had to put out three guys just to look for it." I'd like to laugh and share this with Tomas and I know I never can. "He's so single-minded," she says. "It's what makes him an excellent chef but if something gets into his bubble, he's nothing. And we don't even allow pets."

She pushes me backward. "I won't say anything," I tell her. I'd like to kiss Athena one day. I've just decided this. And this may be another thing I never do.

From my room, later that night, I watch the mountains shining in the moonlight. Rocks splitting the land in two. I come from one side of these monoliths. I feel like the pioneers I didn't quite learn about in school, the ones who saw the mountains and didn't know how to get to the other side. The Rockies can be either a wall or a door. They can inspire awe, fear, wonder. They can stop the rain or make it fall. They can change the weather. They can bend the wind.

PART SEVEN

ROCKY MOUNTAIN HIGH

Denver and the mountains lay ahead of us, mirages emerging out of the golden fog of the tall grass. We drove through the sloping prairie, my foot growing heavier in anticipation of something momentous. The sun kissed the mountaintops; I worried about hitting rush-hour traffic. I tried to associate Denver with food and I couldn't. Denver meant nothing to me except John Elway and skiing and the mountains, and the mountains had become very important. They symbolized something. The sky was clear, a deep azure, heading into Denver. I could see the mountains clearly now, running like a jagged wall in front of us, their peaks dusted with snow. Ahead of them, the skyline of Denver seemed like a small thing, a play set. "I've never seen mountains like this," I told Takeshi, who had already seen them and wasn't as impressed as I was.

"Japan has big mountains, too," he said, almost defensively.

But I was excited, a boy lost in a world of candy. I drove faster. All my sensory experiences were somehow getting transferred to my right foot. "In New Jersey, we have hills and everyone calls them mountains," I said. "Out here, you couldn't even find one of those hills on a map. Over there, we ski on them. It's pathetic."

The sun disappeared behind the Rockies and the sky turned pink. Night descended quickly. Denver shimmered in front of us, like the tree in Rockefeller Plaza at Christmas, and then we were inside the city and the lights made the mountains disappear. "I'm hungry," Takeshi announced. I was, too.

I called Dan and told him we were going to be stopping somewhere. I got off the highway and drove down a busy street, looking for nothing, looking for a place to eat but not knowing what I wanted. I knew Takeshi would hold to form and want a burger.

I called Dan again. He told me to stop at the next place with a good-sized parking lot and right away I knew we wouldn't be eating well because in my mind nothing worth eating can come from an establishment surrounded by a parking lot. A good restaurant to me involves work, especially when it comes to parking. But perhaps that wasn't true in Denver.

We drove by a large park with a banner hung from streetlight poles. The banners announced a zoo. We passed a large museum. I worried about getting too far from the highway and ordered Takeshi to point out the next place he saw. I wasn't seeing anything. You can't look for anything properly when you're driving, especially when everything is unfamiliar. It's like shopping for one specific thing. It never works and that's why so many people hate shopping. The phone rang and I answered it. "So?" I asked Dan.

"A guy from the local paper says there's a good Italian place right down the street, about five more blocks, and they have a big parking lot," he said. He was laughing already.

"I didn't drive all the way across the country to eat more Italian," I said.

"Can you believe it?" Dan asked.

Thoughts of his brother's inedible calzones danced in my head, waltzed into my mouth, and I wasn't hungry anymore. "Fine," I sighed. "Lead the way."

The bus overtook us and I followed it. Seeing the backside of the bus was like seeing the tops of clouds, unfamiliar and strange, and I followed. I kept thinking of pulling a U-turn and just returning to the highway, severing the cord as it were, but I knew I wouldn't and couldn't. I could imagine Dan's reaction, his face, how misshapen it would become with sorrow and betrayal. I saw a vision of Dan seeking military assistance. "I don't want Italian," I said.

"Tell Dan," Takeshi said.

I called him again and told him I would not eat Italian. "I can't," I pleaded. "I have bad memories. There's a Pavlovian thing at work. I can't smell oregano again. The idea of a place that makes red sauce is making me queasy."

The bus pulled into a parking lot. The restaurant looked like it once might have been a steakhouse. Across the street from it was what looked like a family-style restaurant, the kind that hands out balloons to all the kids and where the staff always sing "Happy Birthday" if you ask them to. I pulled in there. I parked and watched as the black bus slowly pulled out of the Italian restaurant's parking lot and made its way to ours. Even the bus looked to be hesitating to cross the street to such a place. I was sure reporters didn't normally frequent family restaurants. Unless they were with their families. Whom I'm sure they missed.

Dan jumped out of the bus and walked quickly in our direction. I lowered the window. "What's this?" he asked, looking oddly insane. He had probably set his mind on a nice veal scaloppine.

"You don't like the nice clown face?" I asked, pointing to the shape that made the *O* in Dot's, the name of the restaurant. Beneath the big name, the words "The Fun Restaurant!" The branding was simple and effective. The sign hadn't changed since it was put up, probably in the early eighties. The parking lot moaned under the weight of numerous minivans. I could imagine the swarms of kids running around inside.

"What's wrong with that place?" Dan asked, pointing across the street.

"Honestly, I don't want Italian," I said. "I'm not joking. I'm sure it's very good. But I'm thinking about the smell and, well, no."

Dan reached into his back pocket and took out his wallet. He gave me a credit card. "Here," he said. "Enjoy your astonishingly mediocre meal. Ask the kids to keep quiet. Maybe you can drink through a colored straw. I'm going across the street to eat something civilized."

"The snobbery, the snobbery," I said in my best Marlon Brando.

Dan boarded the bus. Angie exited. The doors closed behind her and the bus crossed the street and made its way to a parking lot resplendent with shiny sports cars. And not a single minivan. There was a neat sociological phenomenon exhibited by the lots but I was too hungry to think about it. My stomach made grumbling noises. I had to use the washroom. Takeshi exited the Odyssey. I did likewise.

"I hear Denver is full of great dive bars," Angie said.

"I'm sure it is," I said. "But not tonight, dear."

I wanted a cigarette, but smoking in front of Angie, at that moment, felt wrong. Shameful. And I had no idea why such a strong feeling would come over me.

"Mind if I join you?" she asked.

"What have I done to deserve this?" I said.

"The boys on the bus can get tiring," she said.

I held out my arm and she took it and the three of us entered Dot's. A tall woman made up to look like Charlie Chaplin greeted us at the entrance to the dining room. Underneath the getup, I could see the woman was in her fifties, at least. Her nametag said Dot. "Good evening, welcome to Dot's," she said. Friendliness oozed out of her. The kind of authentic friendliness that would soon get annoying. "Would that be three for dinner?" she spoke in a tone that made me feel as if I had just walked into a kindergarten. It was on the ignorant side of patronizing. It was sincere. I wanted to show her the small scar on my knee from when I fell off my bicycle when I was nine.

"Three," Angie said, and Dot looked in a book and then at her map of tables and then looked back at us.

"It's Chaplin night," she said, explaining her getup. "That just means I dress up like Charlie Chaplin."

And then Dot's smile disappeared, slowly, her upturned lips falling like a feather, and I could swear the color of her eyes went from hazel to black, matching the color of the bushy fake moustache she was wearing. "Aren't you . . ." she asked and before she could get much further she stole a quick glance at Takeshi and everything was confirmed. "You are, aren't you?" she said, suddenly shuffling the papers on her little stand. She became flustered. She pulled a Sharpie out of her breast pocket and handed it to me. "Could you sign this?" she asked. She gave me a menu and I signed it. I returned the pen but she gave it to Takeshi. He looked at me, a bit stunned, perplexed maybe. I handed him the menu and he signed it as well. "I'd imagine you want an out-of-the-way table," she said. A bead of sweat formed on what little I could see of her forehead. "For peace and quiet."

"That's very thoughtful of you," I said. "Thanks."

"Would it be too much to ask to get my picture taken with you?" she asked. "With both of you?" She smiled again except this time I saw Dot's smile, not the Charlie Chaplin version she had given us when we walked in. "This is so unprofessional of me, I realize, sorry. But this is so unexpected!" She let out a short laugh. A snort.

"Can we eat first?" Angie asked. "Joe's hungry."

Dot hadn't noticed Angie. Angie wasn't on her radar at all. Her eyes widened. "Of course," she said, studying her map again. "Of course. You must be so hungry. You haven't had a meal since Kansas City, I'm guessing." She pulled out three menus from a slot in the wall behind her. "Please, follow me."

We followed Dot through the restaurant. She approximated speed walking. Families occupied every table. Large tables hosting either extended families or two families enjoying a night out. Children had the run of the restaurant and pink and blue balloons were strung from every chair seating a child. The ceiling was a grave-yard of helium balloons. The volume in the room was like a noisy biker bar that had crashed into a grade school classroom, injuring many. Exasperated parents called out the names of children in a kind of random litany of exasperation. The customers were over-whelmingly blond. The parents were not much older than me and they were fit and handsome in a very all-American way. The smell of the room was a mixture of frying and perfume and kids, that unmis-takable smell that takes over a place when enough kids are in it, the smell of play and dirt and soiled underwear and laundry detergent. It is the smell of people too busy living to care about something as inconsequential as a smell.

Dot took us to a table in a dark corner, on the far side of the kitchen door. It smelled of an unclean kitchen. "No one will bother you here," she told us, handing us the menus. "This is where the staff usually eats. The doors will swing open every now and then but the rest of the customers won't see you." The kitchen door swung open, almost hitting Dot. "You don't mind?"

"This is perfect," I told her, and it was.

"Our specials should be on a separate sheet within the menus and if you want something that's not on the menu just ask and we'll see what we can do." She smiled some more, warmly, exposing her gleaming gums. Dot had that mid-American friendly thing that I often thought of as aggressive. It was an aggressive friendliness.

"Does anyone want drinks?"

Takeshi asked for a Bud. I asked for a Coke. Angie ordered a rum and Diet Coke. Dot laughed. "OK, then, I'll get your drinks and I'll bring a waiter over shortly." Dot's teeth were beginning to hurt my eyes. Light emanated from her mouth. "And if you need anything at all, just ask for me."

I watched her walk away and soon many of the waiters and bus-boys were coming to the table to have a look and say hi. The fathers and mothers, uncles and aunts, the grandparents were bound to catch on soon despite the location of our table, partially hidden from the rest of the room by a serving station brimming with condiments and a touch-screen monitor. A tall blond Asian man brought us our drinks and engaged Takeshi in Japanese. Takeshi sighed and slumped in his seat and signed his napkin. He handed it to the waiter, who beamed and thanked him and left. "He says I'm becoming a star in Japan," Takeshi explained sadly. "My father will kill me." He took a giant swig of his beer and sank into melancholy.

I slapped his back. "Look," I said, "forget your father's business. You return to Japan a hero, do some commercials. You guys have a fierce and lucrative celebrity culture. The money is silly. Irresponsible. You've made it on your own. You've broken free." I was talking like Dan.

Takeshi buried his face in his hands and shook it wildly. "This is all very bad," he mumbled. "Very bad, very bad, very bad, very bad . . ." He repeated it until I was certain it had lodged in my brain, an earworm with a Japanese accent.

Angie raised her eyebrows and attacked her drink. "This is bad rum," she said, making a face.

Takeshi kept at it. He was close to composing a Shintoist koan.

"Plus it's weak," Angie said. "What kind of a place is this?" She laughed at the stupidity of her question.

Takeshi banged his head on the table. It stayed there.

I opened the menu, bemused by Takeshi's reaction, embarrassed that I had suggested he cash in on the predicament, by my hypocrisy, or, worse, by my willingness to say anything. I studied the menu. It offered every possible take on every menu in America.

Salads, jalapeño poppers, burgers, steaks, fish, pizza, Thai spring rolls, pasta, club sandwiches, roast chicken, burritos. This place was everything to everyone and I half-regretted not following Dan and his minions into the Italian place across the street. "Nothing good can come of this," I said. Angie didn't even look at the menu. She knew what she wanted and if the menu didn't have it, she would take Dot up on her offer. Takeshi's head lay immobile on the table. He was pained and embarrassed. I looked at the deli section and found that the corned beef came with coleslaw, a pickle, and fries and closed the menu. I could picture the plastic bag that held my corned beef. I'm in Denver, I should have meat, a steak, something more local, I thought. I shrugged and reached for my Coke and sucked an ice cube into my mouth. And then I went to the washroom and had the most satisfying shit of my life, even while I could hear fathers and sons arguing in the stalls around me. I sat on the toilet for a good fifteen minutes. It was a kind of lost peace. A remembrance of how things used to be. I was alone and marveled at the feeling.

I returned to the table. Dot was hovering, her phone in hand, obviously waiting for a photo. "Well, hello there," she grinned. "Everything go all right?"

I didn't say anything. I smiled, which is all I imagine anyone can do when asked about a trip to the toilet.

"No repeat of Indiana in there?" Dot asked, laughing.

I should have been angry. I should have, but I couldn't find the energy. Angie put her hand on mine. To check my blood pressure, I'm guessing.

I sat down and Dot took a few steps back until she bumped into the serving station. Ketchup bottles rattled. She laughed and leaned backward. The blond Japanese waiter appeared with another phone. Takeshi's head was still on the table. Dot turned around. "Oh, Kenny," she said to the waiter, "could you take one with mine, too?

Thanks." She scooted behind me and put her hands on my shoulder. With that she transformed our group into a family.

Kenny aimed Dot's phone at us. "Say cheese!" he ordered in the exaggerated baritone of a game show announcer.

We said cheese. Kenny took the photo and put Dot's phone down and picked up his and aimed at us. "Say Dot!" he ordered.

We did. We all said Dot. Even Dot said Dot. Kenny snapped the picture. "Thanks!" he smiled. He walked away.

"We're so honored you're here," Dot said, walking back to the station to claim her phone. "It's not every day that we have celebrities in here. We get some of the Broncos sometimes. The older ones. But that's it. We are a family restaurant. We're not hip, that's for sure." She smiled again, hard, a smile that hurt me as much as it should have been hurting her. In her Charlie Chaplin getup, Dot looked like the winner of a struggling mall's Halloween contest. I was craving an empanada of all things. And Hunan dumplings. I had a deep craving for Hunan dumplings smothered in a mildly spicy peanut sauce. "Emma will be your waitress this evening and she'll be with you shortly," Dot announced. "I'll check up on you folks later." She waved and walked away, slipping through the crowd like a happy puppy. She was Chaplin with the film rolling faster than usual.

Takeshi was witnessing his own funeral. That was obvious. "Shit," he said, an appropriate word given the look on his face. "Shit, shit, shit, shit, shit." Angie finished her drink. She finally opened the menu. "Maybe I'll stay," Takeshi said. "Forever. Maybe I'll ride around with you forever. Or I'll work here. Like Kenny. Become blond."

"Don't be silly," I said. "You come from a technologically advanced culture. You knew you'd made the news." I allowed him to wallow in his self-pity, fearing the wrath of a father who was handing him his future. I ignored him because it would be simple

243

for me to feel the same kind of self-pity. And because I didn't want to believe that I would be driving across the country "forever."

"It's not like we're not being followed by a bus full of media," I sighed.

I sipped my Coke and imagined it filled with Jamaican rum. Appleton's. Something that would have pleased Angie. Takeshi dropped his head to the table again. The theater of the restaurant was getting to him, I figured. "They have burgers here," I told him.

"Order me one," he said without looking up. "With fries."

"What can your father truly do to you?" I asked. I couldn't help myself.

"I am embarrassing him," he said.

"This is what we do to our parents," I said. "We embarrass them up to the point we make them proud." Takeshi was unmoved. "You've made it seem like you didn't want that job anyway."

He lifted his head. He shook it slowly at first and then with increasing speed. I thought it would fall off. "That's not true," he said. He stopped shaking his head. "Not excited. That's true. OK. Yes. But I want the job. The company is mine when my father retires. He's built this for me. This is my future. I'll have a good life with this job. A very, very good life."

I had no right to argue this. I knew that. But Takeshi didn't. "Good money doesn't mean a good life," I said. "Does it?"

"Good money gives you a good chance," he said. "A better chance." I wasn't going to argue that one either. Since I was so unsure how true this was myself.

"So call him," I suggested. "Call your father and tell him what happened. You haven't called home once. Call him. Pick up your phone. I've never met a Japanese person who used his cell phone less than you do. If he watches TV, at least he knows you're OK. Right? He knows you're healthy and safe and that nothing untoward is going to happen to you, right?"

Takeshi leaned back in his seat and took a giant gulp of his beer. "I have to go back," he mumbled. He stared off into the restaurant, into nothing, and he rocked back and forth. "I have to go right now." He chugged his beer and slammed the bottle on the table.

"You're panicking," I said.

He stood up and started for the exit. "What the—?" I said. Angie studied the menu. She was indifferent to this drama. I ran after Takeshi and got sidetracked by a little boy struggling to tie his shoe in the middle of the aisle. He had no idea what he was doing. I bent down and tied his shoe, ran through the restaurant, and raced past Dot. "Don't worry, we'll be back," I shouted and left the restaurant and found Takeshi in the parking lot, pacing beside the Odyssey. He was breathing heavily, sweating. What was this if not a sudden panic attack? "What's wrong with you?" I asked, edging closer to him.

Takeshi stopped pacing. He leaned back against the minivan and put his hands to his face. "I'm scared," he mumbled. He dropped his hands. "Suddenly. I saw my life and I got scared. I saw the whole thing." He calmed down and pulled out a crumpled pack of Marlboro Reds. He pulled a severely bent cigarette out of the pack. He lit the cigarette and drew in deeply. He exhaled and relaxed some more.

"Are you afraid of your father?" I asked. I pictured Toshiro Mifune in full samurai regalia. It was a stupid image.

"No, no," Takeshi said, shaking his head. "He's a good man. He works too hard. Shouts. He shouts a lot. But everyone's father is like that, right?" He inhaled some more of the cigarette. "When I go back to Japan, my life starts over. I'm going to work my whole life. I'm going to learn the business and then one day it will be mine. America's my last chance to do nothing."

America's good for that, I thought. "And that's what we've been doing," I said, lighting a cigarette.

Takeshi looked up at the sky and breathed deeply. "I must go back to Japan and become a man," he said gravely. "I'm very lucky. I have a good job in a good company. Fast growth. Cell phones. Ha ha." He mock-laughed, remembering what I had just said inside the restaurant. "Big success story. Everyone wants to know how he did it. He's been on the cover of business magazines. *Asian Wall Street Journal*. Everywhere. When it was all very bad in Japan, with the recession, with layoffs, people like my father became heroes. He showed the country we can still do good things. He wins prizes and gives speeches. Even now." He sighed. He turned and tried to open the door to the Odyssey. He looked at me and I threw him the keys. He opened the door and reached in and took his backpack out.

"What are you doing?" I asked, dumbly. "Japan's always there. Your father, your job, it's all there. It doesn't sound like it's going away."

"L.A.," he said. "I must go to L.A." He fit his backpack on his shoulders. "I'm going to fly to L.A. and then go home."

"Don't do it," I said. I said it for purely selfish reasons, I knew that, but the thought of driving alone, at this juncture, was terrifying. Especially with the Man playing a determined game of hide-and-seek.

"I have to," he said. "What's the expression? Face the music? I'm going home to face the music."

Angie strolled into the parking lot, a new drink in hand. "What's going on?" she asked. She saw Takeshi encumbered by his backpack and her question was answered. "Why?"

"Takeshi's going home to claim his millions," I said, dejected.

"To work for my father," he said, as if this corrected me.

"Dan's going to love this," she said. "I think there are Japanese media meeting us tomorrow morning."

"Please call a taxi," Takeshi said.

I wanted to hug him but I couldn't bring myself to do it. "Everyone has to go home sometime," I said. Except for me. Only then did I realize I was cold. Dot came out and asked if everything was all right. Takeshi asked her to call a cab. "Of course, it's ironic you never use your cell phone," I said.

Takeshi smiled, finally. "I lost it," he said. "And I didn't care. It reminds me of home."

"Let's wait inside for the cab," Dot offered and we followed her inside. We sat on a bench next to Dot's station under posters of Charlie Chaplin movies. On the far side of the room was a cane in a glass case and without walking over to read the plaque I knew the real Charlie Chaplin had used it. That impressed me. "Is it always there?" I asked.

Dot looked at the glass case. She nodded. "It was my father's," she said. "He worked in film."

"So it's really Chaplin's?" I asked.

"It is," Dot said. "And that's why every once in a while I get all dressed up. The kids like it. Their parents seem to like it more."

I looked through a small window across the street at the black bus in the parking lot of the Italian restaurant. I could picture Dan lunging into his veal. I could imagine the amount of wine the reporters were drinking. The cab pulled up and we returned outside. No one said a word. Takeshi got in. He rolled down the window. He looked at me and smiled. He held out his hand and I took it. "Good luck," he said. "I hope you find what you're looking for."

"Me, too," I said.

"I'll watch on TV." He laughed. We looked at each other and smiled. "Thank you," he said.

He shook Angie's hand and closed the window and the cab pulled away and just like that he was gone. We watched the cab disappear into the Denver night and walked back into the restaurant. We entered and walked past Dot and sat at our table. We ordered our food. We ate our meal in silence. The corned beef was an abomination. Angie ate a southwestern-style grilled chicken breast with a salad on the side. She drank another rum and Diet Coke. We shared a piece of key lime pie for dessert. We drank coffee. I felt tired again, suddenly; I felt tired and closed my eyes, cupped my head in my hands. I was ready again for sleep.

And I heard the Man. *North*, he said.

I shuddered awake. *Go north*, he said again. I looked around the restaurant, expecting to see him but everyone was so blond. Angie looked as if she were ready to fall asleep as well.

"Maybe I should have another coffee," she said.

There was no time. Dot came to the table. "And how is everything?" she asked, looking even more ridiculous to me now.

"I need the bill," I told her. "I'm in a big hurry."

Angie perked up. "Why?" she asked.

"No more coffee?" Dot asked. "Free refills!"

"Please," I said and I grabbed her hand. "I have to leave. Now!"

Dot looked into my eyes and an enormous smile came over her face. "Did you hear him?" she whispered. "Did you hear him? You did, didn't you? Right? Here? In my restaurant? What did he say? Is he here? Can I see him?" She scanned the room, looking for the Man, her wigged head and bowler hat bobbing up and down. "Is he here?"

"Joe?" Angie asked.

"Please!" I roared, tightening my grip on Dot's hand.

She stared down at my hand on hers and the smile left her face. I was hurting her. "It's on the house," she said, trying to read me for signs of lunacy.

"Thank you, no, I should pay," I said. I released her hand.

Dot shook her head. "Just tell me what he said," she squealed.

I reached into my wallet for Dan's credit card and now it was Dot's turn for some hand grabbing. "Please," she said, her voiced tinged with desperation. "I need to know. I've followed your story since the start and to think it's playing itself out right here in my restaurant . . ." She put a hand to her mouth. She was going to cry. "Was it important?" she whispered.

I nodded.

"Is he here?" she asked again, her voice creaking.

"I don't know," I told her. "He's anywhere he wants to be."

A tear fell down Dot's heavily made-up cheek. Charlie Chaplin was crying.

"Let us pay," I asked again, stupidly. The thought of paying somehow made sense.

Again, Dot shook her head. "Can you ask him to bless my restaurant?" she asked.

I stood up and stepped away slowly. I thanked her some more. I shook her hand and then ran out. I got in the Odyssey. Angie waited by the passenger door and I let her in. "Call Dan," I told her.

She did and handed me the phone. "They have a marsala that's quite something," he said.

"Gotta run," I said.

"And the calamari fritti is crunchy and light and not at all oily," he continued.

"We're heading north," I said. The background noise of happy reporters came to a sudden stop. I could see Dan with his hand in the air. I heard people shushing each other.

"Where?" Dan asked.

"North," I repeated. I didn't know what else to say. "We gotta go."

"Wait!" Dan pleaded. "What else did he say?"

"Nothing," I said, losing patience. "He said, 'Go north.' That's it. Oh, and Takeshi went home."

Dan relayed the news to the media. I could hear chairs moving. "Take the 25," he said. "Return to the highway and follow the signs for 25 North."

I hung up the phone and Angie pointed out some reporters

running for the black bus. I could not imagine why they still cared but they did and that was their job and it had to be done, just like Takeshi had to return to Japan and do his job, just like Dot had to wear the silly Charlie Chaplin outfit and greet customers with the kind of smile that in its insincerity was sincere.

Some of the reporters stood in front of their cameramen and bright lights and filed their reports for the news. I waved at a camera pointed in our direction. We drove away, past the park with the zoo and the museum again, to the highway and soon found the 25.

"Notice how the public isn't around?" I asked Angie. "Doesn't their lack of presence here indicate diminished interest?"

"It doesn't mean a thing," Angie said.

"I think it does," I said. "I think it means they've had enough."

"I don't think you understand the activity in that bus," she said.

The highway defined a sudden shift in geography. On our left, the Rockies formed a kind of wall that stopped the prairies suddenly like some schoolyard bully demanding lunch money. On our right, the prairies sloped down. Toward the east, toward home. Driving north was disorienting in a way, and felt wrong, and this line of asphalt, this man-made natural barrier between the mountains and the tall grass made it all the more strange.

We drove through what felt like an endless series of suburbs and exurbs, the entire population of Colorado lined up like a strip of Velcro in the shadow of the mountains and then we were out of it, in a place devoid of people.

The landscape was pure here. It was the perfect place for a final meeting with the Man. For a revelation. This must be the place, I thought. It has to be. But we crossed into Wyoming and nothing happened. We drove by Cheyenne and nothing happened. We passed a lot of signs with the word "frontier" on them and then we really were in the middle of nothing and still nothing happened.

"Do you ever get discouraged?" Angie sighed.

I wanted to say yes, all the time, but I didn't for fear of offending the Man. As if saying it and thinking it were different. I wanted to think I could feel his presence in this empty country, that this was his home somehow, that he was watching me, waiting for the proper moment, but I could also hear what my head had to say, the logical part, so shut off this entire time. It was despondent.

My eyes darted about the road, searching, the futility of the whole thing making me feel something, expendable, the victim of the most elaborate joke ever devised. How could this whole thing be made up? How could I be on such a long-winded delusional wavelength? How could I have done this to myself?

Angie was asleep. I wanted to wake her and talk this through with her. She was the only person whose sanity I had never questioned. She could still talk me out of this, I thought, even here, only to realize the folly of such a grand idea. What does one call hindsight when it happens in the present?

The sun rose in the east, which wasn't in my back window anymore but to my right. We passed a small town buried in the wilds of Wyoming. We were the only vehicle on a lonely stretch of road. The only vehicle not going somewhere. With a driver looking for an end. For a beginning.

THE MESSAGE

My office is a dungeon, a dark, minimalist corner amidst the storage and dust of a hidden, forgotten underworld. This is the landscape of the forgotten. Of the not-thought-through. The prettier the public area, the shadier the private. Like a movie star caught by paparazzi without makeup.

I've convinced Athena to hold off on the PR woman. The visit would be pointless. I've read her correspondence, emailed her, and her ditziness is like some kitsch rubber duckie floating in an old-world European spa populated by the outer edges of royalty. Or the members of MENSA. Stupid but sweet, I'm learning. The tagline for the entire PR industry. In the ad world, PR is seen as the lowest common denominator. As well as the biggest threat. Maybe it's the same thing.

The PR woman is the kind of adult who peppers emails with words like "cool" and "awesome." She uses emoticons in place of actual words. The emoticon is a part of the grammar of her writing. Syntax even. Her name is Lindsay. My sense of superiority, as a New Yorker, remains intact.

The research is going somewhere. I can say this with a certain amount of certitude. I have enjoyed the full effects of the spa, my ass has endured long horse rides, I have taken the ATV into the mountains. I discovered there is a day care onsite. Rare are the guests who bring their children along.

I have learned that the owners of this place were lifelong ranchers, are descended from a long line of ranchers, the property having been in the family for almost one hundred years. Two brothers combined their adjacent ranches with the plan of creating a hospitality empire. The brothers hired Athena to look after things while they traveled the world coming up with ideas. One of the brothers, Athena claims, had never traveled farther than Seattle. "They're drinking their way around the world," she told me. "They aren't learning a thing. It's up to me." Not once does she mention her own involvement in any future venture. Perhaps Tomas is wrong about that part. The brothers' wives are no better. Athena could barely discuss the wives. Her contempt for them was as thick as a sheepskin coat.

The staff lounge is the result of a failed experiment in creating, in Tomas's words, an oxygen bar. There are lofts in the stables full of tubing and chrome chairs apparently.

Tomas has added a meat pie to the menu. The filling is made of duck livers and bits of dried salted pork. Small cubed potatoes. Seasoning, including allspice, cinnamon, and cloves. Doused in a red wine–duck gravy. Except Tomas is calling the gravy "jus." No one can order the jus because no one can pronounce it properly. It's one of those foreign words that are not kind to the American mouth. Staff have taken to calling it the "Dork Pie."

In the lounge, between lunch and dinner, Tomas stops by for a glass of wine. He sits by me at the bar. My beer has turned warm from neglect. Before me, splayed out like a wounded animal, all the brochures and PR material this place has ever sent out. It's as if I'm trying to devise something from the entrails of the sacred. "Have you tried the pie?" Tomas asks.

"I'm still partial to the elk steak," I say. And it's true. Tomas pairs the steak simply, with a sweet potato purée and some peas tossed with grated fresh horseradish.

"The pie is doing well."

"That's all that matters then."

Tomas takes the wine glass by the stem and holds it to the light. "I have to say, you worry me," he says, inspecting the wine.

"Oh, stop," I say. "Not again."

He takes the wine in his mouth and holds it there before swallowing. "You're being more thorough than I thought you'd be."

"That's the kind of person I am. Don't forget, I walked here."

Tomas plays with his glass, twirling it. "It just sounded like such a half-assed thing in a way. To be honest. I know what I told you about my feelings on the subject. But I still thought the whole thing sounded like a make-work project. Like Athena going on a fishing trip."

"I was doing fine in the kitchen."

"You were peeling fruit."

"I wasn't complaining. Not yet."

"But still."

"Tomas, honestly, fuck off," I say.

He leans in. "Watch yourself," he says. Hisses is more like it.

"We've had our talk. You've told me your concerns. Yes, if it came down to you or me, you'd win. Of course you would. I know that. So, kindly, fuck off."

I order another beer. Keith enters the bar and our eyes meet and just as quickly he leaves. Tomas takes a long drink from his glass.

Worry like his is so universal it is surprising we ever got out of the caves. People want change. Evolution is good. We may confuse evolution and progress but most would regard forward momentum as a good thing. Except when it's imposed. Like CDs were. I know people who are still bitter about that. "I've heard great things about the pie," I say.

"Because it is good," he says.

"Why wouldn't it be?" I turn to face him. "Why? Why would your pork and duck pie suck? Why would anything coming out of your kitchen suck? You're a brilliant chef. And for whatever reason, I've spooked you something good."

"I just want to be understood," he says. Apologizing almost.

"You told me this the other night," I say. "I got the message. I told you."

Tomas finishes his wine and stands. The bartender comes by and Tomas signs his tab. He leaves a dollar on the bar. "OK. Sorry. I came on too strong. I see you and it's all I think about."

"Great."

"Sorry. I'm just not sure, you know? I don't feel in control. It's not a good feeling, that's all. I'm a chef. We're control freaks. Everything has to be perfect. Or close."

He shrugs and walks out. I down my beer.

In Japan, the ads and brochures emphasize the location, the Wild West aspect of the place.

In California and throughout the West, the PR emphasizes the kitchen, the spa treatments. On the east coast, the PR is more like the Japanese. There are no ads for this place. Anywhere. It's all media coverage. Athena has emphasized the media and continues to host travel and spa writers on a constant basis. The media for this place has been tremendous. The PR woman does her job well.

In the U.K., the PR showcases the kitchen, the location, and, for whatever reason, the wine cellar. In the rest of Europe, the horses, the Rockies, the western lifestyle. Again, no ads. Just an impressive amount of media.

The bartender returns and places a beer in front of me. "Can I ask you something?" I say. He's young, a local, amazingly enough, a student doing a summer job.

"Sure," he says, smiling.

"When you think of this place, what do you think of?"

"What place?"

"The ranch."

"I don't," he says.

"You don't what?"

"Think about the ranch," he clarifies.

"I don't mean in a philosophical sense."

He takes the towel that's slung over his shoulder and starts wiping down the bar. "I work here," he says. "It's the place I work to make some money. It's better than nothing. It's a nice place."

"Great," I say. "Thanks."

"It's not McDonald's," he says. "And the chicks."

"Wonderful."

"It's nice."

"It is."

"But I'm not really your average guy. I'm not clientele," he says. "I live here. Hell, I'm from here. I only notice the scenery when I leave." The phone behind the bar rings. "Excuse me," he says and goes to answer it.

I finish my beer and return downstairs. In my email, a message from Lindsay. The subject line contains four exclamation marks. Denoting the gravity of the missive. Or excessive cheerfulness. The message:

Joe! I thought something about u reminded me of someone! But I'm always saying that about everybody I meet so I figured it was just me being me again! Can u tell me if this is u? See the attached file. It's from *Variety*. (I have to admit I am totally addicted to *Variety*—it's too cool for school. LOL.) This guy Dan Fontana just sold rights to a story about a guy who drove across the country. His name's Joe. Is that u? That would be soooo cool!!! You can tell me, can't u? Now that I know ur someone famous, I definitely need to come up there and talk branding and PR with u! This is soooo gr8t! See u soon!

And this is where I am. In my basement office. With a desk lamp providing illumination. Staring into the computer. Pleased for Dan. Feeling not lost. Feeling off. Just a bit off. As if my sell-by date were yesterday. As if the answer had come to me the moment the buzzer went off. As if.

BIG EMPTY

Wyoming is not a state. It is a place optimistically marked on a map a long time ago now populated by grass and rocks and the odd pickup. Angie counted telephone poles and tried to contemplate a vista where one is surrounded by the horizon. We drove for miles and passed nothing. The interstate headed west again and then we were in Casper and out of Casper and going north. We drove through miles of nature and the only proof of civilization was the occasional sign on the road. We spent hours not seeing another car or town. The view here was 360 degrees with nothing but earth and sky in all directions.

Angie worked her phone. She may have left the black bus but the phone had her tethered to her work. And she did it. When the phone worked that is. Which wasn't that often.

Every turn in the road, every signpost, every rise in the landscape was, I sensed, I hoped, I wanted, a hiding place for the Man. He had to be close. Why bring me to Wyoming if not to make his appearance? But he did not. Driving through this empty place, with both hope and disappointment marked by everything, exhausted me, angered me. I felt bruised. I felt no joy in Wyoming.

We stopped in a spot on the map called Midwest—a village, if that—just to stop, to get our bearings, and the look on my face must have been one of failure. I did not speak. I sighed. Much sighing. Angie and I walked into town and found a quaint general store that sold guns and candy and beer. It was a large shack of a building and had I been a tourist it might have overjoyed me. We bought Doritos and Hershey's Kisses and a couple of burritos the owner had cooked in the kitchen behind the cash. We ate on a bench in the middle of town. We wondered where the black bus was. The cell phones were silent here. The land was big and the sky was swimming pool blue and all of this purity conspired to deny the cell phones a context in which to work. All around us, we could see hills in the far distance rising up gently from the ground like giants being woken up. We were surrounded. The state felt like some great sunken tub. Perhaps this explained its emptiness. I felt uncomfortable stopping for anything.

We bought some gas and got back on the highway. I didn't speak for fear of missing something on the road. I tried to decipher the empty landscape for signs. For clues. There were none. The further north we drove, the further south my spirits went. Angie fell asleep and I envied her. What was she doing so far from home? What would happen to her at the end of this? Would she be content with working her father's trattoria again? What was she getting out of this strange tour of the country? Can you really enjoy the scenery when your job is to keep desperately unhappy men happy, when the locus of your journey is crazed, possibly delirious?

I had felt it before, but in Wyoming my doubts really began to leak out of me. I could smell it. Perhaps it was fear. Or the imminence of my failure. But that thought I'd managed to keep hidden away for so long, the possibility of a ruse, of a self-deception as monumental as the monotony of this landscape, the thought was there now. Constant. On the surface. And my silence wasn't just an attempt to search for signs, but was also a result of my attempts to snuff it out.

Deep in my heart I was doubting myself completely, but I could not bring myself to admit this. I could admit that the trip was a cheap spectacle cooked up by the media to fill some minutes during the summer's newscasts. To Dan, the prize came at the conclusion of the journey. The event only had purpose at its conclusion. To me, this ordeal was a path to the start of a new journey. A new life. That's what I had hoped.

When does desperation become optimism?

Would Dan get his payout? How was this playing in Peoria? We had not driven through Peoria.

My doubts were arrested always by one question: what did I hear? If not the Man, then what? How could I explain that? Did I want to see the Man so badly that I had forsaken everything? Was my life so bad that I *invented* the Man? Was my life so bad? I didn't think so. I disliked my job. Even when it had interested me. This said more about me than the job. I knew that. But what did it say?

There is a Man, I kept saying to myself. There had to be. There was no other way to explain what I had done. The state of my life. There was a Man. And he was playing a cruel trick on an innocent. I apologized for thinking these thoughts.

I had to make sense of this.

The mountains came closer to the road, their peaks dusted with snow, and the towns closer to each other. The landscape was crumpled here, the result of some far-gone geology I would never understand. Around us were signs of civilization. We passed a McDonald's and I thought of Takeshi. Angie was awake now. The cell phone worked again and she spoke to Dan. The bus was miles behind us. She assured him we were on the same road as they were.

We approached Sheridan and passed it. I stopped in a rest area and I fell into a fitful sleep. I tried to conjure up images of the Man.

I couldn't. I slept begging him to tell me what to do. Maybe I didn't sleep.

Angie nudged me awake and pointed out the window at the black bus. It was night now and we got out of the Odyssey. The sky was poxed with stars, each one a tiny hole of light in a black, moth-eaten blanket. Dan got out of the bus, rubbing the sleep from his eyes. I took out a Marlboro Light and put one in his mouth and one in mine. He lit our cigarettes and yawned. Angie yawned. "Christ," Dan said, covering his mouth. "I'm starting to suffer real fatigue. It's an awesome kind of tired. All the time. And my ass is killing me. I'm developing sores, I think. All the guys on the bus spend hours walking up and down the aisle. We've developed a schedule. We watch TV. There's nothing on. The damned thing is a spirit crusher."

"When'd you pull in?" I asked.

Dan shrugged. "An hour ago? Maybe. I'm not sure. I was sleeping. I've lost track of time. Time is irrelevant to everything I do. My blog? Time isn't important. The podcast? Not important. I file a story every day. It's not like I'm doing any live TV anymore. That stopped a few days ago."

"The *Post* is running a story every day?" I asked. I figured New York would have given up on me by now.

"There's a map every day, too, to show readers the journey we've taken so far," Dan said, exhaling smoke toward the stars. "A few hundred words. It's not much. They have to show something for their investment. I'm sure the map's bigger than the story. All the networks have their own maps and graphics. CNN is calling the story 'The Search for America.' They're implying meaning where there's none. The *Post* settled on 'Joe's Journey.' It's flat but the graphic's nice."

"I can't believe people are still interested," I said. And taking in the blanket of silence around us, this was easy to believe.

"I don't know," Dan said. "I don't know if anyone gives a shit.

It's not like we've been gone for long. But the fifteenth minute is fast approaching. Traffic's way down on the website." He stamped out his cigarette. "Whatever."

We stood in silence in the middle of the rest area. I wanted everything to be over. I wanted to end it here. I wanted to find a soft bed and sink into it.

Angie touched my hand and then walked toward the restrooms. In the far end of the parking lot, a scattered assembly of Winnebagos stood lifeless, their occupants no doubt sleeping. "You hungry?" Dan asked.

I didn't say anything. I watched Angie walk away. As did Dan. Before entering the restroom she turned around and looked at me and then vanished behind the closed door. "I'll never have her," Dan said.

"No, you won't," I said.

"It was awkward. I'm not very good in these situations. I tried as hard as I know how," he said. "Meaning it was bound to end in rejection."

More silence. I had never tried. I had wanted to once, a lifetime ago, when a fat bonus gave me the confidence of a thoroughbred. But my laziness trumped my desire and that was that. I never saw Angie's kindness as anything other than . . . kindness. It had been my loss.

"What happened to Takeshi?" Dan asked.

"He lost it," I said. "Sort of."

"He really flew back to Japan?" he said.

"He was going to fly to L.A.," I said, staring at the restroom. "And then home. Start work. His father's got some major concern. Cell phones. Sounded like a very successful, very accomplished man. I'm sure there's great wealth involved. Takeshi decided to face the music. He decided to confront his life. He was sitting there in the restaurant and then he just decided that was it, he was going to grow up, get on with his life. Dive in."

Dan lit another cigarette. "He's going to be a star," he said. "The Japanese have been eating his story up. The CNN guys told me he's caused a bit of a frenzy. Media there were using our feeds. They were set to join the bus. We were happy he left when he did. We have our seats and our likes and dislikes and an influx of Japanese reporters would have fucked things up."

"He doesn't want to be a star," I said. The door to the women's washroom creaked open and closed and Angie did not appear. I grew concerned.

"I heard that some movie star over there wants to do something with his story," Dan said, laughing. "An American journey. He's going to sell his story, I guarantee it."

I looked over to the restroom again and could see a sliver of light from behind the door of the women's side. "Wait a second," I said, my head somewhere else, and I walked toward the light, toward Angie. I was filled with worry and with something else. Longing. I can't think of another word to describe it. I wasn't thinking. I was thinking of a million things. My mind was a hurricane.

I entered the woman's restroom and found Angie leaning against a sink. A sly smile came over her lips. "What are you doing here?" she asked.

"I don't know," I said. And I didn't. "Is everything all right?"

"I think I'm about to get my period," she said and I could not remember a time in my life when a woman had told me such a thing. "We have to stop somewhere for tampons soon. Otherwise I'll bleed all over the car."

Angie had let her hair down. She had splashed water on her face. "I was thinking," she said.

I didn't say anything.

"I've been having this conversation with myself," she said.

We had something in common.

"You know? Don't you?" she said.

No, I didn't. It couldn't possibly be happening. Not here. Not after all this time.

"Look," she said, her hands on her hips. "I've always liked you, and we're in the middle of nowhere. I've been wearing dumpy clothes and I feel like shit." She smiled again. "I want to feel something. I've come all this way. We've come all this way."

I walked toward her. I stopped halfway. I felt like a blind person trying to cross an unfamiliar intersection.

"This whole thing has no meaning," she said. "Your trip. Everything."

She wasn't thinking about me. And neither was I.

I walked to her and grabbed her and she kissed me. My hands eased their way under her shirt and I felt the softness of the small of her back. I lost all sense of myself.

She took my hand and we entered a stall. Her desire for privacy at this hour struck me as odd. The stall was clean, the porcelain on the toilet gleamed. Were all women's restrooms like this? She closed the door behind us and leaned into me and we kissed. She undid my pants and they dropped to the floor. I did not know what to do. She pulled my underwear down and took my penis in her hand. It was hard before her fingers were wrapped around it. She kissed me some more and pushed at me and I was sitting on the toilet. She straightened up and pulled her pants down. I kissed her belly and buried my face in it. I licked her and tasted the wonder of her skin. She stepped away and stepped out of her pants and then pulled her underwear down. She straddled me and guided me into her. "It's safe now," she whispered.

We made love in the stall and I could think of nothing but hanging onto Angie as she clung to me, bobbing up and down slowly, her hands clutching my head, my shoulders, her fingernails digging into my skin. Her inside was soft and tight and wet. I leaned back to kiss her and our mouths gripped each other's, sucking tongues, inward.

We tried to inhale each other's mouths. I could feel our juices running down my balls and then I could hear them dripping into the toilet. Angie breathed heavily and her breath against my face was a warm and happy wind. I stood up and leaned her against the door, holding her up by cupping my hands beneath her bottom. I pushed as deep as I could into her and it was not far enough. I wanted to consume her. She held on to the top of the stall and pushed herself down upon me. A warmth was running down my legs and they felt as if they were about to give out, that they could no longer support the weight of Angie's need. I leaned into her even harder and her back slammed against the door with each of our thrusts. She let go of the walls around us and held on to me, her breathing getting more and more labored. My legs were liquid. My muscles burned. And then I felt my life empty into Angie. She pulled me closer, squeezing me to her. She climbed atop me. She swallowed me up. She pushed herself against me with urgency. I knew I would soon fall over. She grabbed my hair and let out a sound, an operatic note that quickly drowned in her pleasure and soon her body was limp and the only sound in the bathroom was of our tortured breathing, of our mouths taking in huge gulps of air. I stepped backward and sat down on the toilet and Angie collapsed in my arms. She stroked my hair. I kissed her forehead and tasted the salt of her exertion.

"My God," I whispered.

She pulled me out and stood up. She smiled. "Get off the toilet," she ordered.

I did and she sat down and started dripping into the water. I had emptied myself into her and now she was emptying me from her. She looked at me and put her hand to her mouth and stifled a laugh. I looked down to see my penis covered in watery blood. Trails of red flowed from my penis to my balls and down my legs like varicose veins. Drops of blood covered the floor and our pants. The stall was a mess. Angie laughed out loud.

We spent minutes that turned into hours cleaning up. We washed the floor and ourselves, soaked our pants in the sinks. I soaped my legs and my groin. The restroom had sanitary napkins and Angie used them as sponges to clean off the blood. She took a handful for later. We used the hand dryers to try to dry our pants. "Now we can say we actually did something on this trip," she said.

"I guess," I said, feeling strangely shy about the whole thing.

"Neighbors. And we had to come to Wyoming," she said. She didn't mean it that way, but I heard the reproach. Blame. I heard regret and perhaps hints of a future that might have been.

I put my pants on. The clammy feeling one gets at the end of a long walk on a humid day. "Thanks," she said, and she kissed me on the cheek. "We could have done that a long time ago." I stumbled for words.

We left the restroom and walked toward the Odyssey. Dan was sitting on a picnic bench, smoking a cigarette. Jealousy wracked his face. We walked to him. "You guys stink," he said.

"For real?" Angie asked. "Or are you just unhappy?"

"We cleaned up," I said.

"You can't wash that kind of smell away," he said.

I held out two fingers and Dan produced a pack of Marlboro Lights. I took one out and lit it up. "I'm spent," I said.

"Fuck off," Dan said.

We heard clapping and saw the media stepping out of the bus one by one, applauding us. "Care to share your thoughts?" Dan asked.

"Very funny," Angie said.

"Let's go," I said.

I got in the minivan and started it. Angie got in. We did smell. We smelled of sex and blood and something powerfully rank. "Keep the window open," I said.

The eastern sky was a light blue. The next day was approaching quickly. "Is there anything to talk about?" I asked.

Angie thought about this. "Is there?"

We drove into Montana in silence. Angie stared out the window at the grassy hills and mountains that rolled away from the interstate. The sky seemed closer to us and ahead the interstate looked as if that's where it went. A sign told us we were in an Indian reservation of some kind. The land and the sky schemed to inspire thoughts of the Man. We passed signs for Little Bighorn and Custer's Last Stand. Angie took my hand and squeezed it. "There's nothing to talk about," she said dully. Hours later I didn't believe her, even though I had nothing to say.

ACCEPT YOURSELF

Athena says, "Do you know why you're here?"

I say nothing, my silence perhaps all the answer she'll need. "How I got here doesn't matter," I say.

She says, "I didn't say how. I said why."

It is an unfair question. It can have no answer. "I came here to talk about some ideas I'm mulling over," I say.

She says, "I'm curious." She stands behind her desk, arms folded. The questions, I'm assuming, are the result of something Lindsay has disclosed. I don't even care why Athena is asking them.

"I'm here."

She asks, "Are you happy?"

"I believe I am."

Athena lets slip a small, indiscreet smile. She has spoken to Lindsay.

"I got short-hopped, but adjusted," I say.

She says, "I'm not American. I have no idea what that means."

"It's a baseball term."

And Athena makes a face. She's not American. "Maybe I don't care either. Maybe I only care if it will affect your work here."

"There's an irony to what I'm doing," I say. "I came all this way to do something I was doing before. Sort of."

"Anyone who can get away with living an ironic life must be doing something right."

"Irony isn't safe," I say. "It's a dangerous way to live. It can be complicated. Irony is someone else's tragedy. I don't want irony or tragedy. I want things to be simple. And that's why I like it here."

Athena sits in her chair. She fiddles with a pen. "The owners have five other properties across the West. Arizona. Colorado. Washington. One in Canada. In Alberta. One in Idaho. They want to get this place right and then move the brand forward. They want to test all the ideas we come up with here. They are suddenly obsessed by plunge pools. They want to be a luxury ranch and spa brand. Very American. They see equity in a western concept. They know, I know, that this place is trying too hard. It's all over the place. They want to be hoteliers. They want to take their ranching background and make it a luxury brand. A fetish really."

So this is the plan. "So this is the plan," I say. I'm about to be offered a job.

She says, "If they are pleased with your proposals here, they will offer you a job. Director of Marketing. Chief Branding Officer. Something like that."

And so this is the hotel business. I've arrived in the hospitality industry. In the lobby of a brand with aspirations. I'm thinking like someone I might have mocked before. And yet it feels oddly natural. Who am I?

"And you?" I ask.

"I'm along for the ride."

"That's a very American expression," I say. She's withholding the extent of her involvement.

"I just don't like baseball."

A long pause. I am deciding to accept the offer. Lindsay's cloud hasn't lifted. Athena doesn't care. And I can't do anything about Dan's ambitions either. I will be found one day, discovered. Its inevitability is like the rising of the sun. Or death. I will once again attain some status, some middle class of fame. Perhaps I will become the spokesman for the place. Tell everyone I found what I needed here. Every few years a tabloid will interview me for a "where are they now?" feature. Dan's book will get published. A movie will get made. My celebrity will ebb and flow.

I can't decide whether Lindsay's email should feel liberating or not. "I don't know why I'm here," I say. "I understand even less how I got here. There's no answer for it. But I've found myself here and I may have even found myself."

"Lindsay sent me a curious email."

I nod. "It's all true."

"You don't know what she said."

"I can guess."

"Does this mean you'll shave?"

"I'm growing fond of this look."

"I finally Googled you."

I can only imagine what she's found. I can only imagine the type of information, the amount of information, out there. I once held a slice of the public's consciousness. "I don't understand fame," I say. "Or why anyone would seek it."

Another pause. "When can you share?"

"Share what?" I ask. My past? The reasons why?

"Your ideas," she says.

"Am I giving a full presentation? To you? Do I have to do some kind of awful PowerPoint thing? Because I hate PowerPoint." So many questions. I ran away from work to discover answers to the unknowable. And it turns out that I ran to work. To an odd but definite happiness.

"Do whatever you want. Use puppets. I don't care."

I take a long walk. A cold wind slaps my face. I walk to the spa and the wind gets colder, fiercer. It's a seasonal wind, with a certain menace. It swirls around me now and I run into the spa, out of breath. A couple walks by in fluffy bathrobes, each with a cup of herbal tea in hand. They are glowing. The man slides his hand down the woman's back and rests it on her ass. They walk to the desk and a general mumbling takes place. His hand strokes the contours of the woman's back. Their level of contentment is astounding. Enviable. They are in their late fifties. Satisfied. Writing another chapter in their lives. Accumulating stories.

The woman behind the counter walks them through a door that will take the couple to what we call the Wet Bar, an area devoted to hydrotherapy. The couple will shower together, receive a variety of water-based massage treatments side by side. Later, they will enjoy dinner, share a bottle of wine. Retreat to their room. Explore their newly softened skin. Sleep the deepest sleep they have known in months. Tomorrow they will repeat it all. Tomorrow they will seek out the same feeling, the same comfort. Tomorrow they will write another chapter in their life story.

I stick my head out the front door. The wind shows no sign of abating. It's a windy day. I should get used to it.

I'm thinking this place should align itself to a kind of celebrity in a low-key way as it expands. This person and the overall brand should be intertwined. Or it could be a series of people, good mid-level celebrities not yet tainted by the public's expectations and prejudices. All appearing in tasteful print ads shot onsite. People who mean good taste, who mean something. Whose own brands go beyond their own celebrity. To a value.

The ranch needs a new name. I keep calling it Special K. Tomas called it Four Creeks once. That's an evocative name for an overall brand but it doesn't sound western enough. It sounds falsely international and ambitious. I don't know if I'm supposed to brand the future or just worry about this one place, right now. Was Athena telling me what to do or what I should expect?

At my computer, I sketch out an overall feeling for this place. The offering needs to be focused. Simplified.

We all desire simplicity. It's why people come here.

This place should be about people's stories. We crave narrative. We believe we are uninteresting without a compelling story. This is the guiding principle behind reality TV and its replacement, the participatory web. A narrative validates us. It makes us tangible. As the world grows larger, we need to break its component parts down to manageable bite-sized chunks. We live surrounded by more people now, more density, and so we are more anonymous. With our own narrative, we feel a part of the world. Stories connect us. They intersect.

And then this narrative is finally about empowerment. Which is what a spa is about. Luxury is power. The ability to add luxury to your narrative is the totem of everything we strive for. Luxury itself is not a goal. This place is about vanity as well, but again that's not a goal. It is the ability to proclaim your indulgence in luxury. To be vain and not feel shy about admitting it. To not apologize for what you want or who you are. To be able to tell the world that you can experience it. That you have experienced it. And how that experience makes your narrative appear richer and more robust than anyone else's.

Over dinner with Athena, I say, "We're going to need some creatives."

She says, "I understand."

"An agency. More than PR."

"I can recommend that."

"We'll need to create a bible."

"I know the branding game."

"It's a racket, isn't it?" This is most obvious to those who do the work.

"It's necessary."

I cut through my steak. I've been craving Chinese food of late.

She asks, "Will everything change?"

"I don't know."

"Look at what I ate." Chicken marbella. A maple squash puree. Accompanied by a white wine from South Africa. And not a very good one at that. An uneaten profiterole on her dessert plate.

"I haven't thought the entire thing through," I say.

"We need to be thorough."

"I agree."

"They've been drinking their way across the world. They're taking notes. Suddenly they think they know a lot."

The owners are phantoms to me. Athena has no idea when they will return. It doesn't seem to matter.

A waitress comes by and pours Athena a coffee. "The wine is terrible," Athena says.

The waitress takes this in. "Should I tell Frank?" she asks. Frank is the sommelier. He is South African.

"I'll speak to him tomorrow," Athena says.

I have spent the day putting thoughts about this place on paper. I have enjoyed myself. I have used the process to block out my narrative. I can't tell whether or not I have a story anymore. I'm the same person who drove across the country. I'm not the same person who drove across the country. "Tomas told me he doesn't want to change," I say.

Athena takes a sip of her coffee. "He will. He's done it before."

I take another bite of my steak. "How many hits?"

Athena gives me a look, of being spoken to in a foreign tongue.

"On Google."

"More than I would have imagined."

"What did you imagine?"

"I had low expectations."

"And?"

"In the hundreds of thousands."

"Not millions?"

She sips her coffee some more. "Don't flatter yourself."

I'm relieved actually. It's a relief I need. My past is a shadow that I can't outrun. Even when the sun sets, a shadow hides. It waits. My relief is the hope that my shadow recedes into something else. Something less than memory. A small tattoo, perhaps. A tiny scar. A snake that has shed its skin.

ALONE AGAIN

I drove through the endlessness of Montana in a daze. My head was cluttered with what Angie and I had done. By what it might have meant in another time and place. By the road not taken. And the Man. The endlessness of him. The mystery of him and his where-abouts. I searched deep inside myself and he was not there. The relentlessness of the ordeal I was suffering. I felt the force of his hand on the steering wheel. This looked like his place, something I'd been feeling a long time now. And nothing had happened.

Outside Billings, I turned off the interstate and drove through town and past the airport and headed north again. Dan phoned and asked me where I was going and I thought the question stupid and funny and I hung up without saying anything. I drove blindly. I did not see the countryside. I have some memory of mountains. I remember the haze that surrounded me. I remember that I could not really see. I remember that I don't remember. I could have been driving anywhere. I know I drove through Montana but I could not tell you what the roads looked like.

Angie had been sleeping but she woke up now and stayed awake as I drove through the night. We kept our thoughts to ourselves.

There's nothing to talk about, she had said. I drove slowly, carefully. The long road was almost over. This is all I remember thinking. And Angie. I replayed our washroom tango like a loop.

I stopped for gas at a place that was remote and desolate and I remember being amazed by the gas station as it appeared alongside the road. And things became clearer again. The black bus pulled up to the gas station and Dan came out and walked straight toward me. "You trying to get us lost?" he asked. The media got off the bus to stretch, everyone's face puffy with sleep, the toil of their jobs, the inanity of this job, causing them to rethink their lives, relive the many paths that led them to this point, to this remote gas station in a remote part of Montana.

"I can feel him," I said to Dan. "I don't know what that means but I can feel him everywhere." I was lying.

Dan's eyes brightened. "Here?"

"I don't feel as if I'm driving," I said. "I can't explain it."

Dan walked back to his colleagues and told them what I had just told him. They craned their necks to look at me, to look around, to take in the scene, wondering how the visuals of the place enhanced the story, wondering what the event would look like on television. A cameraman came out of the bus and started shooting some footage. It was a nice enough place. Computers were produced to update blogs. Camera phones. The lone gas station set amidst the plains. Mountains surrounded us. The trees in the distance that covered the mountains gave the whole place the appearance of a toy train set. Even the gas station looked like something you could buy in a box. An accessory.

I asked Angie if she was hungry and she said no. The reporters went into the small store and emerged with chips and chocolates and jerky and a giant bottle of soda. I felt sorry for them. I felt sorry for what had become of their diets. I felt sorry for the ones who had children. I felt sorry for the children. I felt sorry for the ones who thought they were signing up for a few days driving along the eastern seaboard and now found themselves in Montana with no resolution in the offing. The only person I didn't feel sorry for was Dan.

Angie ran into the store and emerged with a paper bag. "Can you believe it?" she said. "They have tampons!" She ran to the ladies room and did what she had to do.

We got back in the Odyssey. I drove off. When I felt I should turn onto a different road, I did. I let my hands go off the steering wheel just to see if the minivan would drive itself and it veered toward the shoulder.

We drove. We drove through great forests that edged close to the road and made every bend another mystery unsolved. We drove through Great Falls and got on another interstate and still I did not see the Man. We were heading north, always north, and the further north we went now, the further my heart sank. My disappointment mounted. I was starting to give up hope of ever seeing the Man again. I felt dead suddenly. Or at least like I was driving to a funeral. Mine.

There was nothing ahead of us but rolling hills and tall grass. Ranches. Some forest. Campgrounds. The Rockies were every-where and nowhere. In the distance I could see snowcapped peaks. Lonely mountains sprung out of the plains like popcorn in all direc-tions. I took Angie's hand and she pulled away. "I'm sorry," she said. "I'm sorry we did what we did."

"Why?" I asked.

"It makes everything complicated. I had an itch that needed scratching." She sighed. "That sounds so crude. I'm sorry. I had a moment. I think. I don't know what to think." She leaned her head against the window, her eyes blank. "I needed to. I needed to with you. I wouldn't have done that with anyone else. I felt something. I needed that feeling." And that was that, obviously. "We had our chance once. I think," she said. I felt my heart turn brown and wither up inside me. I had not invested anything in our coupling and now I was because its potential had been taken away. It was now an event. History.

I didn't know what to say anymore. I felt like stopping. I felt tired. And as I drove north, I had an urge to once again lose the interstate and I did. I got off at an exit and turned onto a desolate road that went straight toward the horizon and lost itself there. In the rearview mirror, I saw the black bus continue on the interstate. "Say goodbye to the bus," I said.

Angie reached for my cell phone and threw it out the window.

I could imagine Dan's face at that moment when he'd figured out he'd lost us. I felt sorry for him now, finally, because everything he had invested in me would amount to nothing. Without the end of my story, the money Dan had seen for himself remained a wish. Was his story valuable? He had endured the journey because of the money. The payoff. And now . . .

"I didn't take any photos with that thing," I said. I'd just realized it. Everyone around me had documentation. About my life. About this. Except me.

I drove on dirt roads and over creaky bridges. Past lonely oil rigs pumping away heroically. I remember the Odyssey surrounded by hundreds of steers, angry-looking beasts that seemed to comprehend their collective fate already. We drove through little villages that looked like abandoned movie sets; the road widened, a building appeared, pickup trucks parked in front of feed shops, and then the road narrowed again and the town was behind us. "This is too much," Angie said at one point. "You're lost."

And I remember thinking the concept of lost was inapplicable. I wasn't lost. I was definitely near something, I was no longer waiting for the Man to come to me. To appear before me. I had the sense that perhaps I was going to him. This was his home. There was an energy I could feel, a force, that kept me going. When I turned the steering wheel and drove down another empty dirt road I did so because something was telling me where to go, something was guiding me. I gave myself up completely to this feeling. It was all I had now. Angie was already someplace else. Why she was still in the minivan with me was a mystery. In her mind she was back home. Far away. I was already past tense. She couldn't even look in my direction. Perhaps she was taking it all down. Perhaps she was writing a book in her head.

THE VISITOR

The wind has more bite today. It cuts its way past the layers of clothes, past the outerwear, past the fleece, past the cotton, and gets inside you; the cold inhabits the body like a curse.

Yesterday, I enjoyed a Thai massage and a lithe Hispanic woman dug her toes deep into my back, all the while humming to the relentless pan flute flowing from the speakers. The pan flute lives on in the world's spas and on public television. I was thinking some old slide guitar would work in this environment. Ry Cooder, for example. The pan flute didn't work in Montana. If it worked anywhere at all.

The ranks of guests has thinned out. There are no ski hills nearby. In winter, apparently, the mountains are home to hoofed mammals and semiconscious bears and badgers and wolves and other creatures not worth confronting.

Some of the staff are planning winter getaways.

Athena says the owners would like me to present an overall plan for the branding of a group of high-end ranches across the West. She offers me a three-year contract. I can live wherever I choose. I tell her I'll think about where I'll live. I accept the contract. The pay is remarkable and the taxes here are low. She says, "I think this could be fun."

"Fun is relative," I say, Scrooge-like.

At breakfast, I eat a bowl of oatmeal, consider taking up jogging. I've known people who have considered taking up jogging for years, as if the act of consideration itself makes one healthier. Psychosomatic exercise.

I need to draw up a strong list of B-level celebrities. I might have to employ Lindsay's probable skill at celebrity wrangling. A friend in New York had a well-paid job keeping his ad firm's celebrity clients happy. He was a highly remunerated gopher. His cynicism wore Prada. I should call him.

Tomas joins me at the breakfast table, a copy of yesterday's *Chicago Tribune* in hand. "You can just print it off the internet," I tell him.

"I like the feel of newsprint," he says. "I'm a sense person. Especially touch. I have to touch everything. I like the stains even."

I used to enjoy reading old news. My living room in New York was awash in old editions of the Sunday *Times*. I could pick up any section at random and read. In some ways, news never gets old. Events just add layers of meaning to the original story.

"If the Cubs lost two days ago, they still lost," I say. Tomas is buried in the sports section.

"There's something eternal about the teams in Chicago," he says. "They have their place and they play their roles."

A horn sounds outside, to signal the delivery of today's produce. Tomas looks at his watch and gets up. A truck's horn here makes about as much sense as a lion's roar. There are towns and cities not that far from here. Relatively speaking. But this is the kind of country where your next-door neighbor might live fifteen miles away.

I need a research assistant.

The wind outside is now howling.

At the front desk, the phone rings incessantly with guests making spa reservations.

In my office, I order a large planning calendar for my wall online. I order my favorite pens. A notebook. I read the *Times*. I don't miss New York.

I decide to study the history of Montana. And then the West in general. I'm sure there's more to this place than Lewis and Clark.

I go up to the employee lounge and drink three fingers of Woodford while reading a printout of the Mets' front office problems. Three fingers become six.

I step outside and lean into the wind and have a smoke. I don't enjoy it. I think of Angie and I think of Sophie up in Montreal. And realize I shouldn't. Ever again. If that's possible. I try to concentrate on the Mets.

In the lobby, I run into Athena. "OK," I tell her.

"OK what?"

"I want to live here," I say. "At least for now."

"I'll draw up the papers."

"I'm tired of that trailer finally," I say.

She says, "I have to go," and she rushes off in the direction of the dining room.

Keith walks into the lobby, our eyes meet, and he turns and walks out.

Back in my office, I decide I need a couch. A better light fixture. Perhaps a plant. One that doesn't mind shade. I still don't know what I want to do with the stuffed goat.

Glamorous B-list celebrities.

The power of narrative allows all of us to feel important, to connect to the world, to feel alive. A connection is important for any brand. The consumer wants to see himself in the narrative of a brand. A company without a compelling narrative has nothing to offer in the end. It can't tell anyone what it's about. It can't sell itself because there's nothing to sell. A strong brand is a narrative that helps sell stuff.

The line between two points. The arc. Details that say nothing and everything. Embody values that allow the consumer to imprint their own. Impose without being imposing. Make people feel better about themselves. Associate themselves with things that are good.

The big Afro may come and go but the pan flute is finished forever.

I'm toying with some lines. They are shameless but only because I thought them up:

Find Your Story
Discover Yourself Here
Discover Your Story
Let Us Tell Your Story
Live Your Story With Us

Find Your Story.
The long-range forecast is calling for snow. In Montana, global warming is not so much a threat as a promise.

Athena sends me an email. It is a photo of an island in Greece. No message. Just the photo.

I have started a letter to my mother once a day for the past month. I should get on that.

I could tell her of my happiness. Of how I have found myself in a place I feel I belong. Of starting anew. Of the possibilities and direction promised by the endlessness of the sky. I could tell my parents to come for a visit.

Yesterday, it was announced that one of the horses is pregnant. There was an extravagant celebration in the trailers to honor the news.

A knock on my office door. It's Dan. And he's smiling.

PART EIGHT
LET ME STAND NEXT TO YOUR FLOWER

We drove on dirt roads and one-lane roads and small two-lane roads that passed through a desolate landscape. We drove by small towns that consisted of nothing more than a gas station. We saw oil rigs pumping away on the fields, steel grasshoppers quenching a never-ending thirst. We passed signs for provincial parks and only then did we realize we were in Canada. "When did we cross the border?" Angie asked. There was alarm in her voice.

I drove on, driving toward something, my body driving the Odyssey somewhere. I did not know where I was going. Every turn was a surprise.

Roads would end and I would have to back up and try something else. The land felt emptier than any place I'd ever been. I felt afraid. "Maybe you should turn around," Angie said. "I don't like the fact we crossed the border without telling anyone."

"I'm not turning around," I said. "I can let you off but I'm not going backward. If we're here, we're here for a reason. Everything that's happened to me, to us, has gotten us to this point." I stopped the Odyssey and got out and walked toward a lonely fence. On the other side of it was more of the same, miles and miles and miles of prairie. The fence looked ridiculous here. What was it trying to keep in? Or out?

Angie stayed in the minivan. "Really, Joe. I want to go back," she said through the open window.

"So go," I said. "I don't care. Take the van."

"I will," she said.

"I'm not stopping you."

I stepped over the pathetic fence and started walking.

"Joe, please," Angie shouted. "Don't go."

I don't know how long Angie sat there watching me disappear into the tall grass. I imagine she waited until I was out of sight, until she could no longer be certain that I'd return.

I walked to the crest of a small rise. On the other side of the hill, a deep gully broke the carpet of tall grass. From the top of the hill, I could see the world. I watched the Odyssey driving away, kicking up dust behind it. It faded from view until it was swallowed up by the prairie.

I'd left her. I'd walked away. Once she realized that, there was nothing for her here. She was left with her own search. I imagined she'd try to find America again.

Night fell. I hugged myself to keep warm. The sky was an invitation to a party of stars. To an immensity of awe and wonder. Shooting stars raced across the firmament of what must have been an ancient people's idea of heaven.

I stared at the sky and I yelled at the Man. Who are you? I yelled and my voice echoed out of the prairie and I could hear it go around the world and then it returned and went inside of me. The question lodged itself in me and it stayed there.

And then I felt myself leave my body. I felt myself flow into the wind and above the earth. Time became fluid. I saw myself sitting on the hill and then I saw my life unfold in a dream as lucid as if I'd lived it. I had, of course.

I was in a silent place. The silence was unbearable. I heard my beating heart, the blood traveling through my body, the movements of my muscles. I heard myself think. I felt as if I were flying. And I was. I was in space. I was in space zooming in toward the earth. The earth was floating in front of me, a hazy orb, a single globe, and I flew toward it, out of the metallic effluent and toward the world. I saw the invisible arms of history cut through the people of the world. I saw everyone. I saw the population. I saw all that had come before them, the immolated, the conquered, the divided, the heroic, the millions of acts of cowardice, of surrender, the billions of anonymous lives lived anonymously. I saw the minutiae of history, I saw history, like the thin strands of tissue connecting axioms in the brain, linking everyone, all of whom had either chosen to forget or never knew or even remotely imagined the interconnections that bind them together. I saw the air, the air that sustains billions of breaths every day, the air that holds in it the dying wishes of some great and not-so-great and even vile people, everybody, all inside the same polluted air.

And then I heard the sounds of billions of hands clapping, the drone of billions of laugh tracks on billions of televisions, the failing engines of millions of cars, a trickle of noise that soon becomes overwhelming. It was noisy.

And then I was close enough to smell the smoke, smoke from industry and kitchens, the smell of cyanide and oil refining and curries and seared flesh and the burning of healthy trees. The smell hit me like a blind-side cheapshot. And I braced myself for entry, for the blood-boiling heat of a thousand suns, for the heat that is the final line of defense for a fragile sphere floating miraculously in the numbing emptiness of our collective home.

I passed by colors, colors that melded together as if they were melting. By oranges and blues, lavenders and greens, reds and yellows. I imagined I could hear the Wicked Witch of the

West screaming her death's lament and then I realized, no, I was screaming, I was bellowing, cursing, begging. I was melting.

And then I was falling. Floating was past. I was part of the earth. I recognized the familiar shapes of the oceans and continents. I was feeling gravity's pull. And I fell through the radioactive belts of Van Allen, the charged solar particles that do nothing to keep you warm, rapidly falling through exosphere, thermosphere, down to stratosphere, through a particularly nasty part of the sky called the dust belt and into the troposphere. And then the science changed and I considered topography, geography, geology, hydrology, the brown and green shapes of land unencumbered by lines and divisions. By politics. From the upper reaches of the sky, the world looked good, healthy, natural, peaceful, though I knew better, falling through high, thin, wispy cirrus clouds, pancake-flat altostratus clouds, marshmallow-soft cumulonimbus clouds, I fell, through powder puff cumulous clouds, falling with a disquieting, almost humorous speed.

I fell over the Atlantic and zoomed in. Past islands, bays, hooks, spits, tombolos, narrows, inlets, cays, gulfs, beaches, sounds, harbors, down the coast, past the gray smudges of cities, past the refineries and wharves and ferry boats and sewage pipes, down the East River, which is really a strait, it was obvious to me now, and then I was above land, above the checkerboard pattern of urbanity. I was almost on the ground. I fell past buildings worn gray with age and neglect, past deadened streets where the tireless cars sit on cinder blocks, to the signs of gentrification, the construction cranes, the scaffolding, the new building materials that signal wealth, and then . . . there. I. Was.

I saw myself sitting on the steps. I saw my neighborhood and I saw myself, lonely, sitting, waiting.

And I watched the crowd gather about me. I watched the studied indifference of nonchalant kindness of the people who gathered to watch, to observe, to solve the puzzle that was my act. I watched myself eat lousy pizza, watched another kind woman bring some delectable-looking leftovers in a pink Tupperware container. I watched Dan stare into his notepad, his face etched with the painful realization that nothing would be easy. I watched myself struggle, every night, with the fear of being hurt, the fear of every noise emanating from the darkness, the fear of a man enduring goblins and demons in his fitful sleep.

And then I flew up. I took a look at America. At the continent. At its vastness, so open, so well connected. I saw how the roads in America are limitless; from my vantage they looked like the clogged arteries of an American man. Every village, every town accessible to the larger town, which in turn is accessible to minor cities, that connect to the major ones.

I could taste the wind.

I could see the anguish on my face.

I could see that the sky never ends.

I understood that the air is never clean, not even in America, a place where the activities of everyone I could see is visible only in the landscape, in the large golden squares that demarcate the properties of those whose job it is to make sure we eat. The air carried within it the stench of disappointments fulfilled. The jet stream shot by bringing with it exotic smells from Asia, faraway places, imagined places.

I tried to remember when the world lost its potential for me.

And I saw the minivan. I saw the minivan and the black bus hurtle through the countryside, the story beamed to an indifferent world. I saw the minivan cross the artificial boundary. I saw how artificial the boundary was. I saw how this line does little to the ground, how irrelevant it looked from up above and I thought the arbitrary nature of the thing only pointed to our frailties and failures. I recognized the irony of painting invisible lines, the wasted energy, the strange desire of people to divide, to separate, to close doors, to turn backs, to obfuscate, to commit unspeakable acts. All for an invisible line.

I saw my minivan zig and the black bus zag.

And I saw the bus stuck at a place where the invisible line is defended, actually defended by uniformed personnel, by confused personnel who had no idea where I was. I listened to a dead-end conversation between two spent forces, two impotent forces. There are no answers in these discussions because the questions are regurgitated, repeated, elliptical. One half of zero is always zero.

I dove into the metaphorical hearts of those on the bus. I saw the hardening, the loneliness, the blank realization of futility. I felt it. I felt what it is to hold a heart that beats but is lifeless. I felt what it is to know that everything I have aspired to ends only in failure. I felt the inherent weakness of the world's barely beating heart. I touched it. I put my hand on my chest and touched it.

And then it was morning. The grand vista of the world around me returned. Nothing had changed. I watched the dance of the rising sunlight on the endless grass. I watched the wind come over the distant mountains and then kiss the earth. I thought about the folly of the events that had led me here, about the departure of logic in the absence of meaning from my life. I felt like a simpleton.

I knew that to abandon the adventure here was noble. I began it alone, in my head. And it would end that way as well.

And I walked. I began to walk away, my shoulders hunched, the sun's new light elongating my shadow to make it appear a blackened carpet nailed to my feet. I was profoundly dejected. I thought of the possibilities of promises unkept. I felt tired, tired by a quest I now realized I was not strong enough to undertake. I walked staring straight ahead. Afraid of perhaps seeing the Man riding his white horse in the tall grass, his hat flopping about his head, promising things I now know were not his to promise, his empty hands held skyward.

And I let it go. I just thought about this and let it go, and I felt a floating sickness in me that was enough to illuminate the darkest corner of the most despotic empire. I may have felt freedom. I'm not sure.

The mountains were remarkable. There was a beauty to this place that resonated deep inside of me, that rewrote something, altered my DNA.

And from those mountains a wind rolled across the flat land, a wind that had blown itself around the world since before the land existed, blowing over oceans and seas, mountains and prairies, cities and towns. This was the wind eternal, blowing by me, on its never-ending quest for a final resting place. I watched the yellow-gold flicker of the tall grass bending in the eternal wind.

THANKS

Frankly, I don't quite remember *not* writing or thinking about this book. It has been a long haul and this is a preface to say that it is quite possible (nay probable) that I am forgetting or have forgotten most of the people who should have ended up on this list. So remember that while I may be forgetful, I am never ungrateful.

The first inkling of this book was borne of continental road trips from long ago, one with Doug and the other with Caroline. Photos from these long voyages remain in my possession and they continue to be useful for extortion purposes. It was also a memorable time because I still had a full head of hair.

Then I started writing. Many people read earlier versions of this novel and the insight and wisdom of Timothy Taylor and Douglas Coupland stand out for being most insightful and full of wisdom.

I must thank Dina Yuen for introducing me to Neil Salkind, who sold the book to Jack David at ECW. And thanks are due to absolutely everyone at ECW, including Crissy Calhoun and Erin Creasey, and especially to my editor Emily Schultz, who was kind and smart and encouraging and gentle. Oh so gentle. Thanks to Michel Vrana for proving you *should* judge a book by its cover.

For whatever reason, I listened to a lot of Philip Glass during the endless editing of this work, especially the *Koyaanitsqatsi* soundtrack. So, um, thanks Philip Glass. And then there are the instrumental tracks from the soundtrack to *The Life Aquatic of Steve Zissou*, written by Mark Mothersbaugh. I listened to that when I wasn't listening to *Koyaanisqatsi*. So thanks to Mark Mothersbaugh as well.

Thanks, forever, to the late and great Lou Reed, whose lyrics started this process. And though the project ended far far away from the "man" Lou sings about, this book would be a very different creature without that first and fatal spark.

Thanks, always, to David McGimpsey, who is not just a supporter of my work and drinking buddy, but someone who gets me without being at all demanding. And thus is the best kind of friend.

And thanks to Milo, who has grown to something approaching adulthood during the gestation of this novel and, more importantly, has grown into a smart and sensitive person (who swears a bit too much perhaps, but so do his parents).

And mostly, thanks to Naomi. I'm not easy to live with. But then again, neither is she.

At ECW Press, we want you to enjoy this book in whatever format you like, whenever you like. Leave your print book at home and take the eBook to go! Purchase the print edition and receive the eBook free. Just send an email to ebook@ecwpress.com and include

- the book title
- the name of the store where you purchased it
- your receipt number
- your preference of file type: PDF or ePub?

A real person will respond to your email with your eBook attached. And thanks for supporting an independently owned Canadian publisher with your purchase!